FLOWERING MIMOSA

FLOWERING MIMOSA

by Natalie L. M. Petesch

 The Swallow Press

Library of Congress Cataloging-in-Publication Data

Petesch, Natalie L.M., 1924–
  Flowering mimosa.

  I. Title
PS3566.E772F5 1987   813′.54   86-23024
ISBN 0-8040-0870-1
ISBN 0-8040-0871-X (pbk.)

Swallow Press books are published by Ohio University Press.

for Don

I

Tamsen stopped inscribing the initials *R.W.* in the dust and instead watched her father descend the hillside into the Valley. She was resigning herself to the fact that she no longer loved him. Once he had been the aurora borealis of her life, now he was old and tired. She raked the initials through with her twig, arguing that it was his own fault, he should never have left Texas where he was a hero fighting droughts and banks and even other farmers who didn't have sense enough to dig proper wells. Here he was a hunky. Every day he left the house with a squeaky-looking lunchbox in his hand, wearing those ugly boots from which at dusk he stood at their doorstep scraping the clay and the volcanic rockdust barnacled to the soles. Even his handsome face was becoming rough and mottled from the blasting and shovelling and smelting down of the endless hardrock. He came home rimed with a sweaty grey ash like he'd been dug up from Pompeii. She hated him for it. He ought to have stayed clean and handsome, a cowboy on their bay stallion. That was the way she would remember him. She would blot out the present for his sake. It was humiliating to see him go rattling down a shaft in a cage like a prisoner, sometimes wanly waving—a sad immigrant on a wharf—more often not. She wanted her young father given back to her. She wanted him to lift her again to Thunder's saddle, and the two of them would ride past Spaulding Creek to the Salinas feed store and back again to the farm, Thunder churning the red clay as Reffie gave him a free rein home, the last two miles a whirlwind. They'd arrive at the dried-up burnt-out old farm so hot and thirsty, your own sweat would look good enough to lick. And her mother would be waiting with a pitcher of plain water (*Never ice water if you're real hot*), Reffie first offering glasses of water all around, to her brother Woodrow and her mother and herself, as if it were a party and he just fixing drinks, then drinking right out of the pitcher himself. Tamsen would take the empty pitcher and the glasses and set them down on the sink alongside their pump in the kitchen. Her father would lead Thunder back to the barn, and her mother would open the screendoor for Tamsen and herself. Tamsen listened attentively to the long-ago lost whine and grind of the complaining door while staring with stony resentment at the name which meanwhile was surfacing beneath her twig: *Julia*. And then Tamsen and her mother would cross the threshold within, where it would be, suddenly, shockingly cool. This coolness had always seemed to Tamsen a sign of Roseanne Wingfield's unique power, that outdoors the sun would be bearing down like a hot millstone grinding you to dust between the burning sky and the baking earth, and then you'd go indoors where the shades had been drawn all afternoon, and the small electric fan droned like a tired fly and the quaint white refrigerator that Roseanne had bought second-hand, the one with its round motor on top like a head, stood in a corner of the kitchen, a momentarily motionless robot, and then like a dream which Tamsen had since dreamt again and again, her mother would reach out and there would appear on the oilcloth-covered table a slice of ham, smooth slim and cool as a hand on your forehead, and a glass of milk which sweated cold sweat, not hot, and left your handprint, and above all a canvas cot would be ready on the back porch where after the exciting ride from Salinas Tamsen would lie alone reading, the endlessly pearling string of words uninterrupted except for now and then her father's voice, or sometimes Woodrow's as they dumped the scorched corn with its brown beardlike tassels into the corncrib. Or sometimes it would be the voice of the new baby who would break the silence, two little *ach, ach* cries rather like the scratch of a kitchen match than of a real new person;

and her mother, who just possibly would have been resting herself, or maybe had been in bed with that handsome
young man who was her father, would patter over to baby-
Bobby in her bare feet and all would be silent again except
for the faint sound of the rocker.

Tamsen stripped the remaining bark from her twig,
rubbed out the offending letters, and slowly inscribed her
own mother's whole name in the dust. Then, as if the
talismanic recreation of these letters had, like the ghost of
Hamlet's father, evoked Roseanne Buford Wingfield's ac-
tual presence, Tamsen began silently to explain to the hy-
postatic name that it was not *exactly* that she hated this
strange new place. She could perhaps get used to its towering mountains and giant Douglas firs and blooming cotton bolls of cloud racked by chinooks from the South and
buffeted by Arctic winds from the North knocking the
white bolls open onto a sky streaked in pale pink and pis-
tachio like some velvety Victorian wallpaper surfacing
from a dream; Tamsen might be able to get used to all *that*,
except for the inalterable fact that if they were in Silver
Valley, they could not be with their friends in Salinas; that
even if they had (as Reffie often said they did) the most
friendly helpful guy living across the street from them in
the Valley, then it was nevertheless impossible for that person to be the tall lean laconic man in Salinas that Tamsen
used to think must sound like Abe Lincoln—it was like the
Gettysburg Address just listening to him—he used to let
Tamsen help him in the shearing of the lambs.

So, although their new neighbor was *nice* (as Reffie and
Julia, a pair of awkward matchmakers, had more than
once pointed out) and had invited everybody to go fishing
with him, he was *not* anyone she had known in Salinas.
Therefore, it was quite enough to make you resent his
smiling, meddling neighborliness. What did he know of
her loss? What did any of them Up Here know? Had *they*
ever walked to school only days before *Christmas* with the
morning sun warming you awake from your sleep, while a
mantling movement of the air, almost visible on the winter
grass, stirred all around? Or heard the crickets chorusing

with the throaty water-coolers on the streets of Salinas, blasts of heat rising underfoot as she and Reffie walked all the way to the wonderfully preserved old General Store, kept just as Mr. Henry Williams Senior had left it? Tamsen could hear Reffie's boots striking the curbstone like anvils, feel the reassuring rhythm of his stride, a stride that knew what it wanted and cast a shadow as it moved. And Reffie holding her hand, not to protect her but simply because she was his; leading her around the grain sacks full of seed and feed, past wooden boxes giving off their metallic odor, the nails and nuts and bolts looking strangely fertile and alive as they lay in their little wooden cribs, sensuously oxidizing. Tamsen would stir them with her forefinger, as though they were beans or worms, awed to think that on such odd necessities hinged the survival of their farm; the chickenwire fences and vegetable crates and iron-bound barrels and the feed for the charitable laying hens who, Reffie said, were all that kept them from starving. And what could *he* know—their neighborly fishing companion of Silver Valley, or anyone for that matter—of the fantastic Texas rocks Tamsen would exchange with the rockhounds of Salinas? And the cacti that flourished right in the middle of the rocks, and the hours on end, hundreds of them, of glorious exhaustion in the face of the heat, when it was a bother to breathe, so you did nothing—you held your very breath and sat in the shade of the house reading or contemplating the leaves of the flowering mimosa which was the pride of her mother's life, Roseanne swore she would never leave it; it was a human being to her. And yet Roseanne *had* left it and left them too, and the tree without her precious ration of water had by now probably died. The mimosa, Roseanne would say, was the only person besides their dog, who was allowed to waste water now and then. "Your mother must get up in the middle of the night to steal water for her tree, else it's some kind of loaves and fishes miracle," Reffie said, and Roseanne would smile mysteriously and say *Yes*, that was exactly what she did do, so Tamsen never knew whether she did or didn't.

· 4 ·

The week Julia had arrived at the farm from up North with her new suitcases and the mesmerized look of a bride who believed that love would kill off the bugs devouring the vegetables and protect her sandalled feet from the snakes coiled in the dried-up creeks, the flowering mimosa had been alive and well, its water-sipping lavender flowers blooming luxuriously. And yet (Tamsen often swore to her brother Woodrow that this was true), Julia had not once, not *once*, expressed her gratitude or admiration for such a botanical marvel holding fast its rooty feet in the hot dust of their farm. Rather, Julia had simply sat down under its miraculous shade as if it had been planted there for her pleasure and comfort, solely so that she might come all the way to Texas to do her sewing under it or leaf through the Sears Roebuck catalog looking for warm jackets. Tamsen should have known right then, by the kind of stuff she was ordering from that catalog, that Reffie was going to sell out and move North. And while Julia read the catalog to them aloud, they'd sit there under Roseanne's tree watching the sun go down. Which in itself was quite another thing in Salinas. You didn't exactly watch it, you watched *around* it. You noticed how the sky in the immediate horizon was beginning to soften not darken; how the light changed and changed again, becoming something tangible, a delicate lace or silk tossed over the face of the earth under whose merciful veil the sky was metamorphosing, changing from porcelain-blue to rose then to a fiery umber with a faint filigree of black encircling the light. Because there was never any cloud; no, no cloud at all. That was why the great sky had to bring out the darkness from within itself, an Idea distinct from yet not separate from the light.

And even the silence Up Here in Silver Valley was different, considered Tamsen with exasperation, becoming aware of an emptiness, an expectancy which had seized the hillsides. The miners had now all gone underground, the streets in town would be nearly deserted. Up Here it was the silence of the lonely miners' wives who had sent their children off to school and all their able-bodied men to blast the implacable rock, who exorcised the long loneliness of the day by a furious commitment to hard labor, cooking and canning and cleaning with passionate vengeance, a silence utterly unlike the silences of Salinas where the thermometer might rise like lava over a hundred degrees, day after day, night after night—Tamsen once recorded forty-six days and nights without cease—while the cries of the cicadas rose on the air, their bodies roaring engines of excitement, their legs scraping with longing, their song rising and falling, rising and falling, all through the burning hours. Who needed any other sound? For all their vaunting of their Snake and Salmon Rivers and Columbian gorges, were they even *once* Up Here to hear the sirenic song of the Salinas cicadas, they would throw themselves, mad with homesickness and longing, into their own swollen white waters.

Tamsen could hear the tap water being turned on now, and then Julia bathing Josh in the kitchen sink. She was not sure whether she should feel more angry than relieved that Julia obviously did not even care enough about her to come out and order her to school. Tamsen opted for feeling insulted by Julia's indifference and moved herself to the side of the house, avoiding the bronze and purple and yellow irises Julia had planted. Then with the patience of a scribe in the Dark Ages preserving western civilization by the power of the word, Tamsen wrote:

> Roseanne Buford Wingfield
> Beloved wife of
> Beloved mother of
> Born   Died

Tamsen had heard from the mourners more than once that it was a sad thing for Reffie Wingfield to be left a widower with young children. Yet they had disappeared right after the funeral not returning to grieve with Reffie, but leaving him to his own loss and despair and the resources of the wet nurse who'd brought her own infant along and had sat in the rocker with Bobby: a miraculous twin fountainhead of survival. Tamsen had at once detested this monstrous charity as well as the helpless greed of her orphaned brother so promiscuously and ignorantly nursing at the breast of a total stranger, whose arrival had caused strange things to happen.

Tamsen's own food had become invaded by invisible living Things. Whatever she ate sickened her. She seemed to see what she swallowed going down in endless mucilaginous particles, strung out like sorghum as it oozed down her esophagus; rather like the saliva which bubbled out of the baby's mouth at the breast of the mountainous mother who had had nothing whatsoever to do with his having been born. How could he suckle like that at the breast of a woman he'd not ever seen or heard in his life before? Tamsen had finally decided she detested baby-Bobby too, since he was too stupid to know the difference. At least he ought to have bawled day and night. Instead, after gorging himself with milk till his pale face with its dark eyes resembled a puffy ashen toadstool, he would sleep from supper till dawn while Tamsen and Woodrow lay awake talking, brooding, resenting the awful Power which played such mean tricks. How was it possible that Roseanne Wingfield could be standing in the kitchen one day, ladling peas or mashed potatoes, the sun lying along the brown and white linoleum in amulets of light, and then within a month or so, during the summer it had been, as casually as if she'd gone on vacation, how could she go off into the wild blue yonder of Eternity, *and not even say goodbye*? A short simple operation and a short simple lethal bloodclot had carried her off like a barn owl seeing and seizing its prey. The folks in Salinas had all been struck by awe (it was God's will) and by fear (it could happen to them). *A perfectly healthy woman*, they said, *who would have thought it, and now what would poor Reffie Wingfield do*?

Waving her twig, Tamsen cited her grievances to the absent auditors of Salinas. What "poor Reffie" had, in fact, done:

One: He'd left Texas after the funeral and gone up North where he was supposed to be visiting Roseanne's folks to see would they take the kids until he could sell the farm and get a job somewhere: ride out the economy, he said. And they'd said (her very own grandparents!) had said, *Dearie no*, they couldn't take on *that* much (like they were three gunny sacks of heavy corn or grain), but they'd adopt the littlest one and raise him as their very own. And Reffie had accepted this trade-off—*her* baby brother had become a Buford instead of a Wingfield.

Then (*Two*): After *losing* the farm (he called it "sold"), he hadn't even had sense enough to stay put in Salinas but had started moving around the country like a bum. Anybody could have told him he could live better poor in Texas than rich Up Here (though they weren't getting rich here in Silver Valley either; anybody could have told him *that* too).

And now *Three*: Worst of all, he'd gone and married this Julia, a mere slip of a girl young enough to be Tamsen's sister but too old to be a *friend*.

And Tamsen had decided that she detested Julia too, not for any special attributes, but just for the same reason she resented the undulant hillsides and forests of fir and the pink skies: They were not what she'd asked for, not what she wanted.

She had used to tell God every day what she wanted until she became gradually aware that probably He'd got bored. Anyway, he wasn't listening anymore. What she had used to ask for Back Home was a wife for Reffie just like the one he used to have. There must have been another one like Roseanne *some*where, and if Reffie had waited, maybe he'd have found her. But he'd been in this big hurry to bring someone down home to Texas and then run off to the great Northwest with her—just like any kid wanting to take his girlfriend along for a ride. Tamsen was not ever going to forgive his unseemly haste and it was just possible that God was going to be equally unforgiving and maybe even He had forced Julia upon Reffie in order to speed up Reffie's repentance. Whatever happened would serve him right.

Tamsen now sketched an animal in the dust, giving it a round head with pointed ears, a long tail and great gnashing seines of teeth. The mouth frightened her, it was so open and ugly, like an animal at bay, rather like those big-teethed jackrabbits they killed by the thousand Up Here. And that was another thing. When the rabbits in Salinas had got into Reffie's cornfields and gnawed holes in the squash big as shrapnel holes, Reffie had at first tried fencing in his field, which had turned out to be expensive and hadn't kept the rabbits out either. Then one afternoon in a fit of exasperation, Reffie had taken his hunting rifle, taken careful aim, and shot a half-dozen rabbits. A lot of them, he had to admit, had got away, but then they were so damned fast. As Reffie described to them the soaring parabola the rabbits made as they flew quick as grasshoppers, through the cornfield, it had been easy to see how caught he was between admiration and necessity. But here in Idaho, Tamsen exclaimed to herself righteously, they acted like they wanted to kill every rabbit on the face of the earth and every coyote too, if they could.

Barely a week after their arrival in the Valley, the Wingfields had been invited to a rabbit hunt by a farmer named Phelps, who had organized it. Julia had stayed home to care for Josh, who was just learning to stand by himself, but her brother had gone along with Reffie and Tamsen. Woodrow said that though he didn't find the idea of a bunch of farmers chasing a bunch of rabbits all that exciting, it was an *event*, and everybody was going to it. So they went.

Their caravan had driven straight South toward what they called the palouse, near the Washington border, where the farmers said they were being ruined by a new plague of Egypt: rabbits. The rabbits were costing them thousands of dollars every year, and this year they were worse than ever. A couple of sheep ranchers who had just joined the hunt observed that they devoutly wished as much might be done to the coyotes. Phelps had discussed with one of the sheep men, a man named Ross—a respectable, clean-looking fellow built rather like a bowling pin, with a long slender head and full round hips—the possibility of a coyote drive.

Ross had objected. "No, you can't do that. Rabbits are plain dumb, and scared. But a coyote's too smart. A bunch of dumb bunnies, they're not much more than shooting at tin cans. But just try and outsmart a coyote."

Phelps had narrowed his eyes in irritation. "Don't call them bunnies, they're *rodents*, that's all they are, not fit to be eaten, even. You can get tularemia eating wild rabbit."

It had been a stunningly bright September morning, the sky flawless, a shock of blue. A light mist rose slowly off the hills. The tapestried wheatfields lay spread from one end of the palouse to the other. As far as the eye could see the grain lay golden, undulant, the wheat plowed in whorled furrows like chambered nautiluses. Tamsen heard Reffie's gasp of envy as he pondered aloud the mystery of his own struggle for water in Salinas, while here the farmer had merely to seek for water and it was found, to ask for it and it was given. Their party now headed for what seemed an open prairie. They climbed out of their cars and trucks and stood in the open field surrounded by the silence and the golden, undulant hills. The farmers spoke to one another in hushed voices. Then someone spotted a jackrabbit. They stood in silence, watching as he leaped through the tall grass like a baby kangaroo, his eyes bright and tawny, his long ears vibrating their signals of warning. He gave a magnificent leap, he seemed to soar and hang suspended on air. Then he dropped to his splendid long legs and sped away from them in terror and the shock of invasion.

"Nobody shoot," Phelps said. "You know that, don't you? This is not a shooting range. You'll get your own selves killed if you start shooting. When I give the signal you take your sticks and cover the field. We all head in the *same* direction—so don't go off on some hunting party of your own." He pointed in the distance about a hundred yards. "Ross and me, we built that stockade there. Head the rabbits *that* way, straight into the fence. They'll never get through that fence, believe me."

They believed him. From out of their pickups and the trunks of their motley-colored cars emerged an odd medieval-looking weaponry resembling pikes, maces, lances. Some were mere heavy sticks, thick chunks of split-oak made into clubs by being whittled down at the base; axe handles and spades and shovels and quite ordinary-looking baseball bats by the dozen, as if the most American of games had been transformed. There were jokes now, and some nervous laughter.

Tamsen and Woodrow had sat on the roof of their car, waiting. Suddenly a jackrabbit sprinted away from the direction of the drive and ran instead toward their car. Phelps shouted at Woodrow: "Get him! Get him!" Almost before either of them knew he had done it, Woodrow had slid down from the roof, twisting his ankle as he hit the ground. In a contagion of energy he had struck the rabbit a walloping blow to the head with their picnic basket. Woodrow's strange weapon would have been ludicrous— Tamsen watched as her brother cast the basket over his shoulder like a fishing line—except that his aim was shockingly true. The stunned rabbit fell at their feet. "Good boy," said Phelps, raising his shovel. "I'll finish him." They heard a papery crack of the skull, rather like the crackle of fire in dry leaves. The rabbit fell on its back, its long legs still churning at desperate speed. Phelps turned away to direct the main attack.

Rabbits were now being driven into a corner of the stockade built in the style of the pioneers, meant to protect the frontier folk from Indians and wild animals: very high and solid. Trapped in the angled corners of the stockade, they swarmed and leaped on top of one another, their piping voices of terror sounding through the hillsides. Suddenly Tamsen found herself shivering and retching, she came down from the roof of the car to be sick in the high grass. Woodrow, weeping with revulsion and hobbled by his twisted ankle, ran to fetch Reffie.

He found Reffie at the outermost edge of the crowd, lifelessly holding a stick as he watched the farmers coming to grips at last with the enemy who had kept them from meeting their mortgage payments and was driving them into bankruptcy, preventing their sons from becoming physicians and lawyers and bankers so that they would not have to be farmers and miners like themselves. Seizing Reffie's hand, Woodrow had pulled him toward the car.

"Let's get out of here," Reffie said. And when the engine of their old car started up at once, Reffie uttered the first prayer Tamsen had heard since they'd left Salinas: "Thank God," he sighed. They drove away, the smell of slaughtered rabbits not unlike the smell of the salt sea air, following them on the bright September day.

II

Mornings their sky is azure, the sun dilates through the cloud cover, a lambent eye. A soft fringe of cloud speeds away before this brightness. On Reffie's right, the hillsides reflect sunlight as though light grew upward from out of the boughs of the Douglas firs. On his left the river.

He rises to find a light rime frost on the window. Nothing to fear, plenty of firewood, the windows sealed against the coming cold; the stove checked and ready. He needs but one thing for sure, a hot breakfast: Set the pot for coffee and the blue enamelware pan for cereal. His breath begins to warm up the small kitchen. Good. Reffie shuts the door to the bedroom where Julia lies asleep, hoping to give her a little more rest after a bad night with the baby. He wakes the kids for school—Tamsen first, then Woodrow. *Not too much noise there, Woody.*

Water boiling, Reffie pours a mixture of millet and oats into the pan: Tamsen will watch it while he packs his lunch. Never any trouble getting Tamsen out of bed though she might be half asleep at the stove. Just put the wooden spoon in her hand, she'll begin automatically to stir the cereal, her eyes will slowly become watchful, awake, often it seemed to Reffie inexplicably angry.

For a moment it appears the rime frost is burning, an iridescent fire, rather like a rainbowed oil slick; but it is only the sunlight radiating a few tinted glasses above the sink, sole survivors of wedding gifts received by him and Roseanne in what now seems another life; before Julia, even before Tamsen and Woody. Reffie would rather not think in absolute numbers how many years ago that was, just as he tries not to be too precise as to the thousands of miles he and Julia have travelled since their civil marriage back East: first to his farm in Texas, to watch as it was being auctioned off to his neighbors, then to the Northwest for weeks of job-hunting in Seattle, until finally—at Grampa Wing's invitation, they drove clear across Washington and over the state line into the Valley. Grampa's long standing with the miners' union had tipped the balance; they'd given him a job. The glass, actually, was a kind of bronze color. What had Roseanne used to call it? He could never remember such things, though he had a pretty good memory and by now, the fourth decade of his life, it would seem he had more than enough remembering to do.

Although when he was not in the mine he didn't waste what time he had left of his life by thinking of the Past. It was better to save your remembering for when you were underground. Then, sealed off in memories, you could endure the long day, you could look ahead or behind. *Ahead* often required more daring than Reffie could muster up these days: More and more he opted for looking Behind.

He fixed himself two bologna sandwiches. Often he was hungry enough to eat a third, but with such a short lunchbreak, he'd have to bolt it down, which would make him belch. He hated doing that even though most of the time it was so noisy underground no one would hear it; but a man had to hang onto the decency of certain situations and even of objects: like tablecloths and napkins, for instance, you wouldn't just spit in them. He folded his sandwiches into the brightly colored bread wrappers saved for this purpose and gave himself two apples. They were cheaper here than in Texas, plenty of orchards in eastern Washington. Julia always bought a lot of them. His hand, wistful as a child's, reached into the cupboard for a cupcake: not one left. Disappointed, he tried to shrug away a sense of the Sole Provider's having been casually overlooked. He himself had told Julia never to keep Tamsen and Woody from eating, the kids had got used to a sporadic abundance on their farm in Salinas, being allowed to eat whatever they happened to have a lot of as long as they had it.

One more thing and he'd be ready. On top of his sandwiches he laid two newspapers: one a mine workers' leaflet, and over that, *The Silver Valley News*.

The smell of coffee would reach Julia, she would open her eyes and know almost to the minute how near Reffie was to finishing his breakfast. She would wrench herself awake and be washed up and ready to see him off as he went out the door. Leaving the house to go underground was a kind of surgery he went into that nobody could predict the outcome of, so when he kissed Julia on the top of her astonishingly bright black hair he touched her hands too, lingering at the fingertips. Snapping his lunch box shut was like setting off the Westclox: Julia came into the kitchen, set the baby in the high chair, gave Reffie an awkward hug. Noticing Reffie's still-open jacket, she buttoned it for him, straight to the throat. He understood that this was purely talismanic, meant to ward off pneumonia and other bad things from the mine; so he stood patient as a horse, grateful for the attention, knowing he would unbutton his jacket the moment he was out of sight.

Behind him now the click of the door locking itself into place—though not against burglars and thieves. The other miners swore that there had not been a burglary in the Valley as far back as they could rightly remember. You could leave your car unlocked too, they added, to really impress Reffie. In a town like this, where everybody knows everybody else, nobody would steal anything from you, they said, you couldn't lose anything if you tried, they'd be sure to find it and give it back to you.

Except your life, his friend Smetka had retorted, smiling.

But on such a beautiful day Reffie was not going to think Morbid Thoughts. The miners all joked—at once facetiously and seriously—that thinking Morbid Thoughts caused vibrations in the ceilings; the more you dwelt on such things the more likely the earth would tremble and mysterious canyons open up before you. Cinders had already been laid down the steep incline leading from their hillside house down the path into Main Street although as yet there'd been no heavy snowfall. His son had objected to the cinders because, he said, he wouldn't be able to coast his sled straight downhill to Main Street. What was the use of living where *at last* they had snow—Woody rolled his tongue around the word as if he could taste it—unless he was going to be able to coast downhill? At this Tamsen had turned away in disdain: only a couple of years' difference between them and you'd think it was ten.

Heading toward Main Street Reffie turned right. There was never much traffic off the steep road from his house; he preferred to approach the mine by way of the town rather than by crossing the hillside horizontally to descend by way of an overgrown path. That way he was more likely to see a few folks before punching his clock, store up some faces before going underground. And he liked looking into the store windows, too, seeing the shops open up as he headed toward the mine gate. He'd got into a superstitious habit of forecasting his luck for the day by the kind of company he saw on the way to work: the postman, the grocer, the lady from Ladies Apparel, and especially the school kids. He loved to see them heading for school, their eyes still glazed with sleep, a quiet pride in their walk. The great thing about the kids here, they seemed so free and unafraid, as if they believed that no matter what happened in the rest of the country, they could always survive somehow, living in a hut in the wilderness, maybe, trapping small game and fish from the lake.

But Reffie doubted that it was true, as Tamsen often complained, that this Main Street was unlike any other main artery in America. Tamsen would grumble that there were better stores *any*where, to which Julia would sadly reply that there were more than enough things to buy here, it was having the money to buy them was the problem.

Now at the corner of South Bitterroot and Main, Reffie paused. This was Grampa Wing's favorite view of the town. Grampa had watched the streets of the Valley and the deep levels of the mine grow together. His first job had been in the mine. Grampa had seen how the town grew, first attracting a small seed and grain supply house and a grain elevator along the railroad spur; then had come what Grampa still called a saloon, then a barber shop followed by the still-operating Buckholtz dry goods store featuring (in Grampa's day) the best calico and muslin; and then an elite new specialization for the time—a milliner's shop, now known, as though still partial to millinery, as Ladies Apparel. After that had come a second grocery, and a third and a fourth, and one that sold fresh vegetables brought to the town even in winter, whereas when he, Grampa Wing had been growing up, you might have had nothing but canned green beans and peas or maybe a chunk of hubbard squash. And as for winter *fruit*, Grampa Wing memorialized—forget it. If you were careful, a couple of barrels of apples might last you through the winter. *Now* you have everything, Grampa had told Reffie calmly, staring at him in unconcealed reproach, as though it were something extraordinary, Reffie's being unemployed. Yet of all people Grampa Wing should know better, Reffie considered with shame and resentment, union man that he was, a survivor of the Great Depression.

Main Street proclaimed to him the changes since those days. The town now had more than its share of doctors (one a D.O.), some of them runaways from the California freeways—self-exiled to backpacking in the wilderness; several dentists; at least a half-dozen beauty parlors (probably more, but Reffie hadn't counted.) Exactly where it used to be, across from Ladies Apparel, was the very barber shop which Grampa claimed had been there over fifty years. It still sported its candy-striped spiral totem which still revolved ceaselessly in perfect silence, like some exotic fish undulating in a glass aquarium. Reffie had been in the barber shop for a shave and haircut one Saturday morning when Tamsen seemed about to enjoy some social life in the Valley at last—their friendly neighbor from across the street had drifted into the house unannounced—Reffie had got himself out of the house as fast as possible. On that morning, he'd sat like a Pope or a King observing Arimeo the barber with curiosity to see if he'd show some distaste at the sight of Reffie's stubbled face, which for all Reffie knew might still have a just-visible film of ore dust limning the eyelids. Reffie had stared past Arimeo's handsome young face (a Shoshone Indian, he kept his hair trimmed and glossy as an Italian prince), while Arimeo lathered up the soap and laid it on Reffie's bone-stressed cheeks, the skin fretted with hatchings that had become concave stars (they were the devil to shave). Arimeo, unlike the calumnious reports of barbers on any other Main Street, had refused to engage in conversational banter or gossip or even the state of his health, so Reffie had been reduced to contemplating his own face in the mirror. This however had brought small comfort for his human condition. Rather, the congealed Self and the silence had served somehow to spell out how close to Eternity one always was: His own facial immobility and stark staring eyes seemed even to himself already sepulchral. What he had become sadly aware of as he sat in the barber's chair—though he believed his sadness was not merely, or at least not solely, a matter of vanity—was that what had been scattered streaks of gray in his dark hair, like an untapped vein of ore, had within the past year become a helmet of firm and timeless metal: permanent and inescapable. Looking into Arimeo's mirror he recorded this fact without sentiment or pity, as he would have noted that a dog or horse lies down in the dust when his time came upon him to lie down forever. Still, the eyes astonished him. He might have hoped that in some way his gaze would reflect a little of the hope and pride and even tenderness of his life; reflect perhaps the tone in which he tried to speak to his children, or even what he *didn't* say—his unspoken murmuring incantation of ache and anguish for their survival in a world fraught with danger and worry. His eyes ought to have shown that. And his face ought to have reflected at least some of his own family's crazy-heroic or even greedy adventurism, the pioneer spirit that had brought Grampa Wing to this wild land to homestead, and had carried his own father to Texas; shown maybe some of the energy of his own Texas youth. But no, nothing. From his own eyes he saw—he looked again, still more closely—neither love nor tenderness nor even pity for himself; nor any negative qualities either—neither stupidity nor boorishness—only a great spectral loneliness. Merely a face brooding upon itself as if it were trying to become accustomed to living underground: the face of Lazarus with its stunned look of separation from the Living who silently trod the earth three thousand feet above him.

In alarm Reffie had turned away from the mirror. His own face had made him afraid, though he would not have admitted it to anyone. Turning for relief from this doppelganger, Reffie had focused his sight directly out the barber shop window across Main Street into the window of Ladies Apparel, where bronze or coppery heads with silver eyes, looking as if they'd fallen from a guillotine on some red planet, were gazing at his own still-intact head. From out of their metallic stare they seemed to Reffie to have been weighing his case all along; to have been watching as first, his cheeks were lathered, then restored to a near-normal condition. As Reffie sat returning the stare of these ultra-human heads (his own all-too-human head being meanwhile scraped of debris, as though he were a miner in an accident and Arimeo had been sent to rescue him) suddenly pale hands with glosswhite nails had fluttered around these bodiless Nefertitis. Their silver eyes remained unchanged, but the heads were now quickly transformed. One copper-colored head soon sported a cockaded hat; and the head which only moments before had seemed to bear the tragic mien of the guillotine became transformed by this bit-of-business into a face of mere foolishness. Even the smile seemed to dilate—charged now, it seemed to Reffie, with the cynical allure of a Lady of the Night. On a second head the agile fingers now placed a velvet fedora with feathers, not of course real feathers, like the ostrich or egret of Grampa's day, but imitation feathers resembling the equipage of a whooping crane—a resemblance which reminded Reffie at once of the Arkansas Refuge, and he didn't want to be reminded of Texas at all again, ever—so he rivetted his gaze instead on a full-form model which the efficient hands of Ladies Apparel were now placing in the window.

In spite of the color of the rubbery flesh that one sensed could never decompose—a kind of bruised blue—Reffie recognized the naked form as the body of a girl about Tamsen's age. Around her nubile body, the sedulous hands now flung a fashionable fake-fur beaver coat, and on the silver-eyed head they placed a rakish billed fur cap. Finally, as if to conceal the bruised color, the hands laid a flowing white scarf around the slender throat. After these transformations there was nothing left to Reffie's view except the cold silver eyes floating like metal eggs in a bowl of blue plasticene.

But now *really*, he said to himself, he was no longer enjoying the show: Instead he had begun to think about money, about how much hard rock one would have had to excavate in order to pay for an outfit like that. But the calculation caused his pulse to quicken with anxiety, he found himself breathing heavily, as though there had been a change in the ventilation system of the mine; a man could feel the pressure of it at once. And after he had paid Arimeo he'd decided that barber shops were a luxury he could do without—he'd let Julia cut his hair, at least till he was sure the mine would stay open and if it stayed open, that they'd keep him.

He lingered for a moment longer on Main Street, watching Scott Thorssen raise the blinds of The Red Coat Inn, with its seditious trademark intended long ago to associate itself with the British (it was thought then that the Territory's competition for the fur trade would be won by the British, not the Americans). For a moment Reffie allowed himself the luxury of envying the settlers of those days, when it seemed all a man had to do to survive and prosper was to set traps, kill beavers, and trade with the Indians for furs.

At the curb of South Bitterroot he tamped down his pipe. The sun had now triumphed over the few skimming clouds: The Valley was unveiled. The sky exploded with light. Turning his head to shield his eyes from its brilliance, Reffie caught an angled glimpse of a stand of firs on the hillsides, their long boles serene as cloistered monks. But now his time was up. He must walk quickly and without further pause straight to the main gate of C & L where he would punch his clock: It would be ten minutes to eight.

It was still a matter of some surprise to Reffie to see his name recorded in such clear, legible symbols, as though his name and the time of his existence were information of great import to the world at large. And a strange ritual it was, in which he was hailed daily with this subtle, Delphic message: Ambrose Raphael Wingfield. Nobody had ever called him Ambrose, and only the nurse in the Salinas hospital knew how the name of the archangel guarding our first Garden had been spelled out as Reffie. But the Wingfields had cheerfully resigned themselves to the new orthography, declaring it an act of God. No school kid in Salinas could have survived a name like Ambrose Raphael Wingfield.

This name now leaped to sight and alongside it, the date; with a kind of aggrieved diffidence, as if he were somehow ashamed of the indelible record of the hours of his life about to be contracted to the C & L Silver-Lead & Zinc Company, Reffie punched the hour. The time clock chimed back at him, inveterately cheerful.

He avoided looking at Smetka's slot. He'd become accustomed to working with Smetka and he felt lonely without him. He'd not become friends with any other miner. Smetka was a serious hardworking young man with the troubled look of a much older man. You trusted him. When you turned toward him, you'd know he'd been watching you; but if you tried to acknowledge this in some way, with a word of gratitude or camaraderie, Smetka would shy away. He'd seen Smetka angry only once, when he insisted Reffie leave his pipe in their locker room and Reffie had objected that the pipe was already out and besides he never lit it underground. "All the more reason you don't need it with you then, and *I* want you to leave it

· 21 ·

here!" Smetka had flashed. The two men had stood staring at each other, astonished at the emotion released by the incident. After a moment Reffie had shrugged, laid down his pipe. They'd headed for the cage, already crowded with miners, descending the three thousand feet in silence.

It was Smetka who'd first taught him how to work in the hard rock. When Reffie and Julia and the kids had arrived after the long drive from Seattle, with fourteen dollars in his pocket, Reffie had parked the old Ford in front of what was to be their rented row house for the season and headed for Silver Valley to talk to the boss. Before the week was out Reffie was underground, working.

Almost from his first day in the mine he and Smetka had worked well together. Smetka was quiet and brooding, with a shy smile which came and went around his mouth, while Reffie thought of himself as vocal and angry. He could not forget that Gramp had been an embattled union man in his day, and when he went into the underground city of silver and zinc and lead he could not remain silent. Smetka, on the other hand, who had worked in the mine for years, had learned patience. His temper remained unruffled in spite of Reffie's obvious lack of experience; he was willing to share with Reffie his hard-won knowledge. He showed Reffie his own heavy waterproof boots and told him where he might buy a pair "pretty reasonable," warned him against wandering away by himself to adjoining tunnels, offered to let Reffie watch him until Reffie had learned for himself how to stope and pillar the walls, how to handle the drill. On the very first day he'd taken time out from his own work to show Reffie how to timber a ceiling, using the great logs from the nearby stands of fir. Smetka pointed out with quiet pride that the logs had been treated with the best fire-resistant oil preservative on the market, a technique Smetka himself had persuaded the company to use, and was now used all the time. Above all Smetka had taught him how to drill a hole for explosives, how to set the dynamite and handle misfires: to learn to detonate a misfire, Smetka swore, was the sacred secret of survival.

But there were still some things—Reffie grimly admitted—that Smetka had been unable to teach him, and that was how to breathe in temperatures of a hundred and ten degrees, how to keep his eyes clear of the sweat which ran down his brow. And how to become resigned to his work. He went underground every day hoping the next day would be better, that he would become used to it, that something would happen to the economy so that he could buy some sheep or work the land again, so that Julia would not altogether run out of the hope that their marriage would bring her what he had promised.

He and Smetka were part of a six-man crew who usually worked together at an excavation, each man's skill supplementing that of the others. But since Reffie and Smetka worked so well as a team, the other men in their crew would often work another area of the tunnel, returning now and again to let them know when the explosive had been set and the area was to be evacuated. They would then have to stay out of the area for at least thirty minutes, until the fumes had diffused. At such times he and Smetka would switch to another part of the tunnel, either loading ore into the skip hoist for the smelter or sometimes just working together at the mindless job of shovelling waste rock used to stabilize the walls in stoping and pillaring. While stoping a new wall face they were careful to leave the arched pillars created by the excavation work: the arched pillars helped support the tunnel walls, prevented rockbursts. Working together, he and Smetka had never had a rockburst. Reffie believed this was because Smetka was the soul of caution. A modest man, Smetka merely said of himself that he might not be an engineer, but he knew a shaky pillar when he saw one.

But on this particular day, in spite of Smetka's usual precautions, due perhaps to the tremendous heat generated by the drilling of a new vein above them, there had been a rockburst: The pillars had caved in, and although neither Reffie nor Smetka had been hurt, their access to the first entry shaft was totally blocked by fallen rock. In spite of the dim light, Reffie could see the faint blue veins laminating the volcanic stone.

Smetka had remained calm. On the other side of the crumbled pillar were the rest of the crew. Reffie could still hear their voices, at least he thought they were voices; the roar of the rockburst had left a ringing in his ears. In spite of his faith in Smetka, Reffie's heart was pounding with fear. He assured himself that Smetka knew every raise and winze of the mine; he had spent most of his adult life here in this subterranean city. But as he and Smetka stood aside waiting for the final convulsion of dust and rubble, Reffie began to understand that the crumbled pillar had not only cut off access to the entry shaft but had shut off air from the surface fans ventilating the tunnels through the two shafts. Now one of their funnels of air had been tamped shut.

Smetka was not one to panic. He knew his way to the other shaft. Also, he reminded Reffie, the miners on the other side of the crumbled pillar still had access to the first entry shaft. They would alert the rescue team; the elevator cage would be waiting for Smetka and Reffie when they reached the other shaft.

"But we have to *get* to it," said Smetka. "And fast."

Their flashlights were in perfect condition, so they were able to see well enough at first; they flooded the steam-wet walls with light as they headed for a drift which Smetka said would lead them to the second shaft. "The thing is to keep calm. Try to breathe shallow."

Reffie tried to *breathe shallow*. Their flashlights played along the walls. They were now wading through muddy water, but he was not surprised. Though Reffie's own tunnels were usually dry underfoot, he'd seen the miners working with hoses, the water vapor saturating their raincoats and billed caps, the temperatures climbing to a hundred and twenty. . . .

They approached a drift which led to an exit tunnel. At the end of the tunnel was a ladder, which would bring them to the next level. From there, Smetka said, the cage elevator would be waiting for them, the emergency alarm would have been sounded, rescue teams would be ready at the surface. They would lift the cage elevator at double the maximum speed: risky but necessary. As they stooped to enter the rarely used drift—only the stoped-out pillars were left behind for support—a piping sound, like a pair of whistles, stopped them. Smetka played his flashlight toward the ground. Several terrified mice were plunging headlong down a slight incline. They seemed at first to be merely awkwardly slipping in the clayey deposits; but then one of them gave a desperate leap into the air, shuddered with convulsions and died.

"Suffocated. Carbon monoxide . . . We can't go by way of that drift," Smetka said grimly. Quickly he made a U-turn. *He knew the mine*, his body assured Reffie. They climbed up another ladder, ran as fast as they dared across a drift. The heat seemed to melt their flesh; the sweat ran down their bodies like rain. Smetka threw off his waterproof, then his shirt, leaving his chest bare. In the midst of his deadly fear Reffie noted how thin Smetka's chest was—*nothing but skin and bone*—yet he'd seen Smetka work with a drill that must have been a third of his own weight. That he should be noticing such a thing, a fact quite irrelevant to their survival, was somehow frightening. Their most urgent need was to remain rational, yet these useless thoughts flew about like chickenfeathers. As they crawled through an abandoned excavation, the walls seemed to darken. Reffie could feel the sweat on him, not of heat but of fear. It was a hell of a way to die, thought Reffie, and a homesick longing for his Texas landscape hit him in the midst of a sudden fit of coughing. Then he saw that Smetka had tied a handkerchief across his mouth. Reffie did the same; but it only seemed to make things worse: It trapped the sweat rolling down his face.

But worse than the heat was the strange silence. They were accustomed to drills vibrating, periodic explosions of dynamite. But now there was nothing, not a sound. If there was a rescue party set in motion, if there were sirens above ground screeching to a stop, if there were medics anxiously waiting with ambulances and oxygen, they could hear none of it. He began to fear that the men on the other side of the caved-in pillar had not, after all, been able to walk away from the rockburst to report that Reffie and Smetka were cut off. Perhaps they too at this moment were asphyxiating. Smetka was choking for breath; Reffie tried to keep his own breathing shallow and regular. But they had to move fast, nearly running, and he was forced to open his mouth to pant. The possibility of carbon monoxide in the air made it unsafe to slow down. Yet abruptly Smetka stopped, he seemed confused.

The possibility that Smetka could get lost had astonishingly not occurred to Reffie: confused, but not lost. He waited to hear Smetka assure him that it was impossible to be lost, but Smetka could not speak, he was vomiting.

"Keep going. I'll come later." Smetka leaned against the face of the hanging wall. He pointed toward a fresh vertical cut in the wall face. "They must be working that new vein they found up above us. Push yourself through there . . . then along about twenty feet to your right ought to be another ladder. That'll take you to a loading station. You can come get me. . . ."

Reffie did not waste breath arguing. He managed to push Smetka ahead of him through the fresh cut in the hanging wall. Then with tears of relief he saw that Smetka did indeed know his mine: A new vein was being opened a few yards from the ladder. But the ladder now rose above them, nearly a hundred feet. Looking up, the parallel lines with crossing iron rungs seemed to take on a life of their own, to shift threateningly before his eyes, a grim, ominous leaning tower. Reffie removed his belt from his waist and looped it through Smetka's belt. Smetka opened his eyes momentarily, managed to support himself to the first rung of the ladder. Reffie moved ahead of him, up the ladder, gripping the belt, his hands wet with sweat. Slowly, rung by rung, using his own body as a winch around which he held the belt fast to himself, he helped Smetka upward, a human bucket hoisted like ore in a skip hoist from out of that eternal dark. When, at the top of the ladder Reffie's head reached the loading level, he felt a strong surge of air coming in from the second shaft. Blessed air, more vital than an ocean breeze, surged through the tunnel.

Smetka was still breathing when he laid him in the rail-car. The car made its way down the tracks, maintaining a maddeningly steady pace as if it were carrying a load of waste rock. Reffie tried cooling Smetka down with his shirt, but he himself was so near collapse that it seemed he was merely flailing at Smetka with his sweat-soaked shirt, not helping. When the loading car came out of the tunnel, he and Smetka were lying side by side. Reffie did not even hear the cheers of the waiting men.

Afterwards Reffie tortured himself with the question of whether he might have saved Smetka if he had thought of a better way of moving him up the ladder. But the company doctor said that Reffie could have done nothing—that Smetka's heart had simply stopped. The miners said it was heatstroke. They'd seen it many times.

For weeks after Smetka's death Reffie thought of quitting the mine and going back to Texas, come what may. The stunned, mute faces of Smetka's widow and children when he passed them in the street hurt him as if they had been his own kids. Still, he was angered also by what seemed to him their resignation to grief, as if suffering were meant to be their lot until the Millenium. Until that time, there was nothing for them to do but bury the dead. There had been some insurance, which bore the cost of the funeral and had even resulted in a macabre stylishness in the children, who appeared for a while in their new clothes purchased for the funeral.

But Reffie was finding it hard, for weeks after Smetka's death, to fall asleep nights. Lying on his back, staring at the slant of street light that knifed down from the window shade, his stomach tightened with dread and longing for home. It was one thing, he thought, to talk about dying some day far in the future when you're old and feeble; what had stunned him was the speed and waste of

Smetka's death—the trembling of walls without warning, pillars pulled from their foundations and collapsing as if uprooted by tornadoes. After several weeks of useless brooding and broken sleep, he decided he'd have to risk some money and make a trip back home. Maybe now that the drought had passed over and the grasshoppers had ceased their infernal incantations, he might be thinking about getting another parcel of land. Overriding Julia's objections—"throwing good money after bad"—he took the long bus ride down home, stopping off at a realty company that he recalled Ephraim having dealt with once, about fifty miles from Salinas. The place had a sign out advertising special rates for Texas veterans, and was known in the area to have an inside track on uncultivated land. Reffie introduced himself calmly and confidently—after all he was back home—implying that he would be very interested in seeing some of these lots of raw land he'd heard about. The man behind the desk promptly handed Reffie his card bearing the information that he was Vernon Turner, Senior Sales Representative for Lamar Realty. He was cordial and appreciative of Reffie's interest, and said he wouldn't mind driving Reffie out to some excellent lots the Lamar Company had laid out less than an hour's drive from here. It was what they called a "wild ranch"—the land having once belonged, all tens of thousands of acres of it, to a single family. There were still several lots left in the division, he said, but they were being bought up like hotcakes by the VietVets. The way Turner said VietVets, it sounded to him like a nationality, like German or Czech.

In Turner's silver Toyota they drove farther than Reffie would ever have figured necessary. The trip seemed to prolong itself by some subtle rule of economics by which "raw land," a persistently fleeing phantom, evaded them mile after mile. At least, Reffie hoped, the farther they drove from Salinas the lower the price would be. But the long drive itself turned out to be a serious and delicate operation during which Reffie was to have his head trepanned and laid back so that Turner might pour in the latest astonishing information about The Phenomenon of the Eighties. Reffie sat silently listening, torn between his eagerness to know and his anxiety about knowing; but what he finally understood was that while he had been bursting hardrock at the C & L Silver-Lead & Zinc Company, the land which he had sold off at a loss was now becoming as sought after as oil, due to the remarkable population-shift from the industrial Northeast. But not as land to grow food on. Reffie had thought when he stood beside his barn, watching them auction off his farm along with that of his nearest neighbor, making an enviable doubling of acreage for the buyer, that his land would be taken over by the big farmers, the ones who, unlike himself, banks were friendly toward and ever ready to lend money to so that the big farmer could produce more and more with his ever more expensive and productive machinery. It had seemed at that time that there would be no limit as to how big the more fortunate farmers might grow. In spite of the high interest rates, they could borrow to the moon if they wanted to. It had never occurred to Reffie that one day they too might have to be bought out by the real estate developers. He had never dreamed that the land could get to be worth more with nothing growing on it. He had never conceived of the strange phenomenon Turner described, of levelling bulldozers and sheetrock walls and concrete driveways and "Parades" of homes sponsored annually by the real estate people. Suddenly it appeared to Reffie as he scanned the highway on the right and left that the realtors had flattened every furrow from Salinas to the border. They were excavating whole new villages called Buckingham Square, Shamrock Heights, Westminister Abbey Park and Darien's Peak Village (Reffie couldn't find any heights, parks or peaks in these deserts from which they'd bulldozed every tree, but their names were meaningless to him anyway). What amazed him was that the once rich and splendid land they were driving past (exceeding the speed limit), would never again be available to small farmers like himself who wanted to grow some corn and beets and maybe even some okra, and raise a few cattle. Now as Turner recounted recent events, Reffie wrestled with the concept that high-tech, as Turner called it, had seized the imagination and money of the Texas marketplace. Every man, woman and child, apparently, wanted to be within commuting distance of airports so that they could fly to Dallas or Houston or San Antonio to wheel-and-deal in Hi-Tech, Oil, and Real Estate.

All this talk was making Reffie feel as out of date as a farmer plowing with a mule. With the momentum of space technology, his time had passed. It was bitter news for a man who, when Turner had parked the car and they began walking toward the wire fence that measured off the parcels of land, felt his legs wanting to lope around the land like animals that had been set loose; bitter news for a man who had chopped cotton for extra money, and had watered his okra by hand to conserve water; and who, once during an unseasonable frost, had kept vigil for over thirty-six hours, protecting the young crops from cold, as if they had been children needing blankets and tarpaulins.

As they walked around the land, Reffie listened in silence while Turner—dressed faultlessly in classic Western style—jeans and boots and carved leather belt with silver buckle and a spotless Stetson—explained it all to him. There were actually two tracts of land—one for the Viet-Vets who got their special price, interest rates, and payment schedules allowed them by the State. They'd done their bit for their country and they deserved *that* much, didn't they? Then the other tract was reserved for folks like you and me who might want an extra home. And every lot as Reffie could see had been properly surveyed and fenced off from the others, so there'd be no possibility of confusion as to which was whose. Turner, without yet mentioning the hard facts of money, went on to point out the possible uses for the property:

"Terrific for a dove shoot, lots of dove around here, and you'll find plenty of deer during the hunting season. A wonderful place to get away from the city on weekends."

Not for growing food anymore, thought Reffie, but a place of relaxation for gentlemen from the cities.

Turner at last turned to the subject of money. He described how for about thirty-five hundred dollars Reffie could get a well dug. "But maybe you wouldn't want the land cleared anyway. Maybe you're thinking of it as a place to camp, to rough it with the kids, you know. You could pitch your tent here and the deer will come right up to your stakes."

For some reason the increased urbanity of Turner's voice frightened Reffie. The moment of truth was approaching. He knew he was about to hear exactly what the terms of purchase would be. Reffie took out his little notebook and began to jot down the figures as Turner let them fall into the conversation; softly and invisibly as dust they came down until at last their whole dialogue lay saturated with numbers. Even as Reffie scrawled and added, he knew with despair that it would all cost more than he could save in years.

"Twenty thousand for the land, and then the taxes and the closing costs, and thirty-five hundred for the well, that is of course if you decide to clear the land, though to be honest, clear it or not you have to have water. . . . You can get help pretty cheap, but that's not exactly like it used to be, you know, there's the minimum wage nowadays. But if you were thinking of building a house by yourself—are you handy with tools?—right about *there*, it'd be the perfect spot for one of those old-style houses, you know like Frank Dobie had at Paisano, you ever see it?"

Reffie shook his head sadly, lowering his eyes before Turner's eyes, dark and penetrating as wasps, that were forcing from him these embarrassing confessions of ignorance. No, he didn't think he was exactly the one for building his own house, he wasn't all that much of a handyman.

"Well," conceded Turner good-naturedly, "there's a system to everything, I guess. You got to know what you're doin'. You got to know even which way a tree's goin' to fall so's it won't fall on you." Having now admitted the possibility and extent of Reffie's ignorance, Turner seemed to feel he had said too much and became abruptly silent.

Reffie stood clenching and unclenching the knitted cap Julia had made for him, feeling farther and farther removed from the purpose of his trip.

"I want to take a good look at it," he managed finally to say, adding in the hope of getting rid of Turner altogether, "It's not so far to the access road. I'll walk to the nearest gas station and call some friends of mine—they live not too far away from here. They'll come get me to the airport. I want to walk around and take a good look at the lot . . . before I sign anything." Reffie looked away, refusing to take in Turner's perturbations. It was clearly not acceptable to Turner, he couldn't leave a client out here by himself. But recovering his good manners, Turner declared he had a few errands himself to run; for one thing, he had another land-division to check out about eight miles from here. "I'd have to be coming back this way anyway. I'll pick you up on my way back. In about an hour? Synchronize our watches," he added with good humor.

There was clear relief in his face when Reffie nodded assent. Maybe if somebody tripped over some dried-out old mesquite and broke a leg, he wouldn't be Senior Sales Representative anymore, thought Reffie resentfully, and was surprised at the feeling of loneliness which was already coming over him as Turner shook hands and assured him that as little as five hundred hand money would hold the lot for him, and even the interest rates were not always absolute. "These things are adjustable, you know. . . ."

Reffie didn't know, but he said nothing; he was tired of admitting his ignorance. He stood watching as Turner picked his way to the parked car through scrub brush and rock and withered mesquite. (If there is water under all this, mocked Reffie silently, it must be as deep as a C & L silver lode). Then he turned his back on Turner before the Toyota was out of sight.

Reffie paced slowly around the lot—raw land, which in no way resembled the richness of the land he had managed to revive after Ephraim's death. But everything had been so different then—even, it seemed to him now as he looked up at the sky, even the clouds had been different. As a boy he'd wakened to a sky radiant with great cumulus clouds billowing out. They were like newly discovered continents, those clouds, you looked up and you felt you could sail into them, colonize them, they could become the New World. And then across the road from Ephraim's land, there had been another farmer—Fowler his name was—who had let his fields go for sunflowers, considered rather unusual back then, and not so profitable as nowadays since folks had discovered they were good for your health. And Reffie would cross the road—a road then, and not a highway—and climb the fence around Fowler's sunflowers, just waiting for himself to wake up. He'd always waked up slowly, it was his weakness, he guessed; it was like he needed the sky and the sound of morning birds for him to be truly awake. And he'd sit there, just looking at the sunflowers. The dew would be still visible on the rough leaves, but drying quickly, leaving a memory of moisture like the memory of someone you loved who was now grown and gone. What he marvelled at now was, that as a boy it had not occurred to him there was anything remarkable in those golden mobiles which bent and stirred and bowed as they carried on their eternal surge upward and the invisible life of the roots. What he'd been more attuned to, so early in the morning, had been the rustling and morning cries of birds. Like a changing of the guard it was, the nightbirds hushing and the doves and sparrows beginning to flutter into action.

When he'd sucked the last drop of juice from his peach, he would fling the peachstone as far as he could among the sunflowers; then recrossing the road, he'd head for the barn. It was his chore to let the cows out for the day. Folks might laugh at him but he had loved the smell of that barn; it had had the odor of life, its pungent freshness had been as pleasant to him as starlight. Maybe more so. A man could survive the clouding over of the sky at night, or survive a tornado even, but without the earth churning with unseen life you'd grow nothing but mesquite and stones, like this withered plot of land Turner was selling.

So he'd learned to respect the worm and human waste, a respect he never could explain to the miners, not even to Smetka. You couldn't describe feelings like that to other people, so you didn't talk about it: the haying, for instance. How proud of himself he'd been at his first haying—not yet sixteen years old, but just as tall as the fully grown men in the crew. From early morning until sundown they'd worked in the blazing heat, nobody even wearing a shirt, their bodies filmed over with a gauzy sweat like the wings of dragonflies. They didn't bring in the hay like that anymore—machines did it all.

His mind was playing tricks . . . everything coming back. Maybe it was being out here, walking around the land, hoping Turner would forget to look at his watch. . . . Like he could see clear as day Ephraim buying that one gray Brahma bull, it was enough to make you laugh till you cried. He'd paid a small fortune for the bugger, but Ephraim always complained that the Brahma hadn't caught on to his work, though he and Reffie would go out to the bull every day and rub his great genial hump the way you used to rub a hunchback, for the luck of it, and encourage the dour-looking old fellow, reminding him he was there to make more of his kind. But that old Brahma would just stare at them with his angry eyes. Their nearest neighbor had come to their farm to see the new bull and had commented wryly that though he knew Ephraim hadn't bought the bull for his high I.Q., still—this one didn't seem to know what Ephraim had paid such a high price for. Reffie's mother, rest her soul, had just gone on pickling okra at these remarks. She'd had to pickle it because God knows it wouldn't sell. The market for okra was very unstable; an advertising campaign by a big Louisiana packing company aiming to get Yankees to like okra had failed. Soon it was a pure luxury for them to grow it, since usually they ate most of it themselves. Pickled or fried, his mother could fix it fit for a Cajun prince. Ephraim said he didn't care—they weren't going to survive off okra anyway. For "the Duration," Ephraim had said, they were going to survive by sheep.

Reffie always thought that it was the grazing sheep that had ruined the farm, even before he'd inherited it. Ephraim had decided to buy enough sheep so that his farm work would seem to his draft board an indispensable contribution to the War Effort, and Ephraim would be allowed to stay on the farm and fight the war at home. The Allies needed wool. Wasn't it a fact that Napoleon had lost his war fighting the Russian winter? This idea was Ephraim's successful ploy for survival. The U.S. Army had in fact needed wool, and Ephraim was reclassified. But the sheep, and the goats that Ephraim had later experimented with, had cropped the land so close that when, after Ephraim's death Reffie took over the farm, and later the drought came, there was barely a bush for the dry land to shelter itself under. The world around them simply burned up; the creeks dried into lacerated gullies; the corn fell like armies into dust. Every living thing on the whole farm had seemed to ignite as the sun poured down. He had not panicked though, Reffie thought as he kicked a stone around on Turner's land, justifying himself now to unseen critics. He had inherited the farm; therefore he had told himself that he must also save what was his.

He had faith in neighborliness, and for several years, whenever it was necessary, he had shared the water with his neighbor, Salim. Salim's well had been dug long before the Iranian had bought the land, and his well was in much better shape than Reffie's; the proximity of their two properties had been a source of mutual friendship rather than suspicion, especially during the Year-without-rain, as they afterwards referred to it, when Reffie's well went completely dry. After all, Salim said, they'd been neighbors for many years now; for a nominal fee they would share the water from his well. So long as he had enough water for his cows and for himself, Salim said, he wasn't worried; on the other hand, it was clear to him that Reffie was trying to protect the future of his family. Salim said he understood that very well; he'd grown up among many sisters and brothers in a large family. But since the Revolution, he dared not go back even to visit his parents. As he spoke, he watched Reffie's face anxiously, as if he feared Reffie might be angry with him for mixing politics with water. But Reffie had trouble relating something at once so vast and vague as a revolution with his neighbor. When the Wingfields had first learned that their new neighbor was an Iranian, Roseanne had looked up the location of Salim's homeland on a map, and the Wingfields were surprised to find that Iran was really Persia, a land Tamsen said was famous for carpets and fairy tales.

So in spite of the heavy grasshopper infestation that also came during that time—it was as if the hopping devils could smell disaster in the cornfields, and knew when Reffie would be too distracted to fight back—the farm might have pulled through with help from Salim's well. But Reffie had not taken into account the suspicions of other people who were angry with Salim for obscure reasons, nor the intense hatred for Salim and all his countrymen which had stirred up among the thousands of students from the neighboring universities, all of whom lived within an easy nightride from Salim's farm. The students dedicated themselves to hunting down their Enemy. The fire and energy which ten or twenty years earlier would have been burnt up in fraternity hazing or panty-raids, suddenly turned into political passions. The young people wanted to show each other how intensely they reciprocated the hatred of a country whose terrifying hatred of the United States had been experienced for months on television. Warnings painted in red began to appear on Salim's barn, telling him to go back where he came from; he received anonymous letters and threatening phone calls, calling him a Disciple of Satan. The impassioned young people organized raids; they cut Salim's chicken wire fences; they slashed the tires of his pickup truck; they poured bags of sugar into his gas tank. Still, Salim continued his work—milking his dairy cows, mending his fences, and buying new tires for his pickup while he tried to adjust to the new reality—that after having lived in the United States ten years and become a U.S. citizen, he was now again an alien. He painted and repainted his barn, he enrolled in a nightschool course in English as a Second Language, hoping to correct or at least minimize his foreign accent. But nothing worked. They knew who he was and nothing could change their opinion of him. Again and again, with passionate conviction they cut his fences; his cows wandered lost and bellowing; his two best milkers were found dead on the highway. Salim began at last to consider selling his farm and moving to San Antonio where, hidden away among a large Mexican-American population, many of whom were nearly as dark as himself, he might pass unnoticed. But while he was deliberating, his enemies discovered their ultimate weapon. During the night a couple of daring raiders cut through the new barbed wire (the struggle had escalated from chicken wire to barbed wire), and poured chlordane and bags of lye down his well.

On the day Samil discovered this destruction, he marched over to Reffie's farmhouse. Julia, Reffie recalled, had been standing near the mimosa when Samil approached.

"You know what they did? You will not believe it," he reported in a breaking voice. "It's too much. I can't take no more. I'm going to move away."

That morning it had become clear to them all that Samil's enemies had wiped out not only Samil's future, but Reffie's as well. After a long day's talk, they had agreed it might be a good idea for both to sell out together. Maybe by doubling their acreage and putting it all up for auction together, they could get a fair bid from some big farmer who wanted to deal in grain or soybeans.

"But anyway, we'll have to keep in touch," said Reffie reassuringly. "If I hear of something for you out West. . . ."

"That's right. That's right. We keep in touch," murmured Samil. As they stood up they all shook hands, as if they were already saying goodbye.

Several months after auctioning off the land, they had heard again from Samil. He was waiting on tables at a fine tourist-type restaurant in San Antonio, he wrote. He was earning a good living. It was better than farming. Nobody killed off your livestock. Instead, Samil wrote, the cook cooked them, Samil served them, and people ate them. He reminded Reffie that they must keep in touch: "A mountain cannot go to a mountain," he concluded, "but two people can always meet."

But these soothing proverbs which give you an illusion of comfort while your life is breaking up, Reffie considered resentfully as he stood at the edge of Turner's property watching a couple of idly hopping grasshoppers, were not really much help after your life has actually fallen apart. His back was still hurting him from the long bus ride, and indifferent now as to whether he might yet manage to appear to Turner like a gentleman-farmer looking for rough relaxation in the country, he sat down amid the dust and stones, leaning his back against a fencepost. He noticed that the grasshoppers were not hopping with much energy; they barely reached his knees. Reffie stretched out his hand and caught one; he was surprised at his own gesture—almost friendly, he thought, like a man in a dungeon making a pet of anything alive, even a cricket or a mouse. He held the insect, examining it as if for the first time—its furiously jackknifing legs, its delicately plated abdomen laid together like a phalanx of shields. And how the grasshopper fought him—the enemy—with fear and fury. Its legs lashed out, tiny machines leaping into the void; its abdomen curled and lashed; it wanted to live. You saw how much it wanted to live. The damnfool thing is fighting to live out its allotted time . . . maybe until sunset, thought Reffie. For a while he sat with the grasshopper between his cupped hands, felt the insect beat against his palms like a throbbing heart. After a while he dropped it, chiding himself for his foolishness; but from the corner of his eye he continued to watch it. Feebly it hopped a few feet and stopped. Something had been broken. It rested under a twig, immobile but alert, its antennae sweeping the air.

When Turner arrived Reffie was still sitting with his back against the fencepost watching the grasshopper. Turner's friendliness had evaporated; he was anxious now, Reffie saw, to get rid of Reffie, to cut his losses and begin the struggle to sell the parcel of land all over again. The sheer repetitiveness of this struggle struck Reffie. It's like we're all in the mine, he thought, without anger now either at Turner or the grasshopper.

He thought himself resigned to everything until the next morning as he boarded the bus back to Silver Valley. It was a morning radiant as sunflowers; cumulus clouds glided like white gondolas across a sea of sky. It was the most glorious sky in the world, he believed, and he believed too, with terrible bitterness, that he would probably never see it again.

All the way back to Kellogg he sat hunched in a corner of the bus, unable even to curse, numb with loss. Like Samil, he couldn't take anymore, he was moving away.

III

When Tamsen had told Woodrow that she hated *J.W. (Julia Wingfield)*, he had looked at her in wonder. Like a child, he'd wanted to know *why*. Tamsen shrugged, as if she had some special knowledge. No *as if* about it, she had special knowledge. She described to him Roseanne, *their* mother, who seemed not to be the same mother that Woody remembered.

"You're dumb," Tamsen scoffed. "You never remember anything. You don't even remember her."

"I do. I do remember. She had sort of honey-colored hair."

"*Sort* of," jeered Tamsen savagely. "That's how much you know."

Then, feeling sorry for his ignorance she would construct a portrait for him. Even Tamsen was aware that her portrait was more illustrative than factual. She felt she might be embroidering the truth slightly, but denied that she was inventing. You couldn't invent a mother, you could only describe her. Describing, of course, was totally subjective. She couldn't be held accountable.

Thus when she unrolled her metaphorical charts, catalogues, and illustrations for invidious comparison with Julia, it was easy for her to see who won by a mile. Roseanne had had honey-colored hair, but it was not just the color of honey: it was honey with *sunshine*. She had also had a soft gentle voice which (Tamsen firmly swore) had never once been raised in anger, fear, hysteria or refusal—at least not to *her*, the Firstborn (she eyed Woody suspiciously to see if he might air some sibling grievance at this point; but he merely nodded for her to go on, the way one listens to a story). Roseanne could bake the most delicious biscuits in the world. And when it was pecan time, they would go Knocking Pecans together with the long wooden stick cleft at one end used to prop up the clotheslines. Woodrow widened his eyes at this—he obviously did not remember any pecans at all, not a single one. He shook his head as if at her remarkable if unreliable inventions. But there *were* pecans, Tamsen affirmed testily, wanting to shake Woody as if he were a pecan branch. They fell like bronze nuggets from the trees, all you had to do was fill up your apron and carry them home. She recklessly omitted from this scenario the endless hours at the kitchen table cracking the nuts, then tediously extracting the last stubborn piece of nutmeat with a metal pick, neat and precise as a dentist's drill. After all this wonderful excitement, which you shared with the other beaters *who were usually black*—she pointed out this detail solemnly, as if here were the real Continental Divide separating Them from Us—you carried your treasures home and Roseanne Buford Wingfield— *your mother*—would create a pecan pie which had no more resemblance to pies up here than their black volcanic rock to the luminous red clay of Salinas.

Tamsen had turned away from Woody in disdain. "What could you hope for from a kid who didn't remember his own mother?" she asked the unseen audience.

"That's not fair!" Woodrow objected with tears in his eyes. He was remorseful and furious, partly because (truthfully) he didn't spend much time thinking about Roseanne Wingfield. Mostly he just enjoyed remembering the honey-colored hair.

"It's that you're *willing* to forget," Tamsen scolded. She didn't want him to forget. She had become furious with him when, on their way to Seattle, before they were dumped *here*, he'd climbed into the front seat beside Julia, leaning against her like an itty-bitty baby, while the *real* baby, Joshua, slept beside Tamsen in the back seat. It was hard for her to decide whom she'd detested more at those moments, baby Joshua with his infinitely angelic fatuous smile or Woody who laughed every time Julia pretended to "punch him out" (it was a game they'd invented, as if he'd actually had the breath knocked out of him, which was ridiculous because Woody was a big heavy kid and Julia hardly twig-sized).

Tamsen could have put up with that, but there were other grievances. As soon as they'd arrived in Seattle where her father thought he had a job lined up, Reffie had left Julia and the kids to stand gazing at Puget Sound, waiting for him the whole afternoon. On the wharf, Julia and Woody had at once conspired together in their child-ish enthusiasms, Woody never ceasing to admire the sea and the waterfront and the hills and the seagulls and the new buildings and above all the boardwalk (like they didn't have an ocean in Galveston Bay!) They'd waited and waited while Reffie went to see the timber man who was supposed to hire Reffie in a sawmill or something, Tamsen wasn't sure, and Josh had begun to cry and the sun had clouded over and for a minute or two it had looked like real rain, and *still* Woody had persisted in his pestiferous exclamations of delight over the steamships and cargoes heading for Alaska and the Orient and espe-cially the ferries, standing like patient dromedaries in the Sound, portaging a city full of passengers and cars.

They'd got hungry as bears, waiting in the salt-scented air, watching the seagulls eat popcorn and potato chips and peanuts and bits of bread tossed to them by tourists from faraway places who could never have suspected how hungry *they* were. Julia had some sandwiches in a shop-ping bag (which Tamsen resentfully recognized as the same straw bag Reffie had brought back as a gift from Mexico some years back, and which Roseanne used to take to the General Store). But when Tamsen had suggested they step away from the waterfront and have a bite to eat themselves, Woody had objected, saying it was terrific here with the sea and the ships and all and Julia had backed him up, adding, "Well, probably we ought to wait for Reffie anyway before we eat, and besides it'd never do to take out our sandwiches here. The gulls," she laughed, "are hungrier than we are, and would snatch the food right out of our hands." Tamsen hadn't seen anything so funny about that. She was hungry. And it only made her angrier when, an hour or so later, they did withdraw to a secluded pier away from the seagulls because Woodrow confessed that he too was starving. So Julia and Tamsen and Woody had finally eaten their sandwiches while Little Boy Blue sucked on his bottle and blinked at the sunlight. When Josh began to cry Julia looked nervously at the sky, but it hadn't seemed likely to rain. She changed the baby in the open air and they again settled down for a long wait. Woodrow continued his rhapsodies. They were going to rent a house right here in the city—he fantasized— and he'd learn to sail and also he'd bicycle right around the rim of the Sound. He'd even spotted a hilly road which he was eager to explore at once—but Julia had pleaded with him to remain by her side until Reffie came back (though she had no idea how long *that* would be, she added forlornly), and Woody had instantly obeyed her. It was clear to Tamsen that Woody regarded Julia as their lawful guardian; he obeyed her always. What Tamsen couldn't forgive was that he also loved her. But Woody loved everything.

It was true that if there had ever been a place Tamsen could substitute for Salinas, it might have been this ocean. There was ground for Woody's enthusiasm. What turned her stomach was the apostolic tone, like he was speaking in tongues. Yeah, the water was great, it wheedled you to forget. The sun on it must be like what making love was like, all that quivering on the undulant sea. The very sound of it, stroking the pier seemed to offer solace: You could get used to the death of the world. *Sleep*, it soughed, *forget, forgive*. All afternoon they sat on the bench, their bodies absorbing the silken air. It felt rather like butterflies nudging you with their wings as they alighted and flew away. Dozing, you could forget the desert land you had left. You could begin to believe that with so much water, there was bound to be maybe another Great Flood, one which would not destroy but revive—a watery resurrection after the Bomb.

The sky was so bright it was like something moral; full of cleanliness and virtue, it reflected kindliness and compassion, it said nothing of storms and eclipses and the multitudes who had dissolved in the sea. It made to them all the fraudulent promise that life would now be e-a-s-y, e-a-s-y.

They had almost accepted this fraudulent promise when a squall came up. Suddenly the skies darkened, the winds blew dust, and paper cups left behind by tourists rolled around the pier. Frightened, Julia looked around for Reffie. Their momentary refuge, Tamsen saw, had been an illusion, their silken-skied Paradise was soon to become the eye of a storm; the sea began rocking, not tenderly but threateningly; the choppy waves cast themselves against the pier.

"We'll have to wait in a restaurant on the wharf, where we can keep a sharp eye out for Reffie."

They kept a sharp eye out, while the storm hurled drops as big as lanterns against their window. Julia opened a menu as if to consider what they would order for dinner. But the waiter remained aloof, he'd seen all this before. A woman with three half-washed tired-looking kids was not likely to order Smoked Salmon, Indian Style. Tamsen began reading the menu aloud, astonished at the high prices. In embarrassment Julia turned toward the window. She began watching a young man on the pier who was struggling to secure his boat against the high winds. Her gaze became intense, as if there were something familiar about him. *She's not thinking about us at all*, thought Tamsen with bitterness. Tamsen too looked out. The young man wore blue jogging shorts with gold trim, and a white T-shirt. To balance himself on the pier he had wrapped his legs around the heavy rope; the throbbing rain soaked his thin shirt; through the drenched cloth Tamsen could see the wet whorled hair on his chest. He bowed his head for a moment; now only his legs were visible, thick as tree trunks, the muscles sculptured lianas. Then he raised his head again, flushed with the effort; he smiled happily at Julia and Tamsen who had shared his triumph.

Startled, Julia turned quickly away. "Probably never been sick a day in his life," she murmured in a tone of awe and envy.

At that moment Woodrow spotted Reffie. He was walking like a sonambulist, heedless of the rain. He wore no cap, having forgotten it that morning in his haste to see the sawmill owner. His hair was sopping wet. His poplin jacket was zipped to the throat, his hands were shoved akimbo into his pockets, a manly pose which Tamsen had always admired. He was obviously headed in the direction of the place he'd left them at earlier, because he wasn't looking at anyone and didn't know he was being looked at. Tamsen regarded with shock this person who only a year or two earlier had been for her the godlike Cortés on horseback. There was a strange new look on his face which, because Tamsen had never seen it on Reffie before, took her a moment to recognize: It was the distracted look of fear, she'd seen it once on the face of a schoolmate about to fail a final exam. His eyes were dark and brooding; it seemed to Tamsen that he would willingly have lain down in the waterfront and been dissolved in the rain.

But when he caught sight of Julia and the children at the window his mouth softened, he pulled his head back as though someone had playfully punched him, and tried to smile. He ran in, dripping rain over everyone as he sat down at the table. The waiter came again. He murmured that all he wanted was coffee. The waiter snapped the menu shut and brought him a cup of black coffee, spilling some of it on the table. At home her father would have poured half a cup of milk in with his coffee, but here he meekly drank the black liquid, not asking for anything. Why he's just grateful we're not getting thrown out, thought Tamsen with surprise.

Julia tried to question him. "How did things go?"

Reffie swallowed his coffee before answering. It was clear to them all that nothing had gone well. He'd spent all day going from place to place. Everywhere he'd heard the same explanations: layoffs, shutdowns, housing and lumber industry at an all-time low, loggers furloughed.

Looking frightened, Julia asked, avoiding Tamsen's stare, "Where will we. . . ."

Her father was silent a long time. At last he said, "Let's go back to the car and talk about it."

They talked until it became suddenly dark, and before Tamsen realized what was happening, Reffie had built a sleeping area for them in the back seat, laying down their packing boxes and suitcases. He covered these with a blanket, laid Josh down in the middle and said: "O.K., Tamsen, you and Julia should be able to keep the baby warm. . . ." It was only then that Tamsen realized they were about to begin living out of their car. But she was so shocked and amazed that she did not utter one word of protest.

How does a family of five with a babe-in-arms live out of a car? To learn how you too may do this, write to Tamsen Wingfield, Box 838, c/o The Kellogg Evening News and she'll tell you (Please enclose SASE.)

First, Tamsen explained to her invisible correspondent you learn how to sleep scrunched up into a ball on your side, facing the window, so that when you absolutely have to shift your position, you won't bang your elbow into the baby who's lying between you and the hapless girl who's married your father. You of course knock your knees and knuckles on the door of the car all night long, every time you move. If the baby cries you try to ignore him, it's not your fault that he's crying, *you* didn't come all the way from Boston just to add to the population problems of The Great Northwest, and if he wets (or whatever) all night long, as he always does, so that you can hardly stand the smell, you wrap a scarf around your mouth and breathe into your own CO_2. You try to resign yourself to all this, though you're burning with resentment because you've already learned that the one thing Julia can't or won't do in the middle of the night is change Josh's diaper: Sometimes, though, she will pick him up and put him as close to her body as possible, so that you get what you might call *temporary relief.*

And remember that if during the night you hear people walk past your car, you cover your head so that (hopefully) they won't see anything in the back seat but a couple of bulky shapes which could be anything—laundry, maybe—of the two men who are asleep sitting up in the front seat. (But that's something the cops are used to. Men are always making these long trips somewhere, sleeping in cars). But the really big problem is not (as you, my dear Friend and Correspondent might think), keeping warm when the temperature may drop thirty degrees overnight, or even that for some reason you're always hungry as a bear during the night so that you long for the refrigerator of Salinas with its funny roundtop head as if it were a lover you could hold in your arms. And not the problem of the street light beaming down in your eye, nor the problem which you could never have been anticipated, that both Woodrow and Reffie have an identically odd peck-pecking snore which resounds through the car like woodpeckers tapping the trees. Nor the obvious fact that if Josh so much as peeps or whimpers, both Julia and yourself are awake at once. Nor even the fact that if a policeman should come by and realize there's a whole family living in the car he is sure to tell your father to go somewhere else (but your father doesn't know where—to a police station, maybe, for parking illegally, or to some public assistance place like the Red Cross or Travelers' Aid and your father would rather die than be such a case for public charity). Nor the problem of the wandering teenager high on drugs, and the superfriendly drunk who taps on the window and says, "Hi there, boss, you got a light?" to both of whom your father shakes his head in silence and again checks the doors to be sure they're locked. Nor the problem of your kid brother beginning to snuffle, which Julia says is nothing to worry about, everybody catches a headcold now and then, and besides Woodrow has no fever—a diagnosis which angers Reffie, it's as if her father wants Julia to be more worried about Woodrow; it's as if he doesn't like it that she seems to think of Woody as practically grownup and able to take care of his own snuffles. Nor the fact that every morning your father goes looking for work, leaving them all to wait in the park, and Julia to worry that Woody will wander away and get lost and that then Tamsen will have to go fetch Woody and Tamsen will wander away and get lost and then, "What will I say to your father when he comes back and finds his two kids gone?" Nor the fact that for the whole family they bought only one hot meal of fish and chips every day bringing the order back to the car so that they could split them up into two meals, adding to the fish and chips from their own supply of bread or dough-nuts or bananas which they kept in the trunk along with the instant coffee and canned milk to which they added water (Tamsen or Woody being sent to fetch water from a public restroom); nor the fact that when they are all in desperate need of a bath, they are sent in one by one to the Greyhound Bus Terminal with a comb and soap and T-shirt to dry their hair with, and before the eyes of anyone who passed through, to wash their hair and armpits and even their crotches right there in front of the whole world, who stop to gaze with a mixture of surprise and fear, their troubled faces reflected back at you in the mirror. Nor EVEN what you would surely think was the Ultimate Hor-ror: that, when you've endured all the other burdens flesh is heir to (*except one, except one, concerning which, Fair Cor-respondent, for the price of your SASE, you will shortly learn*), you suddenly begin a lunar cycle which for some reason Nature had thoughtfully delayed, doubting perhaps its usefulness to a girl without a pair of pins to pin to her underpants, to say nothing of the shock of knowing that along with everything else you were now to have this to attend to in the public washbasins of the world. And you're utterly dismayed by this new assault even though

Julia soothes and praises you (as if you'd done something clever!) and buys you a belt from a vending machine so you won't have to use pins, and assures you that nothing will show, no one will see any difference (for some reason your face is burning, you feel sick at the thought that now your kid brother will find out you're even more different from himself than he already suspected). And for a moment you let down your guard, you're ready to be grateful (almost) to this girl whom society refers to as Your Mother, a girl like yourself who's also been enduring this sloppy senseless cycle of blood and cramps ever since they left Salinas, and you're even (almost) moved to sympathy as you recall a moment of intense shyness on Julia's part when the two of you seemed about to share a restroom in a gas station once, and how she had instead asked you to wait outside and hold Josh. Standing outside the toilet holding Josh in your arms for what had seemed an interminable twenty minutes, Josh was so heavy, you had wondered how in the world Julia dragged him around; yet apparently Julia had learned to live like a kangaroo with Josh permanently sequestered in some invisible fold. . . . (*And now, my Fair Correspondent, you have written to ask for information, and the record is not yet complete: Tamsen Wingfield will pay the price of the extra postage should this missive weigh over 1 oz.*)

Not *any* of the above will trouble you, my Fair Correspondent, as much as the searing problem of waking up in the middle of the night needing to urinate. At this point, all you have learned about manners, ceremony, ritual, breaks down. You could open the car door and slip out, but you're terrified of going out alone in the dark to squat down somewhere in the grass which at that hour does not even rustle, even the insects seem to sleep dry and secure at night in their underground burrow. So you are obliged either to relieve yourself in a jar—the top to be securely screwed on after the gymnastic of peeing in a corner of the back seat where it's even impossible to squat—or you're obliged to lie awake and wait for daylight, for fear in your agony you'll involuntarily relieve the pressure on your bladder, a pressure so violent you feel you will vomit and thereby relax the terrific muscular clench of your urethra, and bring on the very humiliation you are trying to avoid.

THIS, my Fair Correspondent, is what it is like to live out of a car for three weeks. If you would like extra copies of this information for distribution, please write Tamsen Wingfield, etc. QUERY FIRST. *Author is planning a change of address.*

But one afternoon when it had been raining consecutively for two days so that Woodrow and Tamsen were not allowed to run free in the park, but were obliged to play an endless game of gin rummy and spelling games and counting games and what-do-you-see games in the back seat until even Woody had got sick of them, suddenly while changing Josh's diaper in the front seat (when Reffie was away filling out job applications, Julia and the baby would enjoy the luxury of the front seat all to themselves), Julia had pricked her thumb and the blood began oozing onto Josh's diaper. As if this had been some signal, he began howling; he did not like lying on his back, he wanted to be held straight-up nearly all the time. While he screamed, Julia fumbled in her bag for a band-aid to stop the bleeding, but couldn't find one. Tamsen regarded them bleakly, not stirring.

"Tamsen, *will* you pick him up a minute?" Her voice was shaking.

With a groan Tamsen reached over and awkwardly pulled Josh across the front seat. He howled louder than ever.

"For God's sake, Tamsen, hold him *up!*"

"Well, whose baby *is* it, anyway?"

The two women regarded each other solemnly, as if some sacrificial rite were taking place. Tamsen wanted to apologize, yet at the same time she wasn't very sorry, she felt the situation was entirely *their* fault, Reffie's and Julia's.

Julia looked away at her punctured thumb. Tamsen saw that blood had seeped up into a small thick bubble.

Tamsen handed the baby over to Woodrow. "Here, *you* hold it for a change."

Julia turned deathly pale, she raised her thumb to her mouth like a child. When Reffie returned Julia was still sobbing softly, her shoulders hunched over. Josh lay stretched out asleep on Woodrow's lap. Woodrow, after a swift kick at Tamsen's ankle, and shaking his head at her all the while like some wise old grandfather, had crooned the baby to sleep.

Her father sank into the seat beside Julia. There were lines of exhaustion in his face; even the back of his neck seemed dried and caked as the land in the dry season.

There was no need to ask him how things had gone, his exhausted bloodshot eyes told them everything. "Say, what's been goin on here?" he asked.

Julia sobbed more loudly than ever. He patted his wife on the back. Nobody explained; they were all too miserable to try to explain the hatred which had relentlessly overtaken them. With a heavy sigh of defeat Reffie said, "I'm gonna call Grampa Wing. See if he'll let us come stay with him awhile. . . . And he knows a lot of folks in the mine, maybe he could get me something. . . ." Nobody questioned the urgency of this final move, which would take them over three hundred miles from where they were. "Now come on all of you, brighten up. We're goin over to that there cafeteria, and I'm gonna call Gramp and you kids are gonna have a hot meal if I have to sell the roof out from under our heads."

This was so palpably absurd that even Julia managed a wan smile. Reffie started up the car and drove them to a cafeteria where at once Julia ran to the restroom. Tamsen did not follow her but instead remained stubbornly rooted at her father's side while he placed a coin in the public phone.

"I want to make a collect call to Ephraim Wingfield," Reffie said.

Her father indicated with a wave of his hand that she ought to follow Julia into the restroom, but Tamsen refused to budge, shaking her head stubbornly. Reffie couldn't argue with her, Grampa Wing had already picked up the phone on the other end and her father was trying to sound first hearty, then light-hearted and insouciant, as if they were all on a lark and maybe the climax of all their travels and adventures (Gramp-willing) was meant to be the lead mines of Idaho. But his tone quickly changed to passionate appeal, to promises and vows, to confession, to total abdication of responsibility—he'd tried everything, he said, and he was at the end of the line; he wouldn't bother Gramp if there were anything else he could do. No, he'd never worked in the mines. "Gramp, you *know* that." Her father's voice was torn between anger and shame. "Why are you asking me that? . . . Gramp, the farm was doin all right, it was the water problem that finally did us in. . . . No, they're all here with me. What was I supposed to do, leave em alone on a farm? . . . It's true, I've never been down a mine in my life, but I can learn. I can learn just about anything. I'm willin to take any kind of work at all, just anything at all. . . . Gramp, you been workin for that company all your life. . . . Maybe now—" his voice purged of all emotion but entreaty, ". . . maybe now you . . . they can help one of your own, your own grandson, for God's sake." Her father had been talking all this time with his fingers gouging his eyes, as if he could bear everything better if he could believe no one else in the world was listening, if this were a private conversation between himself and the voice at the other end. Then he released the tight grip on his eyelids, he stared at Tamsen, as if a full sense of his downfall had finally struck him. Hoarsely he cried out, "Gramp, you just *got* to help me. My kids are goin hungry here. . . ." And for a while there was no voice at all coming through the receiver while Reffie stood shuddering with long dry sobs. Then Grampa Wing said something and her father said, "O.K. Gramp. We'll get there before dark for sure. We got no plans to spend the night in Snowqualmie Pass. . . ." It was a joke he repeated on their way West, but nobody smiled. They all knew by then that Julia would never have survived a night in Snowqualmie Pass . . . All the way to Silver Valley Julia sat in silence, stirring only when the baby cried.

And so *her* father, Reffie Wingfield, had left everything that was good and wonderful in Salinas to come here and bore holes in the ground like a rat undermining a ship. Therefore Tamsen hated every remarkable thing that might be underground in Silver Valley and everything above ground as well that was not where it should be. It should be in Salinas. She was also sorrowfully obliged to withhold her love from Reffie as well, as the First Cause of her unchangeable condition. It was all so wretched—a future without Salinas being a future with hope—that she decided she would not go to school today at all. She would just follow Reffie down the mine and surprise him.

To get into the mine however, would not be easy, she'd have to pass the security guard's booth at the gate. Tamsen stood up, abandoning her inscriptions. With a sudden burst of energy she threw the branched twig as far from her as she could, then entered the house by the back door, averting her gaze from the river: A dumping-river for the mine, acid-tailings had turned the white froth of its waves a murky green.

She now felt herself caught up in the most interesting idea that had come to her since they arrived from Seattle. She moved quietly into the shed adjoining the kitchen where Reffie stored his tools and workclothes. There she found a hard hat and an extra pair of goggles. She imagined herself entering the shed dressed like any other girl, then coming out disguised as a miner. Superman stuff. The hasp on the door of the shed creaked but Julia certainly would not have noticed; Julia never parted the bright red kitchen curtains which hid from her sight the green river and the pile of black slag.

Tamsen found a pair of Reffie's coveralls and a denim jacket; she was beginning to enjoy the morning. Her own clothes—skirt, blouse, and sweater—were soon totally enveloped by Reffie's. She stuffed the legs of the pants into her boots and set the orange hard hat carefully on her head. She wondered whether she should wear the goggles. She decided to save them till she came to the entry shaft, then she would rest them on her forehead. She experimented with balancing them above her eyebrows. It was all rather exhilarating, like being a spy. She set out at once by the hillside path to the mine, estimating that she was following Reffie by about half an hour. This would have given him time to go down the mine. She'd take the next run of the cage elevator.

At the gate she was promptly stopped by the security guard who asked what she meant to do in that outfit, get a job as a foreman? But Tamsen had prepared for this. She explained that she had meant to meet her father at exactly eight o'clock, but she'd got a little behind during breakfast. "And I'm supposed to bring him this—" she held up something that looked like it might be Reffie's lunch "—down to Level 19." She'd heard Reffie refer to the levels by number, she thought that sounded pretty good.

"Yep, well—there's a tour getting ready to go down at 8:30. You can go along with them. Just stand over there by the U.S. flag. You'll see your guide coming. That'll be Mr. Agnell—you know him? He's an engineer. . . . Some big honchos from back East going down with him, looking over the place, I hear. One from Wheeling or Pittsburgh or someplace, they say. Yeah, big honchos. . . ." he repeated with a touch of irony, winking at her collusively: a miner's kid, not an outsider.

Dutifully Tamsen walked toward the flagpole; but when the security guard stepped into his booth to answer the phone, she slid quickly through the half-open gates. Good thing she was so thin, another 10 pounds and she'd have been caught. Even so, as she pushed her way through, Reffie's jacket tore on the gate. He'll be mad about *that*, she thought. She walked quickly to the elevator cage, wishing she had time to leave a message in the dusty sign which challenged her right to be there: WARNING! Industrial Area Employees Only. *Ha! Ha!* she'd have written in the dust.

She waited for the elevator cage to come up, it seemed an interminable time. She wondered why she was the only person going down. Where was everybody? Well, all the better. She'd find Reffie at Level 19 and approach him so quietly, he wouldn't even see her till he heard her voice right beside him saying, "Hi there, Reffie!" He would be amazed. She'd stay and watch him work, that'd give her something really neat for her Social Studies report. She'd call it, "How Tamsen and Reffie Wingfield Excavated Hard Rock in the C & L Silver-Lead and Zinc Company." The cage door now opened, she glided in, leaned against the wall as the elevator shuddered slightly and began its descent. She thought the elevator pretty grubby, and it didn't even give you a smooth ride. She wondered how many men could pack themselves in this space. Stuck on the wall was a placard showing the Empire State Building, informing her that *A ride to the bottom in this cage elevator will take you five times as long as a ride to the top of the Empire State Building*. Well, she didn't want to go to the bottom, she just wanted to go to Level 19. She had thought there'd be signs telling her which level she was at, just like any elevator, but the signs she tried to read as they flowed downward had been worn away by thousands of trips of the cage.

The elevator cage stopped. She decided she'd better get out, if only to check what Level she was at. She was rather surprised at the relief she felt to see that she'd come to a transit tunnel, with railroad tracks. There were about a half-dozen miners here, transferring to a railcar. Their backs were turned to Tamsen. They were climbing into a small railcar like you might see at a circus. The little yellow car reminded her of the banana-act she'd seen once: From out of a midget car had poured maybe five or six clowns with hundreds, thousands, of yellow bananas. The miners in their heavy clothes seemed to her overdressed and awkward, like untalented kids forced to take grown-up parts in a play. Still, it was a real trip to see them climb into these Toonerville trolleys. They stooped over, bowing their heads as they entered; then they sat down facing each other on the benchlike seats. Above their heads was a warning in capital letters, arranged vertically as if the miners were first-graders who read only one word at a time:

KEEP
HEAD
HANDS
AND
FEET
INSIDE

Alongside this warning was a funny cartoon of a miner pulling desperately at a stubborn jackass. In spite of herself she laughed out loud. She would have liked to climb into the railcar with the miners; but she was afraid they might order her back up to the surface, or maybe contact Reffie on some underground phone. Then he wouldn't be surprised and laugh, he'd just be mad at her.

As the men rode away they were quiet and somber. You'd have thought they'd be more jolly, Tamsen thought, that there'd be more camaraderie. She thought she'd noticed her neighbor, Sean's father, on the tram, but maybe under their hard hats it was easy to mistake them. None had been wearing anything over their eyes. Gramp said once that the oldtimers had hated the old-fashioned goggles, and Reffie replied that the young men hated the new, modern glasses even more. Reffie said they hated them because they steamed up in the high temperatures, always between 90° and 100°, you couldn't see your hand in front of you. Reffie said that C & L was what you called a "hot" mine. And then Gramp explained that you have to keep draining the mine 24 hours a day, day and night, even when the men were not working . . . they were always talking about the mine.

Tamsen wondered if she were looking at what Gramp called a sump right now. Gramp was always talking about sumps or slimes. There was a pool of muddy water in front of her, three or four inches deep. Cautiously she moved away from it. Reffie sure was right, it was a hot mine. She was getting warmer by the minute, she could feel the sweat under her armpits. The fun had gone out of her game, she was feeling just tired and hot. A sign now indicated to her that she was only on the Fourth Level. Well, this wasn't working out, she thought ruefully, she'd have to go back to the surface. This Level-business was too complicated, she probably should have invented a better pretext, and taken along a guide to bring her straight to Reffie. Now she guessed she'd just take the elevator back up and go to school after all. She had a pretty neat Social Studies class in the afternoon.

As she was about to re-enter the cage she saw something mysterious as cat's eyes glisten through the dark. It was a vein of ore flowing vertically through the wall, like mercury through a thermometer. She started across the tracks to examine it, walking very cautiously around the pool of water. Here was another sign for the miners: *Respirators, Safety Toe Boots and Hard Hats Will Be Worn Beyond This Point*. Well, she wasn't going beyond this point, she just wanted to see the vein of ore. It surprised her how gloomy and dark it was along the tracks, she'd expected everything to be modern, like a brand-new Mexican subway station, complete with fluorescent lights in the ceiling, and maybe an underground cafeteria. She was disappointed with the mine, it was just a mountain with a hundred miles of tunnels, like Gramp said. She thought of people wandering around in a hundred miles of tunnels, earning a living, making jokes, maybe singing songs. . . . Day and night the trucks and railcars rolled along their Appointed Rounds.

But unless you already knew your way around, the lights along the walls were barely adequate. It definitely was not turning out to be much of an adventure. But this bluish vein in the wall, it was Something Else; it had the mystery of time upon it, the slow bleeding of minerals into the black heart of the mountain. She touched her hand to the wall, it was hard and cold as a corpse. She scraped the vein with a fingernail; a fine dust gathered under the nail, a poignant slate-blue like dead Texas bluebonnets. She scraped some of the ore into her cupped palm. The tiny particles gleamed like the blue Venetian glass of a necklace a classmate had ostentatiously worn to school one day. Tamsen bent closer to examine them; they stirred beneath her breath, then flew, invisible, into the air. Had she breathed a few of these blue jewels into her lungs? She imagined them, sharp and iridescent as diamonds, cutting their way through her cobwebby lungs—deeper and deeper until they'd gone straight through. And where would they go when they left her lungs? Tamsen had no idea. Maybe next year she'd take biology, the first thing she'd ask the teacher would be: Where does the mine dust go after you've breathed it?

She wished that at least she could brag that her father mined silver, not lead. Silver seemed to Tamsen more romantic, it had more of a history, going back to the Spanish conquest and the Aztecs, even. Still maybe this was a safer mine for Reffie; they had had that terrible fire in the Sunshine Mine—more than ninety miners had died. Everybody had been a hero, she wouldn't have wanted her father to die a hero. Nobody knew how the fire had started, just some wood smoldering, then towering infernoes and lungfuls of smoke coming in from the vent system. She wondered where the vent system was down here in Reffie's mine. She took a few steps along the face of the wall, touching what seemed to be a white tube: She could hear air whooshing through it. Why, it's nothing but a balloon made of plastic, about as thick as a tire tube she used to float on out at the Lake, only it was strung out horizontally along the wall of the tunnel, mile upon mile of this sausage-like thing carrying oxygen to men three thousand feet in the earth. . . . She scowled at it, thinking of Reffie. Suppose some madman or weirdo wanted to kill her father? All he'd have to do was slash this tube with his knife. Instantly the fresh air would billow out like falling entrails. She saw how there were patches in the tube where holes had been mended, as if the system were nothing but a piece of sailcloth and they could repair it and put the air back into it if they wanted to.

She thought she could hear another railcar coming through. She turned toward the tracks. The car was approaching very quietly, but she could clearly see the headlight, and now the car itself, yellow and black, like a caterpillar. She didn't want the miners to see her, so she headed back across the tracks to the cage elevator. Altogether, she considered, this had been a bad scene, it was enough to make you forgive Reffie. She thought she was hurrying quickly and expertly around the pool of water, but suddenly the mud slid away from her feet and within seconds she was down, flat on her back. She lay stunned for a moment, tears of humiliation filling her eyes. Those men in the railcar would die laughing when they saw her, a silly girl who'd come down looking for her Daddy and then fell flat on her ass.

But the miners did not even smile, they seemed scared out of their wits at the sight of her lying there. One of them asked in open-mouthed amazement, "What was she doing there?" Taking advantage of the dumb question, Tamsen snapped, "Christmas shopping." But she began groaning with exasperation and pain when she tried to stand. The miners saw then that they had a problem on their hands. "Probably sprained it," somebody said as two of them crossed arms and carried her to the elevator cage. Rapidly they brought her to the surface and within minutes an emergency ambulance had arrived. *Thank heaven they didn't have to sound a general alarm or something: Reffie would have been scared to death.*

She was carried on a litter to the Emergency Room where a company doctor x-rayed her leg and announced that the x-ray only confirmed what had been obvious to him. Tamsen had broken her leg. While he and a nurse began preparations for setting her leg in a cast, Tamsen lay for a while alone in the room, cursing her fate. As if to add to her bitterness, thumbtacked to the wall was another of their ubiquitous cartoons. Above a sketch of a miner, his

arm in a sling, was the warning: WORK SAFELY. DON'T
VACATION HERE.

As they drove up to her home in the C & L car, Tamsen
saw that Julia had just taken Josh out for his afternoon
walk in the stroller. They were nearly at the bottom of the
hillside path when the car approached. Josh dearly loved
this afternoon walk, and would become more and more
excited as he realized he was about to be taken out-of-
doors, kicking his feet and jumping up and down in his
highchair, like a kid on a bucking pony. Feeding him and
bathing him and diapering him and zippering him into his
outdoor clothes took nearly an hour. Then Julia would
rush to get into her own coat before he got uncomfortably
warm. If anything interrupted these ceremonies, Josh became very upset. Like a puppy scratching at the door with
excitement, his desire to be out-of-doors was as demand-
ing as hunger. Now, as the company car parked in front of
their house, Tamsen saw how Julia reversed the direction
of the stroller, pushing it back up the hill as fast as she
could. She was panting when she reached the car. "What
is it? What happened? What has she done?" Tamsen could
not understand why Julia had at first looked so frightened
and then so terribly relieved, as if a broken leg were nothing, nothing at all, compared to what she had feared. . . .
Without a murmur of complaint, but only with that
strange look of relief, Julia had carried Josh back into the
house and laid him down on the sofa. Slowly she took off
her own coat, and undressed Josh. Then turning away as if
with indifference to his howls of protest, asked Tamsen,
"Would you care for a hot cup of tea?"

IV

Comin up here with no job, no seniority, no experience, nothin. Just me to lay it on thick for him with the union, and with a passel of kids in a car that's hardly fit for a museum, much less for drivin through these mountain passes. What else could I do? Nothin but the one thing I swore I'd *never* do, shove my weight around to get my own kin a job where there might be others had more right. Yet here he was my own flesh and blood, son of my son, and a loser if ever I saw one, already bowed down by the times and Roseanne's death, a double whammy, and then takin on this new woman like he hadn't had trouble enough, startin it all over again with another mouth to feed and maybe more after *that*. You'd never know him to be a Wingfield—*his* father had better sense than that. His father was a kid with guts. His father left home to make it big in Texas—Becky and I of course never thought he *would* make it big, but that wasn't the point, the point was that he had the get-up-and-go to go there, which he did—Ephraim Wingfield Junior did. But what did this one ever do to think they owed him a living, I'd like to know? He took his father's farm like a gift and left it to die in the hot sun. That don't take brains, that only takes lack-of-water, what they call *in*anition. And what I learned as a pup on the homestead was that where there's not some, you get some—especially water. So when he called from Seattle, I said to him, "Reffie what in God's name are you doin truckin around the country with three kids and a lunch pail? You better come on over here and see can I find you somethin to do with C & L." And now—you see what kids are?—the kids don't even like it here, they'd rather have gone on sailing paper boats in Puget Sound I guess, and that girl from Boston, so delicate, if she'd seen some of what Becky and me seen, she'd a peed in her pants, that's what. But pretty she is, I'll grant you that, though pale and soft as an egg yolk. And I always thought these new kids knew how not to have any kids of their own before they even had a place to stay in, not livin out of a car with them. Goddam, do you have to hit Skid Row before you know you're in trouble?

I said to him, "Reffie, what we goin do for you? You got a problem, you know that." Thinking of his Julia I almost said, "You got a big problem there too, you know?" And he'd toed the ground like some country bumpkin, not a grown man with a half-grown daughter. And *that's* goin to be somethin to see, I warrant you, watchin that Tamsen ride the broomstick to hell and back.

"I know that, Grampa," he says. "But it doesn't help to make me feel like a bum, you know." I was glad to see he at least had some spunk left in him, enough to speak up and defend himself.

"Well, tell me, how did it happen?" I asked.

He looked at me with astonishment—that young man did, who'd had a richer lode given to him than either me or his father had ever struck in our lives. "Whaddye mean, *happen*? If I could tell you that, I'd be the President of the United States."

You can be sure I snorted at *that* one. It almost put me in a better humor with him, it shot so wide of the mark. "*He* don't know nothin," I said. "Nobody knows a damned thing till he's put in a ten-hour day in muck up to his balls, with his back half-broken and his kids beggin him not to go on strike."

Well, Reffie just stood there, humble and defeated. I felt so sorry for him I didn't know whether to punch him or pat him. "Come on over for supper tonight. I'll show you how they used to cook up a meal in the placer mines. How does Julia like the house they found her?"

Reffie mumbled something meant to sound like *Fine, fine*, but it was clear Julia was not very keen about the house that stands on a hillside about a quarter of a mile from the mine. "She'll get used to it," Reffie said. "It's not that she's been spoiled, you know," he added defensively. "It's just that, compared to Silver Valley, where she comes from is the hub of the universe. Fact is, that's what they call it, the hub of the universe."

Tryin to be good-natured and funny. And what was funny about a bunch of snobs back East thinkin they were the bull's-eye of Creation? But I tried now to be philosophical, forgiving, relying on the comfortable old saws. I sounded to myself like a Farmer's Almanac. "Well, it's good for the kids to have somebody carin for them. A woman in the house for Tamsen."

"That's not what I married her for," retorted Reffie, flushing. "I married her cause I loved her. But it wasn't just love either, it was like she *needed* somebody."

I scoffed at him then. "And you didn't have enough folks who needed you? Takin care of your own kids wasn't a needy enough job for you!"

Reffie began lighting his pipe with shaking hands. I saw I'd gone too far, it was unfair, maybe. Yet it did rankle that this boy couldn't just come out and say he'd wanted a girl in his bed to warm his feet. Ah, if only I was Reffie's age again, I'd tear the place apart before I'd take a pretty young bride and her baby along with me to live out of a goddammed car.

Back in the Thirties, Wing had left Becky in Silver Valley and gone, like his grandson today, to look for work in Seattle and Alaska. It was then that Wing had made the two most important Discoveries of his life: the men from the Industrial Workers of the World, some of whom had taken part in the Seattle General Strike, and the hobo jungles.

Wing had thought then it would be only a temporary

thing. They would be mining again soon at the C & L Silver-Lead & Zinc Company. He was young and strong, and when he'd kissed Becky as she'd followed him out to the bus carrying Franklin in her arms—Ephraim had stayed in school that day as they hadn't wanted him to miss any more days, he was about to graduate from grade school—Wing had settled himself in his seat, looking out at her and the baby named for the new President.

Either he'd be back by Christmas, Wing said, or he'd get a permanent job and send for her. There was no way for Becky to wipe the tears from her face because she was holding Franklin up so that he could see his Daddy, so she had stood there outside the bus window, tears rolling down onto the baby's shirt until, after an unbearable moment of indecision, when it had seemed impossible to Wing that he could actually be going to leave her, that he must get off the bus and take his family home and put Franklin to bed in his crib and then he and Becky and Ephraim would eat spaghetti with powdered milk again for supper (but no matter, they'd be together), when the bus growled, Becky turned her head away in resignation and courage, Franklin began to cry; the moment had passed. Wing was headed due West.

The distance that stretched longer and longer between him and Becky had caused a sickness to grow in his stomach, but it was a plain fact that a grown man with a family had no time to be homesick, he had a job to do, which was to find a job—the rest would be easy. So he hoarded his money and whenever the bus stopped he drank water instead of Coca-Cola figuring every five nickels he saved would accumulate a day's grace. There were still plenty of places a man could get a whole meal for two bits.

It was already late afternoon by the time the bus arrived in Seattle and Wing stood in the station a little dazed. He had hoped to make better time. He'd wanted to be able to check out a couple of fishermen's coves before dark, and now it was nearly four o'clock. He'd have to find a place to flop, but he knew himself not to be the flophouse kind. He wasn't ready to bed down with bedbugs and winos.

There was a Salvation Army not far away, but he didn't feel sufficiently down-and-out for that kind of charity either. Hell, he'd just *arrived*, he wasn't looking for a handout, there were probably guys who needed it more than he did, old guys who maybe wouldn't ever again have a chance to land anything. He saw them now, panhandling, asking *him* for a handout. Resolutely Wing shook his head.

Still it was a new place, therefore a place of hope, and he knew himself to be capable of anything. He'd hardly been sick in his life, he'd shovelled tons of rock a day, he'd helped carve out the mines of Silver Valley from the bowels of the earth, down to where China was supposed to be and back.

A fellow by the name of Emmett Kearney, an old guy he'd talked to on the bus, was now trailing out of the station after him. Wing wasn't sure he wanted him around, though Kearney seemed a harmless enough old geezer. His jacket was as dirty as if he'd been camping out in it, but his face, at least, was not umbered by gallons of cheap wine, and his eyes were as bright as a trout's scales. Still you had to be careful.

Wing was trying to look as if he knew his way around the city, so he announced, "Thought I'd check out Third and Fourth Avenues. Get an idea of what's been goin down. Too late, I'd guess, to go to the employment offices." Wing controlled his tone so that it became a statement, not a question. He didn't want Kearney to think he was inviting suggestions.

Kearney shrugged. "Every day they write up any jobs they got on their blackboards. It's on a first-come, first-served basis. That means if you wait up all night maybe you get an address so you can follow up a lead. When you get there, you find out that maybe five hundred other guys have found out about this same lead. Anyway, you've spent your carfare following the lead, so you fill out the form. They take it and say they'll let you know if there's a fish run or maybe a sawmill going to cut up some logs. But who needs lumber?" Kearney pointed vaguely.

"There's mountains of lumber piling up, rotting in the sheds. You got a place to stay?" Kearney added abruptly. "In case they want to get in touch?"

For a moment Wing considered making up an address, he didn't want to listen to the old man, he didn't want to hear any doom and gloom, he *had* to believe he was meant to be lucky, that unlike tens of thousands he'd get a job here. Faith in yourself was like working in the hardrock, you lived by it, but you could have a rockburst that could crush you.

"What kind of work you trying to get?" Kearney pursued when Wing didn't answer.

"Miner. Hardrock."

"Not much mining going on around *here,*" observed Kearney drily. "Mostly—when they have it—it's fishing and timber. But ships now are just kept in anchor, rusting out. Doesn't pay them to make a run."

Wing tried to sound both good-natured and reasonable about it. "Looks like people would be eating fish nowadays. Maybe they don't need metal out of the mines, but they got to *eat!*" he exclaimed with as much heartiness as he could muster.

Kearney was staring at him in brooding silence as if Wing were some Chinaman who'd just come off the boat and if Wing could speak the lingo Kearney would tell him all about it, and what Kearney would say was, 'Go back to your rice paddy lickety-split.' "Where'd you get *that* idea?" said Kearney at last. "That they got to eat?" Kearney began moving away.

At least he knows where he's going. "Well I got to eat," said Wing in a conciliatory tone, "and you too. If you like—I got a couple of sandwiches left . . ." He pulled out what remained of the sandwiches Becky had packed for him and showed them to Kearney. *Well, you'd think I was showing him the Comstock Lode,* thought Wing and felt ashamed of his generosity, it was such a meager thing.

"I got a better idea. Hold up on those. . . . Just put em right back in your pocket and come with me. I got a place. . . ."

They walked past the nailed-shut stores on Third Avenue and proceeded south of Yesler Way by way of a route that was obviously clear to Kearney, but was an endless maze to Wing. "Hey," Wing tried to joke. "This is worse than being down in the mine. We at least got tunnels!" Once or twice as their path seemed more and more isolated, suspicion gripped him. Maybe this guy was leading him into a trap where Wing would be robbed and thrown from a pier. He began to imagine his body bumping up against the pilings like rotting driftwood, imagined Becky waiting for him. . . .

What he could not have imagined was what they came to: a city of discarded old men.

"How you like this?" asked Kearney, as dusk was descending on the city within a city. Wing, who'd grown up not far from the Snake River, within perpetual sight of the blue Minodkas, stared at the makeshift shacks with shock and dismay. *Nothing but bums and bindlestiffs. Did I come all the way here just to drydock with these losers?* Kearney led him to his own shack, nailed together from sheets of tin which were already curled and rusting at the edges. He and Kearney bowed their heads to enter the door, across which Kearney had nailed a sort of ragged poncho. Inside, Wing saw a couple of empty milk crates and a pair of mattresses—"One to sleep on, and one for a blanket," joked Kearney. Unlike the other shacks, Kearney had covered the ground with broken pieces of slate picked up from wrecking-ball sites. Kearney showed him how well insulated the shack was. "You'd be surprised how warm we keep here." He banged on the walls of the structure to show how firm they were. "See that. Two layers of newspaper, one of cardboard. I'm thinking of getting the walls painted soon as I can find a can of paint left out somewhere. Something lively. We got a guy from Detroit here, he's a good artist. I may get him to do me some artwork. Fact is, we got a lot of talent here, a lot of talent. We're not just. . . ." His words wandered off into the evening air. He offered to show Wing around, introduce him to his pals. Wing demurred, saying he didn't want to trouble anybody. Actually, he was trying to dissociate himself from the place, he didn't want Kearney to think he was going to stay in the camp for any time at all. Tomorrow, Wing thought, he'd push on, he'd land something, maybe find a fishing boat anchored in some quiet cove, just waiting for somebody like Wing to bring him good luck on a run. But he didn't brag to Kearney about what he might do tomorrow, he had the feeling that everything he wanted to say, Kearney had already heard, and Wing didn't want his own illusions shattered; he wasn't going to let these guys talk him out of his future.

"Let's get some wood and build us a fire," said Kearney. "Make some coffee for the sandwiches. But first maybe I ought to show you the toilet."

Wing, dazed and shaken, found himself following Kearney around, asking questions. It was a role he detested— he was accustomed to telling other guys what to do in the mine. But he was on alien turf and he allowed himself to be led like a greenhorn as they walked toward the beach.

Overhead the evening sky was filled with veins of silver, clusters of ore gathering around dark-blue pockets. Wing wished himself a mile underground; he would have preferred a forty-pound jackhammer tearing at his shoulder to this, walking out on the beach to take a piss. He and Kearney made their way over makeshift pontoons of rotting lumber and rusting metal to the wooden outhouses. As they approached, even the salt fresh air could not cover the stench. Wing groaned his humiliation, but to his surprise the beach was astonishingly clean. The ocean winds blew away most of the flies, and the men searching endlessly for trash or driftwood to keep their fires going left the sand clean, if deserted-looking.

They found two friends of Kearney's waiting for them when they got back. Kearney introduced them as Hackett and Grogan.

"Seen you brought a newcomer," said Hackett. "Thought we'd ask, can he help build us a coffin?"

"A what?" gasped Wing. "I'm a miner, not a carpenter."

"You don't need to know nothin about carpentry to

build a coffin," Hackett assured him. "Nothin but a box."

"Yeah," added Grogan, "and if it don't fit too good—no problem."

"Whose coffin?" Kearney asked. "Who died?" Wing realized from the question that Kearney had been away for some time.

"The redhead," said Hackett. "Guess you knew him better than I did. The one used to work in the lumber camps. The one said he used to be a friend of Anna Louise Strong. Of course every Wobblie around here," he added to Wing, "says he used to be a friend of Anna Louise Strong. But *I'm* the only one who ever saw her, I'll bet you. Saw her talkin to Lincoln Stephens one time. I used to deliver stuff to that newspaper she worked for, the one really got her into all that trouble, *The Call* . . ."

"What about Red?" interrupted Kearney. "What are they going to do about burying him? Did he have any kin?"

"No, no kin at all. But a bunch of us oldtimers want to have a kind of reunion. We figure we got at least thirty bonny fide used-to-be IWW's in this here camp alone. We gonna give him a regular send-off. Get some of the old guys who were in the Nestor Building when they wrecked the office. Play taps, sort of. Anyway,"—addressing Wing—"if you could lend us a hand? Even though you're *not* in the carpenters' union."

Kearney objected. "You're already asking this man to give you some of his time. And we haven't had supper yet. We're going to eat soon as we get this fire going."

The men immediately offered to share their day's assets: Grogan, who had a paper permit allowing him to use the breadline, pulled out what was left of his lunch; Hackett claimed to have saved out what a housewife gave him while he was door-to-dooring that morning; but the contents of the stained bag he pulled from the pocket of his blue canvas jacket, on which Wing made out the faded black letters HOSPITAL, had the look of leftovers from a patient's tray, complete with paper napkin. Nobody in the camp would have spent a nickel on paper napkins.

They sat around the fire exchanging stories. Kearney had

built an excellent fire in a trashcan, leaving ventholes for the smoke to escape. They fed the blaze with dried driftwood, boards of rotting lumber or pieces of coal Grogan had collected along the railroad ties.

"What happened to Red?" asked Kearney. "When I left he was on the wagon. He couldn't take a drink without it making him sick as a dog. He should have gone into the hospital. You can't cure an ulcer on booze."

"Don't any of us know exactly what *did* happen. He was sick, he was drinking too much, as much as he could get, and I guess he started bleeding."

"The hospital finished him off, you know that!" exclaimed Grogan with contempt. "He should never have let them take him to the hospital."

"Well," observed Hackett, trying to mollify him. "You pick up a man in the street, he's about to die of pneumonia out there, he's not about to complain about what you do with him. They found him on Washington Street, they thought he was drunk, but he'd probably just fainted. His ulcer was bleeding him to death."

"Well, what then?" Angrily Kearney shoved a piece of wood into the trash can, which began burning more quickly than he wanted it to, so he tried to snatch it back from the fire. The hot ashes blew onto his shaggy jacket and he began brushing them off, cursing furiously. "Damn it all to hell, can't even find a decent piece of firewood anymore, and all that stuff rotting, rotting, rotting in the yards. I'm going to *rustle* me some lumber pretty soon, they don't watch out. . . ."

Grogan shrugged. "Yeah, then you'll be warm enough. They'll lock you up till this here Depression is over and done with, till *you're* over and done with." Kearney glowered at him, his silence acknowledging the truth of what Grogan said. "Anyway, are you listening to us or you going to burn yourself *up* tryin to keep warm? They picked up Red on Washington Street, and that's all we know. There wasn't a *thing* wrong with his heart, he only had this itty-bitty ulcer . . ."

"What you mean itty-bitty? He was hemorrhaging," contradicted Hackett. "Listen, Grogan, you got to stop being one of these persecution nuts. They've stopped shooting down Wobblies, you know. They don't give a damn about us anymore, cause we're all dying like rats anyway."

Grogan remained surly. "You'll never convince *me* they didn't black bottle him."

"What's that?" Wing felt obliged to ask, though he didn't want to listen to the answer. He was trying to concentrate his efforts on what he would do tomorrow. But the fire, the hot coffee, and the aimless, richocheting conversation, along with the strange futureless society in which he found himself—a society without hope, responsibility or higher aim than to get through the day—had paralyzed his will. It was as if he were caught up in a dream where all the scenes and talk were out of his control; but at least, however terrifying the events, he need feel no guilt about them. He need only lie there and listen or force himself awake.

"Kearney," Grogan was saying, his voice rough with bitterness. "Explain it to this guy, what a black bottle is."

"I don't know what it is, I only know what they *say* it is."

"Well then, say what they say it is!" exclaimed Grogan fiercely.

"*Who* says?" Wing felt suddenly exhausted. He thought with deep grief and longing of Becky and the kids.

Kearney slapped the soot from his hands. "The men here say, especially the older guys who were here during the General Strike, they say They're trying to get rid of us all. That they don't want us or need us anymore, and as soon as they get the chance—the old men say—They're gonna poison us off. . . ."

"For Chrissake, who says that? You guys gotta all be crazy here. . . ." Wing half rose to his feet, as if he were going to leave them, but no one took the slightest notice. He squatted down again on his heels close to the fire. *Like some Shoshoni living in something less than a tepee.*

"It's those damned interns, they don't care about you. If they don't actually poison you (which *I'm* not saying they

· 71 ·

don't)," added Grogan, "they sure as hell don't encourage you to take up your bed and walk. They'll bury you there—bed right on top of you."

"And what's this new guy doin here? You bring him?" asked Grogan abruptly of Kearney, as though Wing were deaf and dumb and couldn't speak for himself.

"Lookin for work," said Kearney, glancing in apology at Wing.

"And you said that with a straight face too, didya? Hee hee hee," nickered Grogan, looking up at the sky while taking out his sack of Durham. Curving a piece of wrapping paper cut down to size, he shook the tobacco in as into a chute. "Smoke?" he offered Wing in a dour but conciliatory way.

Wing shook his head. "Never took it up. A smoker in the mines is more dangerous than dynamite, cause you're apt to be more careless with it."

"So you're a miner. And what do you think of the Industrial Workers of the World?"

The phrase detonated around Wing's head. *Aw, these guys are just a bunch of reds. Should of known that.* He weighed his words before answering. He didn't want to alienate these men. "I'm for the WFM. Guess people like to fight for theirselves, right? Like the auto workers, the garment workers, you know? I just don't see how you guys can believe there could be *one* union for everybody."

"You'll find out how there can be—when you get hungry enough," Grogan said. "What do you think you're sittin on your ass for right now, except you're already in the Big Union—the International Union of the Unemployed?"

"What about that National Recovery Act that's gonna let everybody organize?" intervened Kearney with an air of compromise.

"Recovery! Sounds like a hospital ward to me! We're not going to recover from this till they figure out what to do with fourteen million people with nothin to do. And you know how they're gonna do that?"

Wing said he didn't know.

"Well, you'll find that out too. You got any kids—boys? *You'll* find out."

Suddenly they all became gloomy; they were all men separated from their families. Grogan said he hadn't seen his wife in over a year. "But I'm gonna go back East for Christmas if I got to ride the rods." One by one the men began taking out their worn wallets and exchanging snapshots of their children, their wives. Some showed cards from employers who had asked them to call back in a week or two; the cards were mottled with small black moldspots from the rain and fog of Seattle.

The exchange of snapshots had cast a despairing mood over them all. They began to knock out the fire, saving any half-burnt pieces of wood for morning. Grogan seemed to repent of his manner toward Wing long enough to give him some advice. "Nothin here in Seattle, boy. If there's anything left to get, it's up in the North country. You can take a ferry and be there in a few days. I mean, if you got money to *get* there . . ."

The following morning he and Kearney rose early. They didn't stop to make a fire but ate a few saltines and a tin of sardines Kearney said he'd been hoarding for a special occasion. Kearney gave him some directions and a few warnings—not everybody could be trusted, he added, looking away. Kearney said he was reluctant to pass judgment on the rest of the world, but he knew for a fact that one man in the camp had been robbed and cast into the sea after winning a pile at a card game. So if Wing had any money, he should sew it up good in the lining of his pants or his shirt.

Before starting out for the employment agencies Wing asked if he could borrow one of Kearney's books, *The 42nd Parallel*; it looked to him to be pretty interesting. He might read it, he said while waiting around for an interview. "*Interview?*" echoed Kearney, shrugging as at some childish fantasy.

Wing hesitated. His question seemed, even to himself,

ridiculous. "What kind of address do you think I should write down? General Delivery?"

"No need to do that. Anything you have sent here, the postman knows me. We got an Unemployed Citizens' League that helps keep us honest. We got a vigilante committee, a mail committee, a food distribution committee, they handle all the stuff from the city relief, and a sanitation committee—keeps guys from pissin in the ocean—you're welcome to stay here long as you want, Wing," Kearney suddenly interrupted himself. "But my advice would be the same as Grogan's. This is a city of old men."

"Aw, come off it, Emmett. You're not even fifty."

Kearney stared at him with a bitterness so deep that his voice did not even show any emotion. "You don't think fifty is old?" After a moment he handed Wing his copy of *The 42nd Parallel*. Wing weighed it in one hand, considering whether he wanted to be carrying anything not strictly necessary. "An Atlas, is it? Any good maps?" Wing flipped it open.

"A novel."

"Oh, a novel," said Wing, losing interest. "I never read that kind of romantic stuff. Just give me a good plain horsethief anytime. You got a Zane Grey?"

After a week in Seattle Wing had to admit Grogan and Kearney were right; there was no work for miners. Nor for carpenters, plumbers, fishermen, or professors. The morning he stood in line with a Doctor of Philosophy who was trying to get a job in an unemployment agency writing job resumes for the unemployed, Wing decided to risk all and take the ferry to Anchorage. But it would be turning cold fast and Kearney warned him that if he was going to try the last frontier, he'd better hustle. He'd freeze his ass off if he got there in the dead of winter. He looked down with a strange mixture of pity and contempt at Wing's jeans, rubbed thin at the knees. "Goddam, Wing, we'll find you some warm clothes before you go." True to his word, Kearney went around the camp, bartering coffee, cigarettes, and some commissary-issued cans of lard in exchange for a pair of old rubber boots and a coat many sizes too big for Wing: it fell right down to his ankles. Kearney comforted him. "Under that big coat you can wear whatever else you got. You can sleep in it if you need too. A big coat with plenty of pockets is all a man needs in this world". Kearney almost grinned. He told Wing a story of a man who'd camped out on the park bench for weeks, everything in his coat pockets, till the police found him one morning drunk and froze-to-death. "It's not being hungry that kills you, it's drinking to keep from *thinking* that gets you in the end," added Kearney philosophically. "Here, have another Zane Grey, a gift from us folks back home."

They walked together to the Sound, where Kearney stood with his pipe in his hand, like a small flag a patriotic child might carry to a ship christening. Now and then Kearney would raise the pipe in the air and nod encouragingly. Wing could taste the fear in his mouth as he waved goodbye to Emmett, drifting farther away than ever from home and the land he knew. The ferry was soon navigating through the gleaming water of the Sound, and Wing (like some Gold Rush miner, he thought), was heading for the last frontier.

It was a cold, miserable trip, there was hardly anyone for Wing to talk to. Apparently folks had given up rushing to the Northernmost flank of the country for jobs. They were hunkering down where they were born, hanging on to local identifications that might qualify them for relief. A migrant like himself, Wing considered ruefully, was sure to be feared and detested, since it was plain as day that he came to take work that might be given to one of the local folks; or else, failing to find work, he was in their eyes just another vagrant: nothing was held in greater suspicion by folks raised on thrift and providence.

It had begun to rain almost the moment he set foot on board, and afterwards it was his invincible belief that it rained all the way from Seattle to Alaska. The few fishermen on board who were also headed North were glum and uncommunicative. He saw no women except a couple of young girls from whom Becky would have averted her eyes, they were naked to the hams and painted to the eyelids. They seemed to be making a little money on board—god knew where they took the men they disappeared with from time to time. There was one other passenger on board, who looked to Wing to be one of your "pink shirt" gamblers. He claimed to be playing for pennies, but every now and then Wing noticed green money going under the table. Wing touched-for-luck the few bucks he had sewn into his red flannel shirt. He swore to himself not to take the shirt off until it was padded thick as a quilt with money.

But his biggest problem at the moment was keeping warm. Even with the long coat Kearney had got him, he felt frozen to the bone; obviously they were not going to waste heat on a few die-hard fishermen and a couple of chippies, so Wing paced up and down, going out on deck when the wind was not coming directly down from the Arctic. He began a letter to Becky, but he didn't know whether he'd have the courage to send it—he was so ashamed of his handwriting. Damn it all, if only his folks could have sent him to Boise to school. . . . But there was no sense in complaining, he was a hell of a lot better off than *they* had been: homesteading, cutting down the everlasting sagebrush, fighting the black volcanic rock, planting potatoes and beans and corn with no fences to keep out the ranging cattle. They hadn't even had screens in their windows during those first years on the land. Every day his poor-sainted-Mother would spend a half hour before dinner killing flies so the men could sit down to eat a meal without being buzzed to Perdition.

Settling into a sheltered corner of the deck, Wing tried to find comfort in the fact that he, at least, had a neat little house back home in Silver Valley, which he partly owned, and which he was hellbent not to lose to the banks; and he had two terrific boys, smart as whips, and a wife who'd never once crossed him in his life, and was right now maybe needing him, so what was there for *him* to do but stand up and be counted? Carefully he constructed word after word of his letter to Becky, adorning the big capital letters with graceful flourishes, and altogether admiring his own handiwork so much he almost forgot that he was near froze-to-death, had only a few bucks in his pocket, and that only God knew how he'd make it back to Silver Valley. If he failed, he might as well cut bait and run forever, Becky would go on welfare, and maybe be better off without him. But he wasn't going to fail, he was going to Do It. At that moment, surrounded by fjords and mountains and forests of firs as dense as the day of Creation, Wing vowed he would beat the odds or die.

When at last the ferry docked at Anchorage, Wing lost no time in looking around for a flophouse or Salvation Army; he headed straight for the beach where he rightly guessed there'd be another tent city, not as big as the one "Back Outside" as they called the States up here, but sufficiently crude and open as to let a young man like Wing try his luck with the rest of them.

But as soon as he laid his eyes on the place Wing became wary: These were a different breed of men—Last Chance hoboes, ready to steal your blanket while you slept and leave you to freeze. When Wing arrived, nobody spoke to him. He was relieved, at least, that they didn't exchange conspiratorial glances, that it didn't suddenly occur to them that by joining together they could finish Wing off in a minute and bury him in the snow till Spring. Diffidently Wing placed a tightly-rolled newspaper into the fire. Nobody thanked him or acknowledged his presence. He wanted to ask if it were possible to bed down somewhere in the camp, but he was scared to. Bed down with whom? He wouldn't want to sleep under the same roof with any of these guys. Wing decided that the next best thing, for the moment at least, was to find some public building—a post office or hospital or even a bank—where he could warm up without worrying about who might put a knife in his back. So assuming a harmless, indecisive manner, Wing began backing away from the fire. Unlike the well-built fire Kearney had so carefully tended, here they indifferently tossed whatever refuse they had handy. As Wing turned away, the dark smoke billowed toward the limestone skies.

There was still plenty of daylight left, so Wing was not feeling as anxious as he might have felt back home that the darkening wilderness might isolate him before he'd found shelter. But he was colder than he'd ever been in his life and he saw no so-called public buildings. He did spot what appeared to be a cheap sort of lunchroom with steamed-up windows. It had to be warm in there.

Wing sat down at the counter and asked for an order of fried potatoes. They'd be cheap but hot and would keep his belly feeling full till his luck improved. But when the potatoes were set in front of him, he was disappointed; they were cottage fries, mealy and greasy. But at least they were hot, that was all that mattered. He began eating slowly, letting the heat of the place warm him up. As he ate he thought about the potato, what a plague or godsend it could be. As a child back home in southern Idaho, he could remember a sea of potatoes extending across his parents' homestead. When it came time to harvest, every man, woman and child would be bent to the ground. And always, it seemed, they were rescuing the potatoes, from the late blight or the first killing frost or before they became nearly worthless on the market—farmers in Idaho were getting forty-five cents for a hundred pound sack that folks in Chicago would pay six-fifty for—he and his father had once stood beside a veritable mountain of potatoes, enough potatoes to feed a regiment through the entire First World War. But it hadn't paid to ship them, so they'd been left on the ground to rust and sprout . . .

. . . Potatoes . . . with their milky-eyed sprouts that sacrificed themselves like saints and grew to a greater blessing. That could be baked or scalloped or creamed or mashed or made into a cold vichyssoise fit for a Prince, or a hot soup fragrant with parsley and a squirt of lemon—a soup that could warm you to the bone, better than brandy it was for giving you joy without hunger. And even the raw potato, it too was a blessing, it could cure a cold, excite women, bring the rheumatism from out of your *knuckles; its frothy enzyme could wear away a wart. The very skins held a secret power, full of the good growing stuff you needed to keep your teeth from falling out, while within the brown green or purple sacs were stored up all that protein needed for hungry schoolkids: like Abe Lincoln who'd warmed his hands on the way to school with the benevolent potato, then warmed his belly with it at lunchtime. . . . Goddam, potatoes BREATHED. They could change the temperature in your storage bin. And like humans, they could sicken and die, the rot smelling worse than a corpse. Not even formaldehyde-dipping could cure them of the cancerous black rot. He'd seen his mother scrub her hands over and over trying to wash out an odor as strong as ether.*

The tasteless lunchroom potato had made him homesick—not for Becky and the kids but for his own childhood home. Lord, *that* was a wilderness—a sagebrush wilderness, without trees. He hadn't even seen a tree till they made that trip to Salt Lake City. And then the miles and miles of sagebrush that it'd been his job to cut down for firewood; what a blaze it'd make: one big firecracker and you were right back to chopping the brush. That insatiable pot-bellied stove would devour all his hard labor at one gulp. . . . But he'd kept the fire going. With temperatures at forty below to have let the fire go out would have spelled a quick hypothermal death; or to have let the red-hot iron belly of the stove crack from overheating; or to have failed to adjust the damper before going to sleep could also have meant death. And to have fallen into the Canal while getting those endless buckets of water for the potato fields might also have meant death. And bringing in the hay for seventy-two hours like his brother had once done might also have meant death. And walking to the one-room schoolhouse in a snowstorm might well have meant death. And going up to Silver Valley to work in the mines, having received all the booklearning he was to get in this life, without his folks, living in a boarding house alone while he worked a man's shift in the mines from the time he was sixteen, that also might have meant death.

But it was obvious that God had meant that Ephraim Wingfield should survive. Because here he was now, eating potatoes in a joint where it looked like possibly they still spit on the floor. . . . At this moment Wing slid the last piece of potato into his mouth. It was quite cold now, but he savored it nonetheless, sweet to the taste as an after dinner crème de menthe. Feeling more cheerful and reconciled—his reverie on his folks' homesteading days had somehow given him new courage and an almost patriotic sense of his heritage—Wing moved toward the cashier at her register singing softly:

> Potatoes are cheaper
> Tomatoes are cheaper
> Now's the time to fa—a—ll . . . in love.

A pretty woman, Wing was thinking.

"Fifty cents," she said.

He glanced quickly around the walls for a price list in order to correct this error. "Whaddye mean, fifty cents? All I had was an order of fried potatoes."

The cashier glanced over her shoulder toward the kitchen. She raised her voice slightly. "Fifty cents. You ate em, you pay for em."

"But how can that be?" No one had even brought him a bill.

"A *miracle*," she said. "Every day of the year we got miracles here. Guys come in, they eat, and they *pay*."

"I never paid half a buck for an order of fried potatoes in my whole life. I could buy a whole hundred pound sack for that much."

"Yeah? Well, I guess you got a whole new life ahead of you. You better pay now, this not the Salvation Army."

Wing looked around him for somebody to complain to about this outrage. But there was only one elderly man in the restaurant who looked steadily down at his coffee: *not going to get involved*, his profile said, plain as day.

"I could of got a whole dinner for twenty cents." Wing had the humiliated feeling that he was just babbling.

"Yeah, where? Back in the Forty-eight? Well go get your-self one then. But in *this* country, you pay for these pota-toes."

The cook, who also seemed to be the owner, now came out of the kitchen. *Big as a brown bear,* thought Wing. Ridic-ulously it made him think of an old refrain: *Snap your fin-gers honey, I declare. . . . It's a bear, it's a bear it's a bear. . . .*

"This guy givin you a hard time?"

The cashier shrugged, tore out a sheet of red-lined paper from a checkbook, wrote 50¢ right in the center, looped and noosed it around several times with her black pencil, then stuck it on a nail and waited for whatever was going to happen to happen.

With maddening calm she asked, "Call the police?" It was clear to Wing that she had absolute faith in the huge hand which now touched hers reassuringly.

"Yeah. Give him five seconds, then get the police."

"Hey wait a minute! I didn't say I wouldn't pay. I'll pay . . ." Wing hated the sound of his quavering voice.

"You fucking well better pay, or Mr. J. Edgar Hoover will be on your case in just five minutes!"

The goddam thief has a sense of humor, thought Wing bit-terly as he laid two quarters down on the glass counter. He tried to keep his fingers from trembling with rage as he surrendered the price of a hundred pounds of potatoes. The cashier picked up the quarters one at a time, using her nails like tongs, and tossed them into the register where they made a bright clinking sound like horseshoes hitting a stake. Wing was now in such a hurry to leave these robbers—before he got mad enough to yell out some ugly insult that would set him up for an assault charge—that he went out leaving Becky's letter on the counter. He rushed back in again almost immediately for his letter, but the cashier said she'd never seen any such thing. Wing how-ever, spotted a corner of the opened envelope in the trash, fortunately he'd not been so crazy as to send Becky money in an envelope protected only by a U.S. postage stamp.

But he was taking no more chances—merely for the sake of keeping warm—on confrontations with the locals. He walked back to the bus terminal, determined to stay there all night. He'd have to pretend he was waiting for a bus. He inquired at the window about a round-trip fare to Fairbanks. "And how long do you think you'll be in Fairbanks?" asked the clerk, who seemed to be just trying to be helpful; but Wing had become distrustful of personal questions, and answered him evasively. "Well," the clerk said, "your problem will be comin back. You want a round-trip ticket and here it's not yet full winter. But in a few weeks we won't be runnin any more buses between here and Fairbanks, so how would you get back?" Wing replied that he thought he had something lined up, at least for the next couple of months. But just to be certain, he added, he'd try to phone the guy in Fairbanks before making that long trip. Every hour or so Wing got up from his seat in the bus station and dialed the number of the pay phone in front of him: His charade seemed to convince the clerk that Wing wasn't just another bum trying to spend the night in a warm place. He let Wing wait out the night till he could call Fairbanks again in the morning. Wing dozed, one eye on the clock. As soon as dawn broke through the windows—a strange purple sort of dawn that seemed to intensify the cold rain falling ceaselessly—he hiked out to the canning factories without stopping to eat. He was almost the first man in line. The smell of coffee made him feel sick, he could feel the emptiness of his belly like a cold swamp. When a vendor came by hustling his hot watery coffee, Wing gambled another nickel for the sake of his future.

At eight o'clock the employment office opened. The men waiting in line were all told the same thing: A guy came out to announce that they were not hiring here, but there was guaranteed work on Kodiak Island . . . Wing wanted to punch the guy in the face, but instead he laughed a short bitter laugh, like a barking dog. Raging with anxiety and anger, he and several others who'd waited in line, hiked back to the pier and caught the next ferry out to the Island. Eighteen hours later Wing was down to his last buck, but he had a job.

It was no Cozy Cannery. On the Island they worked with fish brought directly from the sea, cutting and slicing, bagging and freezing, and shipping it to the *table d'hôtes* of the world. Seven days a week for seven weeks Wing cut his way through thousands of pounds of flesh, most of it pale and pink as flamingoes; his heart palpitated irregularly from the bennies he took to keep himself awake on the double shift of sixteen hours, and by the time the weather had turned bitter cold so that it was becoming impossible for fishing boats to go out on a run, Wing was coughing up an oozy phlegm, iridescent as caviar, from chronic bronchitis. For weeks everything he touched or wore or ate smelled of fish. At night he dreamt of a fish, lying inert till he attacked it with his long-bladed knife, but as he hacked through its milk-white bones, the fish would suddenly come alive; its eyes would open as if it had been merely asleep, not dead, and opening its mouth, it would become a talking fish, a remonstrative, rebuking, cunning, wheedling fish, that always outsmarted him. Leaping from his clutch as he tried to grip its glistening body, it would swim across the conveyor belt, evading him, always evading him, so that every night he dreamed he'd lost his job due to his own incompetence, and would awake in anguish to the daylight that had scaled the walls of his roominghouse while he slept and had painted his room a soft pink salmon color.

In spite of everything he stuck it out, he endured; he saved more than he spent until, when the seasonal lay-offs began, his shirt was solidly padded with money, and by the time he again boarded the ferry for Anchorage and Seattle—navigating through icy waters within sight of icebergs that had once seemed majestic to Wing but now were merely menacing—Wing had saved enough to hunker down in Silver Valley with Becky and the kids to make it through the longest Depression in history.

But before the ferry returned to Seattle, it stopped once more at Anchorage, and Wing knew he had a thing to do. He had worked like hell, hardly spending anything on himself; but after a few weeks he'd bought a heavy lumberman's jacket and a fur cap which covered his head to the eyebrows. He'd also let his beard grow thick and curling around his face. The beard and the fur cap seemed to expand his entire body size: he looked fifty pounds heavier. Then for the final effect he'd bought a pair of cheap sunglasses—even Becky wouldn't have recognized him, he thought. He checked the departure time for Seattle, synchronized his watch with the ferry's banjo clock, and walked into Anchorage. He headed straight for the joint where he'd paid the price of a hundred pound sack for one potato.

He had chosen the busy noon hour, the place was crowded. Wing sat down at one of the small tables beside the window. He ordered half a fried chicken and some fried potatoes. He saw that they were the same sort of potatoes he'd eaten weeks before, razor-thin, weighing altogether about two ounces. Slowly Wing ate one or two slices, concentrating intently. Then unobtrusively he slipped the chicken into a paper napkin and shoved it into one of his pockets. From another pocket he drew out a small package, fastidiously wrapped in tinfoil. He set the package on the table, unwrapped the tinfoil, and carefully slid the dead rat onto his plate. Then he stood up, cursing loudly. His chair overturned with such force that Wing saw with satisfaction that he'd cracked the window: *that'll bring in cold air like a flood in a mineshaft.* "Christamighty, it's a rat, a goddam rat!" he cried at the top of his voice. Gagging and heaving he rushed out of the restaurant. He stood for a few seconds at the curb, continuing to gag. (*Bigod, I should have been an actor, I missed my calling. They'll be talking about the fried rat in that clip-joint from now till kingdom come. . . .*)

He had it all timed down to the wire. Within ten minutes he'd run like hell back to the ferry, they were pushing away from the pier, and he was heading back to Seattle. He stood on deck waving and waving to the vanishing shore as if he were leaving a thousand friends behind, shouting triumphantly, "*Goodbye Alaska, for now and forever!*"

So, when Reffie arrived in the Valley after his big bust, his *failure* in Seattle, toting his baggage and kids with him, Wing had been exasperated by his poltroonish figure. Talk about being out of work, who knew better than Wing about *that*?

V

In Massachusetts Julia O'Gorman Wingfield had not known that the rest of America was different from Cambridge. She had dimly realized that there were people who believed in the existence of a Brahmin folk whose parents trusted that their sons would go to Harvard, but that they would not, while studying in the university's great libraries, become so liberal as to marry a Catholic girl like herself.

In truth, these sons were not ever much in danger; for it had not once occurred to Julia that one of them might marry her. She had not ever to her memory spoken to any of those scions whose venerable ancestors had created the culture and chaos of Cambridge she so admired as she walked home from school, following Trowbridge to Massachusetts Avenue and straight through the heart of Harvard Square to Watertown. The young men who glanced at her as she passed might have been so many Lords discussing the Poor Laws in Her Majesty's Parliament for all their relevance to the O'Gormans. But one thing Julia had clearly grasped was that though the O'Gormans lived only two miles from the Yard of the great university, neither of her parents had ever set foot in it. Therefore, it was not theirs, it was not hers.

What was hers, however, was a quiet corner of the big cemetery which was about a mile from the house into which the O'Gormans finally settled, following three convulsive moves after Julia's father had lost his job. It was in this house that her mother had announced, rather like Brigham Young upon seeing the great Salt Lake, "This is it . . ." and the O'Gormans had never rented another house. Towards June, in the last weeks of the school year, as final exams were approaching, Julia would stop at the cemetery every day. It was a wonderful place to study. In high school, she had enjoyed studying, hoping to impress her teachers, hoping to impress the Big Company she imagined she'd one day work for; hoping (even) to impress the blind boy, Angelo Viggiano who sat beside her punching his perfect mastery of the Ablative Case into his metal plate. On afternoons in early spring, when Julia had reviewed the vocabulary lesson assigned daily, Julia would sit in a sort of a trance, listening to Angelo's stylus pick-and-choose, steady and determined as a bird tapping a cage. While Miss Sullivan was assuring them that Caesar's conquests had rendered unto Western Civilization a culture which was The Best the Western World Has Ever Known except for, of course, the Greek, Julia would sit, pretending to study, pondering what these wars and encampments in Britannia could mean to Angelo, and how all this was going to help when he had fulfilled his ambition to become a District Attorney so that he would be able to prosecute those (as he had told her he intended to do), who committed heinous crimes leaving people crippled or maimed forever.

Julia would sit watching Angelo's fingers. They had a life of their own. They thought and ruminated and stopped short, then ran again, swift as sandpipers, across his metal beach. When he had finished a page he would—with a brisk snap of the spring lock—remove the page from its metal plate. There would be a moment of solemn silence in the classroom, and Miss Sullivan would give out some arbitrary grammar work. Obediently their class of college-bound teen-agers would bend their heads to their workbooks for the last quarter of an hour while Angelo—who would later have his exercises read to him by his sister or mother—would sit quietly, his hands resting on his knees, motionless as a guide dog, his chin at an angle, his head turning almost imperceptibly on its axis as he listened to the silence which for him (as Julia could understand, merely by shutting her eyes), was not a silence at all but a shuffling of papers and perhaps the knicking sound of the sweet lemon lozenge against Julia's teeth, and the soft scraping of the window shade which rose and fell, rose and fell. And the air. . . . Julia took it all in for Angelo as if they had entered together some secret seraglio of the senses: The air for him on that June day would have been charged with the odor of chalk, earthy and poignant as the veiny mineral fragrance of broken stone. . . .

Julia had not known then that theirs was a Civilized Classroom, that indeed they were all of them supremely Civilized there in the hub of the universe, that they were Civilized in special ways that only they could understand because Michigan, Wyoming, Kansas and Texas and certainly not Silver Valley (as Julia was now learning to her grief) did not even know what it was they lacked. But whatever else Julia's high school may or may not have been on that day, the sky had been flawless, the air radiant. Only retrospectively, when Julia had come with Reffie thousands of miles from home to the C & L Silver-Lead and Zinc Company, had Julia reflected upon this miracle of breathable air: air *frissonante*, as Miss Sullivan might have said, and how with one grim assault Reffie had been deprived of it all; how now when he came out of the mine and took in the air and the sunlight he looked like a dying man looking upon his loved ones; or rather, Julia amended, trying consciously to use and preserve the little learning she'd gained before her marriage—like Leeuwenhoek, seeing for the first time the myriads of visible creatures under his microscope.

Even Texas during those first bridal months had been better than Silver Valley; Julia would have preferred not to move again. But it seemed as if from the very beginning of her marriage she'd been doomed to wander, never stopping: from Boston to Texas to northern California to Washington to this dirty mining town over three hundred miles from a real museum or library or theatre or. . . . How different was their marriage, hers and Reffie's, from the O'Gormans who, having had the historical good fortune to immigrate from London to Boston After-the-War, had anchored themselves there for life. But of course for Julia's parents the future—as they would have both asserted—could hold nothing worse than the past they had left behind in London, because as an Irish working man, her father said, he'd been worse off yet in London than if he'd stayed in Dublin. In Boston, at least, by virtue of her strong back and young arms Julia's mother had swept into the kitchens of the gentry, polishing their parqueted floors, answering their gleaming phones—learning to say "Williams' residence" rather than "Hello". Her mother had learned, too, to sleep in a third floor alcove with the youngest of the Williams' children until a year after marrying Walter O'Gorman she was "blessed" as she always insisted on calling it, with a child of her own. Still, Mrs. O'Gorman had continued to work for other people even after she married—learning to inflate *soufflés* to just the right weight of breathable air, and to walk three Dobermans as if they were her own children, feeding them dainties which she would have marvelled to have seen on her parents' table in Ireland.

These stories of her parents' early married life had been repeated and stored up till Julia's arrival in the world while the Walter O'Gormans were being blessed first with a daughter, Elisabeth, and then with another girl who died in infancy—leaving her mother as totally devastated by grief as if this child were not to be followed by five other O'Gormans who would break her mother's heart over and over as they left home. But since there had been so many O'Gormans, it was all the more amazing to Julia in retrospect that she had been permitted to study what she wanted to, learning *Useless* Things, as her parents would sometimes observe with an unconcealed pride that was not without anger—anger not directed at her, but at the ruthless Cataloguer who defined and separated out dreams from necessities.

One of these *Useless Things* was the Latin Julia was listening to. They all knew Latin to be a superfluous luxury, just as certainly as if her lessons had arrived in a box from Filenes' labelled *Fragile*, at the bottom of which lay some filagreed Useless gift which, when unveiled and held up to the light, would break in one's fingertips like the iridescent dry wings of insects. But her father had seen how passionately Julia loved it. He had personally visited her high school principal and after considerable haggling they had scratched Business English from her schedule and substituted The Foreign Language Requirement for the College Track. As a result Julia's future had been irreversibly forged. She was to be a Vocational-College Track student, a permanently hyphenated person.

But on that June day she could not have imagined she would ever be concerned about the "idle luxury" of her education. She was listening to the silence which had concentrated itself in Miss Sullivan's class. Twenty-seven sixteen-year olds now began watching the minute hand of the old clock as it moved forward in an absent-minded spurt, every two and a half minutes, falling downward toward the pricking hand of four (Why was 3:20 the established moment of their liberation? The Seniors said it was because they were still young and stupid and needed the extra hour). Before the day was officially ended, the blackboards would be washed and all the windows would be shut and locked. Because of Julia's love and loyalty toward Miss Sullivan, she would assist her in these chores. But for the past quarter hour Julia had been almost totally preoccupied with the faint breeze from a nearby window, watching the rise and fall of the gold-glinting hair on her own arms—a sensuous distraction which made her feel like a traitor to Miss Sullivan and all *haute culture*.

It was also one of Julia's little tasks, particularly on Fridays, to check every desk to see that no one had forgotten his lunch box or baseball cap or notebooks or chewing gum wrappers; and once Julia had found a condom, neat as a bullet, hidden in a corner of the desk. She had stood for a moment, more in wonder than in surprise, grasping the overwhelming fact that there were boys in her class old enough to engage in sins of this nature (that there might be girls who were also old enough for sin was still unthinkable to Julia). And while Julia and Miss Sullivan worked at their tasks, Angelo, who was waiting for his sister to drive him home, would be carefully packing his books—books which always seemed to Julia so heavy and cumbersome that to this day she had not stopped asking herself how one had the zeal and courage to learn *any-thing* when one needed a grocery cart just to carry around the reading assignments—huge volumes studded with Braille like carpenters' tacks.

But on this June day Julia had carelessly set aside all such burning questions, and when her chores for Miss Sullivan were finished, she began her slow walk home-ward. Overhead the sky was a tortoise-shelled vault; the sun offered sensuous promises for the rites of Spring. As she stopped in the Square to listen (as she loved to do) to the arcane conversations around her, she overheard a heated argument—which took place without so much as a glance at her apparently invisible presence—about some blazers which had been ordered but had not arrived in time for a special event. She drifted onward, dealing rather deftly, as she thought, with her lemon sherbet and her books until the sherbet was quite gone and she had reached the cemetery. She piled her books beside her on her favorite bench. Blue and yellow crocuses, daffodils, purple amaryllis and scarlet geraniums ablaze with life, spread before her. Everywhere there were sparrows—on the tombstones, among the flowers—chirping ceaselessly with an anxious, determined joy, as if they had promised to sing till the dead rose again, asking *Did-we-do-it-right? Did-we-do-it-right?*

It did not occur to her that the sparrows' refrain or even that the cemetery had anything to do with herself. It was a beautiful cemetery, that was true; but like the faces of the very old with their lives of passion or complacency sculp-tured forever on their brow like walking epitaphs, what could all that have meant to her? No—what she had proba-bly been thinking if she had been thinking anything at all in those retrospectively glorious days of her "youth" was that this was *her* quiet Spot where she could easily do her homework—even taking out her notebook to begin, looking away from the bright flowers, as if they would always be there for her to see. . . . With so little sense of her own mortality she might have gone on for another year or two admiring the passionately flowering geraniums placed beside the graves and might have gone on forever admiring the intaglioed carvings on the marble tombs. *Yea, Lord,* she confessed ruefully afterwards, *I might have remained in paradisal ignorance forever if Hollis Michael Hearne had not also been there that day.*

He had stopped, recognizing her with an air of injured surprise, as if she were trespassing. For her part she was gratified that he remembered her. Although he was a member of the school's debating club, he rarely attended meetings. This of course had been understandable since he was a Senior, and everyone knew that they had many senior activities competing for their attention.

Without exactly understanding what she was guilty of, Julia had felt obliged to excuse herself. "It's a nice place to do homework," she said.

He stared in angry amazement. "What *kind* of homework?"

Feigning an insouciance she was far from feeling, she had recited a few lines from a Shakespeare sonnet. She wished afterwards it had been Gray's *Elegy*, it would have been more appropriate, but she had become nervous, her heart beating with a strange excitement, and she'd been unable to remember exactly how Gray's *Elegy* started. . . .

Still staring, he observed: "And you find this just the right place for that kind of stuff?"

Was he being ironic? Did he mean to be witty? Was she supposed to smile? A babble of merriment rose to her lips, but she managed to stifle it just in time.

"You didn't come to . . . *visit*?" he added, still with shock and anger, as if it were an outrageous insult that she used this place as a bower to recite verses in, not regarding it as he said later, "as a charnel house where people lay shovelled in over their ears."

"I *like* to come here," she admitted, though she had sensed it was certainly not what he wanted to hear. She also sensed that her admission would evoke a strong reaction, maybe he'd not walk indifferently away, but stay with her to argue. . . .

"*Like* to come here! Christ, I can't think of a place I'd rather not be. It's just you lucky people with the blue sky in your eyes—" he now looked more closely at Julia's blue eyes as if to confirm her guilt "—you people who imagine mausoleums and crypts and bones and catacombs and pots of geraniums on Veterans Day make a romantic background . . . for *verses*. Suddenly he pulled out his handkerchief and wiped his eyes. "Damn you. Damn you all—"

Shocked and hurt, Julia had wondered whether she should call out to a policeman passing by, or whether to take Hollis Michael Hearne in her arms. She knew she *must* not take him in her arms, however; so she had begun to pick up her books slowly, one by one, as a signal that she thought it was time for her to go home, but she did not leave. It had seemed pointless, anyway, to pretend to be going home after Michael had abruptly sat down on the very spot where her books had been, as if he thought she'd picked up her books so as to make room for him.

He said he was sorry he'd spoken to her that way. He blurted out that five years ago his parents had been killed in an automobile accident and that, actually, he hated cemeteries. He hardly knew why he had decided to come here today. His voice faltered and stared at Julia as if he expected her to tell him why he had come. But Julia, stunned into silence, could only stare into his dark, angry eyes. After a long silence he added awkwardly. "I live with my sister . . . But she's sick now.

"Oh. . . ." murmured Julia, looking down at the earth.

He pointed vaguely toward his chest. "She's had surgery twice . . . and now chemotherapy, which if you ask me, is making her sicker that she was. She has two kids," he added grimly, again looking searchingly at Julia as if she might have some answer to this enigma.

"But who will—?" She didn't know how to raise such a question. She couldn't imagine her own family without her mother—laughing or crying or making tea or warning her daughters of the treachery of "men," meaning of course, only their father.

"They'll go to a home, maybe."

"Home? Whose home?"

"*A Home*," he said almost contemptuously. Plainly her ignorance was boundless.

After a moment's silence she managed to ask: "Is she . . . doesn't she have—?"

Mercifully he interrupted whatever circumlocution Julia might have discovered.

"No. He left her when they were but tiny babes. . . ."

This odd expression for some reason rendered Julia speechless. Everything about this Iberian giant now nervously shoving back his black hair, was new and surprising. Julia could think of no way to express her sympathy. But it was he who presently suggested they walk back to the Square and have a coke somewhere. She could not help noticing as they left how he strode impatiently ahead of her and did nothing so awkward or romantic as to offer to carry her books. It had seemed to her then his blunt way of asserting that we must all make our own way in this life, that as far as he was concerned, he had neither the time nor energy for any burdens other than his own.

Although only two miles separated Julia's sheltered home from that of Michael's sister Nancy, it might have been the Bering Strait: culturally, the two families were continents apart. Compared to the O'Gormans, this remnant of the Hearne family were beggars. While it was true that the O'Gormans lived in a rented house, they nevertheless faced the world with lace curtains in their windows and a white cloth on the dining room table in the center of which her mother firmly supported her personal concept of Good Taste and Beauty with a bowl of waxed fruit, vivid as a Renoir. To emphasize the relationship her mother had a Renoir print framed and hung above the dining room buffet. *Whereas*, Julia observed, at Nancy's apartment they didn't even have a dining room, much less a dining room table. They ate standing around the kitchen stove or seated around the coffee table with its ornately carved legs, on

which Michael and the children precariously balanced piz-
zas and popcorn and potato chips and cokes—Trevi foun-
tains of coke—and occasionally when The Check had
arrived—Julia presumed it to be Nancy's welfare check but
never asked—there would be a feast: little cardboard boxes
with metal handles filled with foods from the local
delicatessen—cole slaw and macaroni salad and potato
salad and barbecued beans. Julia was afterwards to recall
that during the year in which Michael had besieged and
occupied her girlhood, she had never seen him except at
one emotional extreme or another—pushing food or the
table or even people away from him so *abruptly* that everything, it seemed, rattled and overturned—or laughing with
such tender joyous abandon that tears came to his eyes.
These moments of joy, however, were rare. Most of the
time he and Julia sat around in the local drugstore while
Michael cursed the very coke they drank, wondering
whether he should try the merchant marines (but he dis-
trusted the tyranny of sea captains) or go to Florida or
California where it was understood there were still for-
tunes to be made (but he hadn't enough money even to
stake himself to such a risky venture, he would add brood-
ingly), while Julia would nod sympathetically, not really
understanding this dilemma of impotence, wanting with
all her heart to comfort him.

Since arriving in Silver Valley it had now and then occurred to her that if she had really understood Michael's
desperate need, she might have then advised him to "go-
West": he might have found a new life, perhaps, in farming or even in the silver mines. But no—she would always
be forced to admit—not in the mines—not any more than
Reffie, would he have been able to work underground
miles from the sun. Every week that Reffie spent underground still seemed an inversion of his nature as monstrous as taking a sailor accustomed to the wide, wide
sea—to the cliffs of Dover, to ports, to viaducts, to the
Acropolis, to medieval towns clustering like honeycombs
around the Adriatic sea wall, and harnessing him, a blin-
dered mule, to grind the eternal corn. . . . Poor-Reffie (like

herself, Reffie but a two-years' bridegroom, had become a hyphenated person) was meant for the outdoor life, and they'd hoped they might eventually put aside enough from his job at C & L to buy some land. That had not happened . . . but, at least, she consoled herself, neither the O'Gormans nor the Wingfields had been cursed by tragedy the way Michael's family had been.

When, reluctantly, Michael had finally taken her to visit the mother of "these two devils," as he called Nancy's children, Julia was totally unprepared to find a young woman—*walking around*, Julia thought, *just like me and everybody else who expects to live maybe another fifty years or more*, waiting for a miracle that would save her for Joel and Wendy. Julia could no more grasp the fact that Nancy was terminally ill than she could imagine her own death, until one afternoon as she and Michael and Julia walked slowly down the corridor to the visiting area of the hospital, they stood shocked and frightened while Nancy stood trembling in the hospital corridor, unable to proceed further. Leaning on Michael they had slowly made their way to the bay-windowed visitors' alcove, where long sheets of sunlight dazzled down through the curtains. Nancy at once folded herself into the first chair she touched with a look on her face such as Julia had seen in photos of exhausted mountain climbers within miles, yet, of the top. It was then Julia began to understand Michael's rage.

What Julia had not understood, and which remained to this very day one of the holy mysteries, was that Nancy had talked, not about Eternity or the immortality of the Soul, or of the terrors of the Dark or of the suffering of the Innocent, of the injustice of a God who tested his worshippers with these unequal contests of Will, but about the lack of paper cups in the dispensary, so that patients were frequently obliged, Nancy said, to wash and reuse their own waterglass in the bathroom, under conditions likely to be somewhat less than sterile; and that Nancy's daughter Wendy was having a lot of trouble with her teeth, she ate too many sweets, but then the child had always loved sweets. Nancy recalled with a sudden smile of pure vicarious pleasure that when Wendy was only five years old her daughter had prepared a chocolate pudding by herself—not ready-made pudding, Nancy added with pride, but a confection of cocoa and sugar and cornstarch and milk, and that now Wendy already knew how to make divinity fudge, and that the dentist at the university Clinic had said that Wendy should have a few teeth removed to make room for the new ones coming in, they were crowding each other, and that the way it was going, it was likely Wendy would need braces.

Or again, on another of Julia's rare visits, the conversation had revolved about food: about what was or was not eaten there, and which patients refused to eat vegetables or meat or to drink milk according to the vagaries of their appetites or religious consciences. But the meals, Nancy hastened to reassure them, after a glance at Michael's angry face, were excellent here: though to be sure on Sundays dinner was eaten late, very late, because the cook who, by the way used to know Michael when he was a boy, and was now a dietitian, went to Mass first and made it back just in time for everybody to have dinner before the scattered Sunday visitors arrived.

At the word "visitors," everyone's voice seemed to become muffled. It was not easy to explain why there were so few visitors. Even Michael seldom came to visit, and he now turned to look out the window, opening and closing his hands as if his fingers ached. After a while Nancy turned to Julia and asked her about "school," as if she were a child like Joel or Wendy and she, Nancy, had to put herself out in the conversation to make Julia comfortable. Julia winced, wishing she knew how to be at once entertaining and interesting and sympathetic and yet utterly silent, so as not to disturb the meditational murmurings of Nancy's voice. Julia felt as she did sometimes at Mass, that to cough or speak would have been on her part a sign of spiritual emptiness. . . . But having made a weak effort to include Julia in the conversation, Nancy seemed to resign herself to the inequities of the situation and began to talk. She talked as if she were talking for posterity and Michael were writing down every word for her children and her children's children—talked almost without interruption except when she was stopped, sometimes in the middle of a sentence, to gasp for breath. Her voice, even as Julia and Michael sat listening, seemed to have become at once deeper and less audible.

When, after their visit Julia had asked Michael why he himself had been so quiet—apologizing at the same time for her own mesmerized silences which she feared had not helped Nancy one bit, he had replied with a broken voice that his sister was so changed. In less than a month since he'd last seen her, she was very much changed. "It was a shock. I didn't know what to say. I wanted to smash the place to bits. Why aren't they saving her? What's the damned medical profession *for* if they're not going to save her? It's all a colossal lie," he said. Nothing would save Nancy nor himself either, and turning fiercely upon Julia, "Nor *you* either, you better believe it!" Julia had thought for a moment that he simply hated her for having had the good luck to inherit her mother's splendid physical health. But it had been only his agony, as he later explained, at witnessing (again) the Inexorable Intruder face to face. The Nancy he loved was already irrevocably changed—her face seamed with new lines, her eyes which had always been so clear and bright, shot with red from sleepless nights or perhaps from crying. Even her hands had grown cracked and leathery, and when she'd stared at him there'd been a new bewilderment in her face, as if she could not understand how her very own brother could continue to be as he'd always been (weren't they the all-too-same flesh and blood?) Nancy's fingers had prodded the small green fern which sat spreading its leaves on the hospital table. She'd pushed her fingers deep into the clay pot of earth as if anxious to feel the knotty certainty of root and stem, and when she'd lifted her fingers she'd seemed to stare in sorrow and unbelief at her earth-soiled hands. . . .

"And meanwhile we're talking about Wendy's teeth and chocolate pudding and whether the goddammed cook goes to Mass. Julia, it all makes me mad as hell." he added in a shaking voice.

Julia nodded. *Of course. No need to explain. Stupid of her to ask.* She continued to nod long after he had stopped talking, agreeing with him from the bottom of her heart. She felt she would burst into tears, but instead she leaped up on her toes, just high enough to break off a slender redbud branch and whip the air with it as if whipping all Michael's invisible enemies, while she and Michael passed one bus stop after another forgetting to wait to take one back to Julia's house, until somehow they had arrived at the room in Davis Square that Michael had rented about a month before, when his sister's illness had taken a serious turn for the worse and the children had been sent to foster parents. And it was easier than all words and explanations to let Michael hold her hand, gripping it as though he meant to fold it lengthwise and put it in his pocket. Without asking herself what was the meaning of all this, feeling only that it was nearly the end of summer and Michael's sister was dying, they had stolen up the stairs very softly because Julia had known even then, without ever having been told that if Michael had a girl in his room the landlady would throw them both out with a great hue and cry about his Religion and her Respectable House. So without letting go of her hand, they had slipped into Michael's room.

And if Julia had been surprised by Nancy's home which had had neither lace curtains nor tablecloth, her heart was melted and shaped to warm wax taking on Michael's image forever at the sight of the room in which Michael slept and paced the floor and maddened himself with thoughts of failure and eternity. It had a bureau and an orange crate filled with books and several hangers in the closet. It had a small metal bed near the window with a striped spread which Michael now ceremoniously pulled back and folded neatly at the foot. The sheets were clean and unironed. Julia was all her life to remember the laundry marks on the pillow case, the rough texture of the sheets on her bare back and the solemn way in which Michael had begun to make love to her, leading her first to sit in a hard wooden chair where he knelt and removed her shoes and stockings. Julia had noticed a dark smudge across her instep where the shoe had rubbed, and she had tried to hide it, but he had taken her bare feet in his arms, weeping, "Dirt and sweat—only the dead are truly clean." And thus they had comforted one another.

Julia had been taught all about Sin, nothing about its power. She had not understood why it was so hard "to resist the Devil." She now discovered why. It was because the Devil spoke like the angel he was; his fingers were soft as velvet and curled into the conches of one's body like a warm, trembling creature seeking life, not destroying but creating. The devil laughed like a cherub, his mouth an open dipper of fresh water; the devil spoke from a chest that was a stream of Irish laughter. He deliberately, it would seem, wore threadbare shirts so that from the moment he loosened his worn leather belt, the bare flesh beckoned to be coaxed and solaced. And his sex was beautiful: how could it be denied? It bore the banner of strong youth, the succulence of flowers, the tender probing figure of a billed ibis. She worshipped his sex, it was obedient to her touch and adamant to his will. She had no desire to resist it. If this was what had destroyed the great but erring Abélard and Héloïse how was Julia to resist—she a mere girl who had never before suckled at the honeyed mouth of an Irish bard? (Michael claimed to *be* an Irish bard though he had never, he said, composed any song but murmurs of admiration as he moved through her thighs, flexed, silent and stirring as sea anemones.)

So it was a Sin, of course. She didn't need the parish priest to tell Michael that it was sinful—the most elementary teachings at Julia's home would have taught her that. But what she and Michael had to weigh, with a most un-Celtic pragmatism, was whether theirs was a sinful condition which they should end at once in the mutual poverty of marriage, or whether it would be wiser for them to wait until Michael at least—Julia's future had seemed still so far away as not yet to need consideration—had finished his education, which he'd not even started, having only recently begun to think about Boston College.

"*Wait? Wait?*" Michael would exclaim as if the word were a curse, and drawing her into his arms he would protest, "I can't wait. I can't wait another minute." So they would forget to wait for money, jobs, education and the future and would begin instead to wait for the most unbearably heightened moment to begin to sin again. Thus, as her parents would have described it, Julia *fell* into sin as into a well, again and again.

It was Michael's small room which was ever to be thought of as their "lovers' bower" as Michael called it. Perhaps this was because of the ineffable lash of poverty which lay upon it, like a healed wound in a beloved body: the narrow, metal bed with its concave mattress, the comical floor bulging from a thousand scrubbings, the wood so warped that the boards creaked and rolled beneath their bare feet like barrel staves; the tiny wash basin which their passion taught them to use with perfect indifference to its cracked bowl and throaty drain, but with absolute and jealous attention to their own bodies as they prepared themselves like Nero's catamites anointed for an Emperor's love. Julia had preferred that ugly room to all other places on earth, because it had proved again and again that their love was Prospero's wand: It turned the dusty curtains to purple velvet, the trough of mattress to a Sybarite's marble tub. Even the cobwebbed light fixture in the cracked ceiling above them was a miracle in that it did not fall but remained suspended, like the Earth revolving endlessly in its sphere, but which held firmly in the hand of God, trembled but did not fall. . . . Julia would sometimes blink at its dim light from where she lay, and when she opened her eyes, there would now and then be revealed to her a thread of light across which a very busy, frightened and intelligent insect hurried to and fro, hunching its small back and pausing now and then as if to listen to the turbulence below.

Abandoning themselves thus to love, they had believed they had only Nancy's mortality to brood over and the problem of whether to marry now or in the future. But suddenly the future—at least so far as the O'Gormans were concerned, disappeared. After twenty-eight years, Julia's father was out of a job (who needed foremen where there was no one to supervise?) and Walter O'Gorman was expected to start all over again as if the intervening years had been nothing and he were still a lad of eighteen, full of energy and hope and promise and love and married to the most beautiful young girl in the world who was also full of energy and hope and promise and love. The only difference was that since then they'd had six children.

Julia learned of this new calamity upon arriving home from school one sultry day. In silence and concern she had put down her books. She had thought at first that perhaps her mother had fainted because her mother was sitting on the floor leaning against the sofa and her father was offering her a glass of water. But it was simply that in wonder and shock, her mother had sunk down to the earth, as though in sudden realization that the earth was their true and certain ancestral home. O'Gorman, overwhelmed, had taken her in his arms to console her, but she had remained stunned and silent, too shocked even to weep; it had been her father rather, who'd begun to sob with anger and guilt (what had he done wrong that he should find himself unemployed at his age?). Eventually they had all joined her mother on the floor, shunning the chairs as being perhaps too civilized and comfortable for such a disaster. Like the desert Indians reduced to subsistence, to whatever scraps of bone, leather and desert cactus they might survive on, the O'Gormans had begun casting off the dispensable.

Thus, while Michael was waiting to get accepted at some nearby college (several had already rejected him as not having satisfied one or another of their requirements), and while Julia's parents were grappling with History, she and Michael were meeting every afternoon to express their long litany of complaints, but ending always with caresses and reaffirmations of their Great Good Luck: They were so lucky, they said, so lucky to have each other. What else could they ask of the world?

The world had other things in mind for them, however, and by the end of that long year Julia was to learn more about the way of the world than she was ever to know again. Indeed, the next eighteen months brought such a crescendo of catastrophes it was as if a bored and resentful God had decided to test the O'Gormans in order to see how far he might try their faith in his orderly universe.

Walter O'Gorman had been separated from his work the way he might have become separated from God—at first gradually and agnostically, with a sense of lingering vulnerability to events should He after all turn out to exist; then with bouts of hope that perhaps it was not, after all, a necessary and permanent separation, that this Fall-from-Faith was not irreversible, that the housing industry would revive and interest rates would fall and the auto industry would recover and the mills would open, and plants would begin to hire again and even office workers who'd been only temporarily (they'd been told) laid off would be recalled to their typewriters and calculators and computer terminals, and the O'Gormans would again begin to plan for their children's future; time would again pass quickly and imperceptibly until eventually the children were all educated, the mortgage paid off and the O'Gormans would be permitted, thank God, to begin the process all over again with the same hope, the same energy, the same waiting for their future, for their grandchildren.

But none of this happened. Instead Walter O'Gorman's faith spiralled downward. No call came to deliver him; it was as if he had been excommunicated from Work forever. Nevertheless, week after week they had waited for the promised miracle to happen until at last, just before Christmas O'Gorman had consented to Julia's mother taking in a couple of foster children. In spite of their enlarged family and reduced circumstances they had tried to celebrate Christmas as usual. Their Christmas tree had stood perky with popcorn balls and ornaments made by the

O'Gorman children at other Christmases and sacredly preserved for over twenty years by Julia's mother. The two little boarders sat wide-eyed and frightened at this strange new turn in their lives: The State had given them over to the O'Gormans for nurture and education, and they were overwhelmed by the presence of the O'Gorman children. For the sake of the newcomers Margaret had played to the hilt their annual Christmas "drama," which consisted of pretending to be prepared to wait all night for the paunchy St. Nick to arrive. Since the O'Gormans had no proper chimney, Margaret had explained to them that probably the poor fellow would have to climb the wooden stairs (it was really a fire escape) to the rear of their house. Then she had served some cinnamon cookies to go with the hot cocoa, and they had all settled down to wait, until at last around eleven o'clock when the children were perishing for sleep, Margaret had nodded significantly at Julia and announced that she thought she'd get ready for bed. Almost simultaneously there had been a knock at their door and moments later a sack had fallen onto their porch, knocking against the storm door.

But even such romantically heroic efforts to preserve the joys of the good old days failed as, months later, O'Gorman was still making the rounds of the employment offices. In the past four months since his unemployment checks had run out, he had changed his approach. He began offering his services in all areas, in *any* area. But he was no longer a young man; his excuse for being out of a job grew frothy in his mouth: He had trouble swallowing his saliva as he explained all this to the Personnel Managers.

While her father was slogging the pavements, Julia abruptly learned that disasters may come not only to wary, world-wise immigrants but to the bright-eyed new American generation without a trace of their foreign culture in their speech. Julia had barely walked down the aisle of her high school auditorium, diploma in hand (she had included her seldom-used middle name, Irene, and the change had made the document seem as if it were an honor meant for someone else, while at the same time the embossed Gothic letters made the paper seem as ornamental and useless as a medieval manuscript) when Michael had called to tell her he would not be able to take her to the senior dance. Desperate perhaps to prove that some things were still right in their crumbling world, Julia had lavished so much attention to this *rite de passage* and her disappointment was so great that at first she could not comprehend what he was saying. Even his voice was blurred. He sounded as if he were in a foreign country. She had stiffened to receive the blow. He was going to tell her, of course, that he didn't love her anymore, that was the way it always was, wasn't it? But to her shock he began speaking to her in language that was a strange mixture of love and legalese, explaining that "under the circumstances" and "without, of course, wanting to scare you" but "nevertheless it would be advisable" and "of course even x-rays aren't always foolproof. . . ."

"Michael, are you all right?"

"Yes, yes. I've got just a touch. . . . Small as a dime. It's you I'm worried about. They wouldn't even have noticed it, but they made me take another physical if I was going to use the gym. . . ."

It took a while to sink in. They were supposed to go dancing and make monumental love in honor of the first high school graduate to have fallen in love with the Irish bard, Hollis Michael Hearne, not rushing panic-stricken down to the city Emergency Room to take x-rays of Julia's lungs. Michael's extreme concern for her health even seemed some romantic role her bard had fallen into. She couldn't believe there could be anything wrong with Michael, he seemed so splendidly healthy; therefore it must be some tender hoax meant to intensify their love, and all would be made right again with a potion of Oberon laid on their eyes during their next sleep. . . .

But their eyes remained open all that night. While Julia's parents assumed that they were gaily dancing the night away, she and Michael had sat in the car he had borrowed for the evening, while Julia wept. At last, coming to a decision, they had arrived at the Emergency Room in all their senior prom finery. Michael had explained to the astonished nurse in attendance that there had been no accident, but that he felt he *must know at once* whether he was guilty of . . . guilty of having exposed his fiancée. . . . *Why that's me*, Julia recognized with surprise, and she was always afterwards to remember the wave of joy that came over her at the recognition—a joy followed almost at once by the cold, inquiring voice of Survival. Was she willing to risk death for the pride and joy of that title?

But on that night such questions had been overcome in a wave of promises. It was true, they were forced to admit, that like Abélard and Heloïse they would be separated; but they would also, like the lovers of old, *write*. They would fill entire galleons with cargoes of letters and then, after a few months—or maybe a year at most—of the wonderful new treatments for tuberculosis modern medicine had now, Michael would again be ready to take on, first the University, then the World.

And she had kept her promise, Julia was ever afterwards to be able to prove, because Michael had kept all her letters, eventually returning them to her. . . . Yes, she had written galleons of letters to her lover in Ward Six of the sanatorium. Because writing long letters was her only reward for her day's work at the Fall River cotton mill, her only relief from the long loneliness during which she was home with her family only on week-ends.

But Julia had begun to understand as early as her first week in the mill that she was not composing these threnodies and epithalamiums for her lover but for herself, that they were compensation for another day of involuntary servitude.

Julia was not yet seventeen and she had already been in love. She trusted God. She loved her country. She believed she had received a decent education which would endear her to the hearts of the middle class. She considered that her spoken English was excellent and that she was "highly articulate," as the recommendations in her personnel file indicated. In short, she was young and believed herself to be eminently employable. For her father, on the other hand, there appeared not to be a crack left in the mortised economic wall into which he might burrow and survive. First he had been obliged to see his eldest daughter, Elisabeth go on welfare. For years after Elisabeth's husband had deserted her O'Gorman had "helped her out a little," so that Elisabeth might feed and clothe herself and her son. Then he had been forced to allow his wife to take in the foster children, a bitter blow to his pride. Finally he had been forced to stand aside and allow his youngest daughter, Julia, to go out to work; it was the last humiliating blow for him, and it always seemed to Julia that her father became a broken man after she went to work in Fall River.

When she had first brought up the idea of taking a job rather than going on to college, she had not mentioned the small cotton mill which had survived the historic migration of the textile industry, first to the Southern states and then to the developing nations of the world who were exporting their cheaper textiles at an ever-increasing rate. Julia knew they were hiring again at the Fall River mill; there had been a brief revival of production since a new generation of fashion-conscious, upwardly mobile young people had begun to opt again for natural fibers over synthetics, especially for summer clothing to be carried abroad in the suitcases of tourists seeking warmer climates. The Fall River plant had based their hopes on a recent advertising campaign that offered a product that "breathed" *Wear The Natural Fiber They Wear in India*, it advised.

When Julia had first brought up the idea of working away from home, she had not mentioned the Fall River mill because she was beginning to understand that she had been (until now) the relatively protected daughter of a hard-working Irishman who, by the sheer strength of his will had kept them, though often precariously, in their social class. Her father, Julia had come to realize, would not consider working in the mill a job suitable for a daughter of that class. And Julia herself, when she had taken the bus out to Fall River to fill out her application, had felt rather the excitement of a social experiment such as a journalist might have felt rather than the embarrassment of becoming déclassée. As she'd filled out the form, she had not really believed she would be working there. She considered that she was merely making a reconnaissance trip. Nothing, finally, would ever come of it, her father would regain control of their lives, their world would be secure again. Meanwhile O'Gorman let it be known that he would take any job, any job at all, and one day he proved it.

One Friday night in January—Julia was to remember it all the more clearly because it was three months to the day before she had met Reffie—O'Gorman was called to the phone and instructed to rent or borrow a truck and drive to Providence, where he would carry some caskets from Providence to Arlington. Eager to earn a day's pay, O'Gorman had set the alarm for five in the morning. On sudden impulse he wakened Julia and asked her to come along with him: he needed someone to talk to and help keep him awake, he said. It was impossible, she knew to refuse an invitation that was also a command, so she had reluctantly put on several layers of clothes and settled herself in the cab of the truck. It was an old truck, the heater did not work, it took half an hour just to get the engine going. During most of the ride there, there was ice on the windshield. Every fifteen minutes or so her father would stop the truck and rub furiously at the windshield with his gloved fist. As they drove through the slowly-breaking dawn, he explained to her with gratification that this one day's work would pay nearly a whole month's rent, they'd be back in time for supper. Julia merely nodded her approval, which he seemed to need. The early morning cold was knifing, it harrowed the bones and left one gasping. But she knew it somehow to be her responsibility to assist her father in this arduous ceremony which would exorcise him of his guilt. He was profoundly ashamed of being a burden on the womenfolk he felt himself bound to protect. From time to time as he drove he would clap his heavily gloved hands together to restore the circulation. Julia thought about Michael, about, how in spite of his will and his dreams, his body as a biological organism had succumbed to defeat. Perhaps though, there was solace in defeat, perhaps it was an immense relief never again to be wrenched about like a harpooned whale in this titanic struggle for survival. At the moment for Julia the thought, merely, of sleeping again in a warm bed was like breathing in some pain-killing air which would put you to sleep forever. "It's really not far," her father repeated several times. "It's just that on account of the ice we have to go slow." They went slow. The drive took over three hours. By the time they'd arrived, the other men in the crew had gathered outside the employment office. They had brought their own tool boxes and shovels, in case they should be needed: they carried their shovels on their shoulders like rifles. Around their necks they had wound towels into which they breathed, warming themselves with their own breath. "Well, me hearties," called out her father in parody of himself, "Where's the work? When do we start?" The men had already begun to straggle out to the truck: no one spoke of taking time for lunch.

Maybe, her father had said afterwards, maybe if they'd just stopped to have a bite of lunch first, he'd have had better stamina, the thing wouldn't have hit him so hard, he might have mastered his feelings. Instead, Julia saw how her father's eyes scaled over with revulsion when he understood that the caskets which they were to ship from Providence to Arlington were not new, but had lain underground for years; they were to be carried to their new resting place in Arlington where the bodies would be transferred to shining new insulated caskets. O'Gorman began coughing nervously; he ordered Julia to stay in the cab; but there was no way she could keep warm in the truck, Julia had ignored his order as being a mere formula anyway and followed the men to their work. She heard her father protest as the men chopped at the ice that this was not the work that should be done in the dead of winter. One of the men retorted that it was better now than in the heat of summer. Then her father protested that it was a sin to move these poor souls from their holy resting place. The foreman of the work-crew growled at O'Gorman that the move had been approved by both dioceses. Nobody had a right, the foreman said to her father, to preach to men who had to earn a living, "Do you want to work, Walter, or not? Why don't you just admit that your stomach's too weak for the job?"

O'Gorman had tried to stand up to this challenge, but beginning to gag violently, he was forced to stand aside. He stood apart from the other workers, white and trembling, not even watching. Abruptly he turned to Julia, "Let's go home." Back into the cab they went. The sun was high in the sky now and they both felt much warmed and more comfortable, yet they did not speak a word to each other on their way home. Her father sat slumped over the steering wheel as if he'd been drugged and tied into an electric chair. When for a few seconds they slid over a stretch of icy road, his body jumped in the air as if in fact he'd been electrocuted. They pulled out of the skid, and it was only afterwards that Julia realized her father had not even expressed alarm. O'Gorman returned his rented truck to the garage, then he went to his room and sat watching television hour after hour for several days. When he finally emerged, he asked Julia, "How much are you getting for that work in Fall River?" After that he never spoke of it again.

All day Julia stood on her feet, surrounded by deafening machinery. The cotton dust flew in the air like hail, a desert storm of dust. The other operatives were obviously her friends or wanted to be (they smiled at her wanly from time to time) but in the deafening roar she was unable to speak loudly enough to be heard. The very effort tired her. Finally, she plugged her ears with ear plugs. From her self-inflicted silence she gazed around her with amazement and something like terror at the other operatives working with her in the midst of No Man's Land while the machine shook the air in continuous explosions; it was a bombardment sufficient to produce shellshock.

However, there was one melancholy consolation, Julia learned. She had become An Adult. When she came home on weekends her mother awaited her with a special tenderness and a new furrow of solicitude in her brow. Indeed, she hovered over Julia at dinner with such concern and guilt and love that Julia would hurry away from the table to keep from screaming out that it was all a lie, it was not "employment," it was Hell-on-Earth, that no human being in the whole world should be subjected to it, much less a girl like herself who was in love with the Irish bard, Hollis Michael Hearne; a girl who wanted only to sit in the park and read Latin poetry and who never—*never*—in her entire life had been subjected to such tyranny as that of the ruthless, mindless, omnipotent Machines.

Then one Saturday evening after a particularly wretched week in which one of the machines had broken down and an operative who had been suspected of wanting to stop the machines had been fired, and another operative had announced that she was suffering from an illness Julia had never heard of before called *byssinosis*, and still another had announced with great joy that she was getting married (the two announcements taking place on the same afternoon, as if they were somehow related), and her mother had silently set before Julia a huge bowl of fish chowder, Julia had begun weeping over her bowl. Without asking her what was wrong, her mother had observed with a terrifying bitterness that she'd tried to soften with a smile, "Well, you can always marry a Rich Man and that will be the end of it."

Julia had stared at her mother, gathering up the horrible woman's-option as though it were dried faggots meant for their double burning. She realized that her mother meant nothing humorous by it; it was her way of giving advice.

Julia had turned her head away with shock. Where would *she* be today if her mother had listened to the cry of the moneychangers instead of to Walter O'Gorman's lyric call? Julia did not at the time, however, make this point to her mother; she continued instead writing to Michael, who always answered promptly, so promptly that when one evening upon returning to her Fall River room after a sweltering day at the mill she found a great bulky letter waiting for her, she'd felt an odd twinge of envy. *He* had nothing to do all day but rest and get well—whereas *she*, from day to day, barely had time to bathe, wash and iron her clothes for the next day, and pack her lunch before it was time to sleep and work again. One weekend when she was at home and visiting her sister Elisabeth she'd found herself dozing over the letter she had been writing to Michael. Suddenly she woke, startled to find herself leaning on the railing of Elisabeth's front porch. Her head ached from the pressure, her pen had rolled down to the sidewalk, she felt too weary to finish. She'd risen from her chair and gone home to her parents' house to sleep, feeling nettled and guilty, forgetting even to say goodnight to her sister and Rolande.

The next morning she'd wakened an hour earlier to write a letter of love and fealty to Michael. But when she returned to the mill the following day, she'd felt overwhelmed by a new and different kind of rage. She looked around at the other operatives. Though bound to their labor by invisible ropes, they seemed not so miserable as she. The blinding truth struck Julia that what made the work bearable for them, was they did not believe it was *their* work, they believed it was meant to be the work of others, and that they themselves would soon be liberated from it. It was all part and parcel of her mother's advice. The women were waiting to escape from the mill into marriage and the sooner the better.

But this revelation had only intensified Julia's sense of abandonment—by Michael, by Walter O'Gorman, and even in an obscure, unacknowledged way, by her mother. Her feelings of isolation were crushing her when one afternoon Reffie had appeared at the mill. He had come to Fall River to arrange for the legal adoption of his youngest child by Roseanne's family, and while he was in Fall River, he said, he was visiting the mills. It was a way of life, he said, which was so different from being a farmer in Texas.

Julia had noticed at once, in spite of his awkward silences, how his gray eyes took in the total environment as he asked a few questions of the foreman—who, she later learned, was actually related to Roseanne in some way—showing him around the mill. Reffie had stood staring at the foreman without blinking his eyes, as if this were an unforgettable moment and he wanted everyone's face to be engraved on his mind forever. Above all, Julia saw how he saw *her*. It was only two o'clock in the afternoon, so she was not yet utterly at the end of her strength and her perceptions. He had turned toward her and asked how long she'd been working there, and how did she like it, and how old she was. . . . Then Reffie had asked the foreman if he might try out Julia's work for a minute, and then, asking Julia if she'd mind, had very gently and politely asked her to stand aside. And somehow it had been Reffie's asking her to stand aside while he tried to do her work for her, leaving her free, if only long enough to take out her handkerchief to wipe the dust from her eyelids, which had so deeply moved her. Only a few moments it had been, but the relief of it had been like an hour of rest. His momentary acceptance of her burden had become for her the symbol of his presence there. It seemed plain he had been sent to deliver her from the Machine.

And Reffie had continued to stand beside her, watching her, clearly unwilling to leave, while the foreman had shifted his weight nervously as if he feared some contagion of mirth or restlessness would seize the other women—who were in fact watching the scene as closely as they could without slowing down the thundering Niagara of their own work, watching with girlish amusement and curiosity as Reffie tried to outwit and outwait the foreman so that he could speak to Julia again. Julia had allowed herself to burst into laughter, and then she had burst into tears when she realized that it was the first time in the eleven months since Michael had abandoned her that she had laughed at anything.

Since that time several of Julia's somewhat less than tactful but well-intentioned friends had asked her why she, a young girl, had married a widower with three children, a man who had neither money nor friends nor even much education, and who, when Julia met him, had not yet set out on a new career but had already begun to fail at an old one. At such questions Julia would at first become angry, then overwhelmed by guilt, because what she could never explain—the bitter root of the Unmentionable—was that Reffie had come into her life at a time when she thought that everyone had abandoned her, a time of despair and therefore (in retrospect) a time for mistaken choices. Without looking back, without asking her parents what they thought of it, without even having met Reffie's children, she had flown into his arms where she believed his love would at least bring warmth and comfort at time of greatest vulnerability. When Josh was born, the Wingfields celebrated with a small party. They had been back in Texas by then, and Reffie was already fighting to keep the farm.

Still, all had gone reasonably well, Julia considered, and this in spite of the loneliness, the struggle, the isolation, the strange landscape with its hillsides that cast out the sky; in spite of the baby whose birth had exhausted her and who had been frequently ill; in spite of the responsibility of two children for whose welfare she had been relegated authority without power. Although Woody flew to her bosom for consolation, Tamsen—who should have been her friend and companion, whose adolescent terrors and misconceptions were only a few halting steps removed from her own—Tamsen was growing more alienated every day, wearing an air of *nolo me tangere* which frightened and intimidated Julia: she had not the courage to break through it. After what they had endured together in Seattle—they had seemed for a while two women against a world they never made—Julia had thought they would grow to be friends. Tamsen had seemed to become more sensitive to what it meant for Julia, too, to be isolated in a strange new place. During the weeks in which they had prepared together for Christmas, walking almost daily to the mall to buy things for Reffie and Woody, they had shared the pleasure of having money-in-hand almost for the first time since the farm had been auctioned off.

Thus their affairs had been settling into a domestic calm when one afternoon, upon looking out the window, Julia had seen a familiar figure outlined against the afternoon sun. She had thought for a moment she *must* be mistaken, it was only the brilliant sunlight and her maddening loneliness. Hollis Michael Hearne could not, would not walk into Silver Valley wearing a heavy new overcoat and carrying a suitcase as if he meant to stay. Yet there he was, standing outside their house, gazing at the shining windows she and Tamsen had cleaned only the day before. It was where they had decided to set the Christmas tree so that it would be visible from the street.

Julia's first impulse was to draw the shades, bolt the door and hide in the bathroom. Let him knock till guardian angels blew their horns, he would never know she was at home. But the ridiculous paradox of hiding from Michael overtook her at once. He wouldn't be standing there if he didn't know she was inside. In joy and terror she had flung open the door, scarcely aware that her hands were clenched into fists as if she meant to beat him should he touch her.

"What are you *doing* here?"

He smiled sadly, deprecatingly, as if he were a drifter down on his luck and she was the polite lady at the door about to let him chop wood for his dinner. "Just came looking to see if it was true. Everybody told me it was true, that you'd given . . . everybody up to go cattle ranching in Texas and goldmining in Idaho."

"Not gold. No gold at all. Just lead, mostly." She was still standing in the doorway as if to block his entrance.

He glanced around at the other miners' houses, at their foot-high wire fences, at the frozen chrysanthemums in their front yards which faced other front yards almost exactly like it. If he had looked over her shoulder he would have been able to see the South Fork of the Coeur D'Alene River, its acid-tailings polluting the riverbed.

"I think I liked Davis Square better than *this*," he observed adding, "Isn't there a park . . . or a cemetery near here? I thought I saw one as I drove in. I need a place to rest a bit before I go on."

The fear of his staying in Silver Valley became now the fear that he would not stay. She managed a broken laugh. "Are you O.K. now, Michael, are you really O.K.?"

He shifted his suitcase from one hand to the other. He patted his chest with tender irony. "Sound as a bell. They've got lots of stuff nowadays, you know. Nobody has to die anymore," he added, echoing the phrases they had heard over and over again from the physician when Michael had been admitted to the sanatorium. He was smiling with joy because he saw that he had brought tears to her eyes, which told him what he wanted to know. "Aren't you going to ask me in? It's cold out here. Must be about seventeen degrees."

She had forgotten that it was cold. She herself was scarcely aware of the cold wind that swept in from the door. "No. No. You can't come in. How could I?"

"You mean, how could you explain who I . . . was?"

Her silence indicted her, she knew. She would have given years of her life to have had the right to ask him in, to have sat by his feet and to have taken off his shoes, his socks, as he had done for her.

"I have a baby," she said at last. "A baby boy."

"I know that. But you didn't name him for me, did you? I sort of hoped you would." After an electrically charged silence he said, "Is there a room to rent hereabouts? I'm going to need a place to stay."

The daring of his intentions stopped her for a moment. She gasped, "Why are you doing this? Why are you staying here?"

He looked at her so intently, she felt her breath stop. "The climate is good," he said slowly. "A good dry, healthful climate, they tell me. Isn't that reason enough? What more reason do you need?"

"Michael, you can't do this to me. You can't just set your

life down right next door to my life. I'm married to a kind, wonderful man. I have a beautiful child. I have three children whom I . . ."

"Yeah. So I heard. Big family," he said laconically. "Will you walk down the street with me a little way? I think I'll try the McKinley for tonight, till I find me a room. Good hotel, they tell me."

"*Who* tells you? How long have you been planning . . . *plotting*?"

His voice changed suddenly, becoming angry, "Ever since you left me that day . . . scared to come back to see me. Not that I blame you. It's a contagious disease, right? People *do* catch it. I explained that all to myself again and again. But I was also thinking, all those months, 'When I get out of here, when I get well again, I'm going to *stay* well. And I'm going to find Julia. We'll get married.' "

"Michael, I *am* married, And not only married but. . . ."

"Yeah, yeah. I heard you," he said with a serene smile. "You don't have to keep saying it. I can count. *Three* kids. For somebody hardly out of high school, that's a hell of a lot of family to take care of."

The wind was blowing her hair. The cold air must be reaching the crib where Joshua was napping. Yet she stood at the open door, unable to conceal her joy.

"Put on a coat and come out."

"I can't. The baby . . ."

"Phone somebody to come over and stay with him. I'll wait for you at Larchwood Cemetery. You know where *that* is, don't you?"

This was more than she could bear. "Oh Michael, how could you, how could you do this to us? What shall I do?"

"Well, you could let me in out of the wind . . . for just a minute? While you get a neighbor or somebody to come stay with the baby."

She nodded, the tears streaming down her cheeks. As he entered the house, his boots left pools of melting snow beside the door. She stared down at them, powerless to move now that he stood beside her.

"Michael, I can't believe . . ." she said, as his mouth trembled on hers.

"You will," he said.

The moment Mrs. Parranni arrived Julia fled down the streets of Silver Valley to Larchwood Cemetery. Michael was already waiting for her, reading the names on the tombstones with a scholarly air of detachment, as if he hadn't come thousands of miles in the dead of winter to track her down.

"Lots of Italians settled here, didn't they?" he remarked cheerfully. He began reading the names aloud as if they were some sort of poem he was reciting for her sake. "Rinaldi, Vergobbi, Bottinelli, Biotti, Comolli . . . Lutro, Marco and Orlandini. And see—here we have some names right out of Queen Elizabeth's day. "Stubbs and Quince and Corrick and Webb. . . ." He looked at her appealingly.

Julia shook her head. She refused to be swayed from her conviction that he must go, he must go *at once*. It would be *ruinous* for him to stay. Why had he done this mad thing? she reproached him. When she'd left him, he was a sick man.

"Thou hast said it."

"Michael, be *serious*."

"I *am* serious. I'm *deathly* serious. I was sick for a year. I went through agonies of loneliness . . . but worse, of jealously. Now it's my turn to be happy. And where better to be happy than—?"

He opened his arms to her, and with a faint cry Julia ran to him. As Michael gathered her up in his arms Julia heard in the distance the inquiring trill of a bicycle bell. Its echo hung for a moment suspended in the crystal air, then fell silent.

VI

In the Shoshone Public Library Tamsen glanced at the big clock for the fifth time and then down again at her book. *Lewis and Clark were the first white men to enter what is now Idaho.* She sighed with resignation. Every school system wanted the same stuff. In Texas she'd been asked at various times to write an essay on the Battle of the Alamo, on the life of Stephen F. Austin, on the German immigrant population of New Braunfels, on the architectural structure of the rotunda of the State Capitol, on the Mexican-American War, on the Undocumented Migrant Workers, on the founding of the great University of Texas, and—twice—on the War Between the States. One smart kid had actually written an essay on Barton Springs, The Best Place To Go Skinny-dipping, and had got an A for his subtle pornography.

But ever since her leg had got so casually broken, she'd decided to at least *appear* friendly, tractable, and resigned. During those weeks Julia had been attentive and kind; Reffie had patiently driven her to school every day, and even Woodrow had run errands for her, carrying her things while she cautiously picked her way along the hillside on crutches. These attentions had evoked a new and shattering sense of her own helplessness, a helplessness which had been sweet too, cunningly sweet, like the lure of the Devil must have been when folks believed in him. Much of the time when not in school Tamsen had lain on the sofa, reading, surrendering the best light in the house which came from the living room windows only when Josh was set down on the floor to play. Then she would hobble to her room, avoiding dinner. She seemed to have lost her appetite along with her mobility. The fruit preserves Julia had bought from a farmer had not stirred her interest, though "made fresh from Lewiston cherries" nor the trout Reffie had caught "fresh from the lake," and especially not the sinewy-looking peanut butter Woody had brought home from some county fair "freshly ground from peanuts grown in eastern Washington." Maybe it'd been the sheer "freshness" of everything, oozy and sluicy as placentas or as those slimy Man-of-wars they'd seen on the Galveston Beach, but it'd all turned her stomach, honed down by indifference and nausea, she'd lost fifteen pounds. For a week or so after her return to school her body had seemed so lightweight and ethereal she might have lived on air. Her mind was clearer too. Like she could probably write this term paper in a day if she really wanted to, it'd be easy. The fact was, she found history more interesting than life. Real life was full of colossal bores—your family in their different disguises of love—offering you peanut butter. Whereas in history the details leaped up from the page, sensational as a tabloid.

. . . The Indian woman went on horseback to get assistance for the white men who were enemies of the Nez Perce—a distance of 26 miles.

Silly Indian woman, selling out to the white men. Like Malinche to Cortés. If she'd been an Indian woman she'd have let those white men boil in oil before she'd have helped them against her own people. But actually—the most interesting discovery since her accident had been, not this new clarity of mind, but a certain newly perceived *vulnerability* on the part of Julia and Reffie. Julia had been so upset by Tamsen's refusal to share their thick soups and cheesy lasagnas and crusty beef-and-potato pies that she'd burst into tears, leaning against the sink. "What'll I do if she won't eat, Reffie? The *child*" (Italics Tamsen Wingfield's, Tamsen parenthetically informed the silent library) "refuses everything I fix for her." And Reffie comforting her, "You'll see, she'll pick up. It's sitting around here all day with no exercise. You'll see, everything's going to be all right." And Julia wiping her eyes, "I guess I'm exaggerating things. I think I'm going a little crazy here. It's all so strange." Confessing, "I get so *home*sick." And Reffie staring back at her, helpless, unwilling to move again. Since his return from his failed trip to Salinas, he had begun talking as if they were going to stay in Silver Valley forever.

Unable to take any of us back, thought Tamsen. We're like on the Mormon Trail, we've set our faces to the West, and we can't go back, even if we all die or go crazy. . . .

Even before the turn-of-the-century Idaho was allocating money for an insane asylum.

Well, that was far-sighted of them. Who needed it more? Tamsen inquired of the antique library clock. She looked around at the turn-of-the-century library. It had in its reading room, three solid oak reading tables, eighteen straight-backed chairs (also of oak), and a deacon's bench along the windows. In spite of herself Tamsen had become fond of the Shoshone Public Library. She was not sure just how this feeling had crept up on her. Perhaps it, too, had had something to do with her accident. Every afternoon she'd hobbled down here from school to wait for Woodrow or Reffie, who'd carry her stuff. It'd become Tamsen's special place. Of course when *Julia* had seen the place, she had stood amazed; she'd said it was no bigger than an *alcove* at the Boston Public Library. Well, what could you expect from Eastern snobs? Though Tamsen too had to admit the library was smaller than the one in Salinas. Still, she preferred being there if she had to be *any*where in Silver Valley. Everything was so out-in-the-open, like a stage, she could see everybody, and nearly every book in the reading room from where she sat.

The Coeur d'Alenes, the Pend d'Oreilles, and the Kootenais were already living there when Lewis and Clark came to northern Idaho.

The main light came from two windows reaching nearly to the ceiling. People tended to sit on the ladderback chairs along the windows as if they were attending a pie social. There were also several beat-up looking armchairs (donated, probably). Here, nearly every day at the same hours, the "oldtimers" came in to read *The Kellogg Evening News, The Kootenai County Leader, The Coeur d'Alene Press, The Sandpoint Daily Bee, The Daily Idahonian, The Lewis County Herald, The North Idaho Press* and *The Wallace Miner*. She'd heard the librarian apologizing to an oldtimer once for not having a newspaper from his far-flung village, explaining to him that there were over seventy newspapers in Idaho, and the county couldn't afford to carry them all, at which the old man had grumbled that, in *that* case, he couldn't afford to carry the county *either*, and had walked out complaining about his taxes. Men like him—rarely did Tamsen see any older women—would sit at the tables, the newspapers spread out in front of them, wetting their thumbs as they turned the pages. Some would sit all afternoon in their plaid flannel shirts and windbreakers and worn jackets or raincoats, reading the details of lives, obituaries, weddings, parades, Alcoholics Anonymous sessions and Senior Citizens Meetings that were as familiar to them as their own gnarled hands; they could have written the obituaries themselves.

Under conditions of extreme hardship the Pend d'Oreilles would bury their children or old people alive. . . .

In addition to the light from the windows there was a white globe in the ceiling which cast a soft light around the tables and books. From time to time Tamsen would look up from her reading and rest her gaze on the heavy oak tables which might have been brought into the county in 1890 when the Territory first achieved Statehood. They'd carved out the State from everywhere else around them—from Montana and Utah and Oregon and Washington, with no special reason for existing, thought Tamsen with a grimace, no wonder they had to build a nuthouse before the State even got started.

But the ancient oak surfaces were surprisingly un-harmed: no crude notchings with penknives, no hearts carved within hearts. The heirs of the pioneers were above all taught to respect property. One of her classmates at Kellogg Junior High had been procedurally arrested for in-eptly pocketing a key chain (the kid had had a thing about Chief Joseph, whose head he'd seen bobbling from the loose end of the keychain), and was sternly handed over to the Juvenile Authorities; you'd have thought he was a horsethief. The other people standing by in the store were ready to hang him from the nearest tree. This respect for other folks' horses carried over. You could take all the books you wanted out of the library just by signing your name and address. There wasn't a kid in the county who'd have stolen a book. Rather, they were all growing up to be Abe Lincolns. They'd have walked four miles in the rain to return a borrowed book. Still, in spite of her-self, Tamsen was grateful that awe or fear or both had kept the tables so flawless and golden. She squinted at the mel-lowing wood which caught the surfaces in a slant of light.

The cedars of the bottomlands in Idaho are truly gigantic. The Indians frequently carved out their trunks for use in canoes. Some of these great trees, especially in the Clearwater district, have been growing a thousand years.

As she ran her hand over the table she noticed how the turquoise ring her mother and Reffie had bought her one Christmas in Juárez seemed ready to slip off, her hand was so thin. But that was great, she was still too heavy, another five or ten pounds and she would have been as lissome as a fern or willow. She wondered for a second what it would be like to be a delicate perpetually-reclining invalid, your veins like blue glass in your pale arms. She'd be so light Reffie could carry her from room to room. She'd be like Elizabeth Barrett Browning—then someone would come and rescue her, taking her back to Salinas where she'd sit sipping iced tea under the mimosa tree.

In some parts of Idaho you will find the beautiful bracken fern. These exquisite plants have been said to make a tropical paradise of some favored areas. . . .

Tamsen looked up at the sound of students now arriving from the Senior High School. They seemed, every one of them, to be bursting with health as they flung their down jackets carelessly over the backs of chairs. They looked as if they'd been wearing hiking boots since they could walk; the nylon surfaces of their jackets rustled with self-sufficiency. Boys and girls alike seemed to proclaim that they could shoot a bear if need be, build a fire, cook a whole meal in tinfoil, hike ten or twenty miles over snow-covered mountains, backpack from Moscow to Missoula as calmly as kids in Salinas might hop into a pickup truck to get groceries.

But there were also former city folks up here, running away from Newark or Detroit or even (unthinkable) Houston, living in cabins or huts like oldtime prospectors. Those two, for instance, who'd come in to return a stack of overdue books. . . . Tamsen heard them complain about having been back East to visit his family in Chicago and how glad they were to get back to Bonners Ferry "even if we do have to come all the way here to get books." Tamsen watched them with deep envy: they seemed to her so free. The bearded young man was wearing pants sewn from rectangles of thick woolen khaki. From an army blanket, Tamsen thought. When he lifted a fold in front, Tamsen saw that there were no zippers or buttons. As he signed his name, Tamsen saw that his nails were black with dirt. Although his face glowed with health, his eyes were still city eyes—brooding, suspicious, reluctant (Tamsen heard) even to give his address.

The girl with him, who seemed not much older than Tamsen, was carrying a baby wrapped in a rebozo, like a Mexican-Indian woman. But this smiling, curly-headed blonde girl with the pure-blue eyes of Easter eggs was no Indian, she could only be, Tamsen mused, a Norsewoman from Minneapolis or an excommunicated Mormon from Salt Lake City who'd chosen to go primitive in Bonners Ferry. Tamsen's Social Studies teacher, in a tone of unresigned complaint, as if something should be done about it at once, had pointed out that there were probably four or five thousand people living up in the wilderness, some to escape the police.

Tamsen listened shamelessly to every word. The only "alternative culture" people she'd ever seen had been the street people she'd observed when their whole class had visited the Texas State Capitol. But the kids in Austin had been very different. Set adrift in their flowing saris and thong sandals, they lived by selling their artwork or panhandling, seeming to trust their livelihood and bodies to the sun. These two seemed a new and hardier species. Meeting the girl's gaze—an intense flash of white and blue—Tamsen dropped her eyes to her book.

One of the most beautiful animals we have in Idaho is the antelope or pronghorn. This graceful creature can run at astonishing speeds when it is escaping its traditional enemies. . . .

Tamsen would have liked to ask them lots of questions, like how, exactly, did they live up there with no running water, no plumbing, no doctors or hospitals, and how did they educate their kids, or maybe they didn't bother with that at all? Julia had said there were lots of custody cases up there, parents hiding out in the wilderness with their kidnapped kids. (Imagine loving your kids that much, thought Tamsen jealously. Reffie would never hide *her* in the bulrushes; more likely he and Julia would just hand her over to anybody that'd keep her, like baby-Bobby bartered over into the custody of those weird grandparents Tamsen had never seen.)

For a moment the Bonners Ferry couple seemed to have a problem over some book, but it was just a case of the library's not having it in right now, something called *Natural Healing*. So, no doctors up there in the new Paradise. Suppose you broke your leg, who'd set it? Now to Tamsen's delight the couple were sitting down at her table, right across from her. The girl eased the baby onto the table as casually as if it'd been a puppy. But maybe it only looked casual. Lots of things we used to do in Salinas looked easy to other people, like folks who thought all you needed to do was put a seed in the ground and it'd grow, they didn't count the thousands of hours you walked through the furrows worrying about every little leaf and praying for rain.

The smiling librarian now brought the couple two books she said might interest them. Tamsen glanced quickly at the titles: *The Legume Legacy* and *High-Protein Vegetarianism*. So that was how they did it. O.K. with Tamsen. After watching those rabbits bludgeoned to death, she thought she'd never eat meat again. But how did they take care of that baby when he was sick? And what, Tamsen asked herself, glancing again at her book, did they do for heat when it was twenty below zero?

Idaho takes special pride in its natural resources. Among these, as everyone knows, are our great forests. Unfortunately, we are using up these forests at an alarming rate. Within another quarter of a century, if our present rate of lumber consumption continues, we will have exhausted one of our richest natural resources.

Tamsen flipped the book open to its cover. The book was already forty years old. Well, Reffie Wingfield and Family had arrived just in time for the Final Depletion of Everything. Even the C & L Silver-Lead & Zinc Mining Company. Reffie said there was a time-and-motion study man around the mine all the time now, somebody supposed to be scientific and objective about it all, sent out by the United States Bureau of Mines, but from Reffie's point of view all that data and statistics and stuff were bound to work against the miners. There was open talk among management people about the "cost effectiveness" of C & L and wouldn't it be better to go somewhere else? Gramp said he hoped they all went to hell if they shut down a mine that had been here before Idaho was even a state.

The three great lead mines of Shoshone County—the Bunker Hill and Sullivan, the Morning, and the Hecla—employ thousands of people in northern Idaho, making a major contribution to the prosperity of the area.

The young couple whispered, something about the state flower, the syringa. They smiled shyly at Tamsen, looking from their book to her, as if to include her in their conversation. Apparently Indians had used the syringa stems for just about everything—the women had used them for babies' cradles and the men had used them for smoking, letting the beetles eat their way through the stem from end to end. *Good* Tamsen smiled back at them, nodding with what she meant to be smashing sarcasm. In the 21st century everybody will get high on grass through a syringa stem cleaned out by insects. Then the couple began talking about the edible bulb of the sego, "how the heroic Mormons had survived on it in the desert." Were they perhaps Mormons after all, or just looking for edibles on which to survive? Tamsen wondered. But she was beginning to get bored; the trouble with studying in a library was that it made you aware of time. She'd looked at the clock a dozen times in the past hour. It seemed as if each time she learned something new about the State-she-was-in (now, *there's* a pun) the hands of the clock slid into a new slot of time. She could spend her whole life here, taking notes about other people's lives; she could stay here till they dropped the Bomb, they'd excavate her afterwards, like the three-toed Pleistocene horses found in Snake River Valley, or more like those petrified trees found in Santa Creek. Like the trees, she'd have been buried maybe five thousand feet in lava. She'd become an object of scientific study and amazement, a petrified Tamsen Wingfield. Look at this delicately-formed (*lissome*) fourteen-year old, or maybe fifteen. See the jewelcases where her eyes were laid, see the slender bones of the hand; and this perfect skeleton was (they'd say) surrounded by eighteen petrified oak chairs and three petrified oak tables. They'd reconstruct an entire history for her. Tamsen Wingfield must have been of royal blood, they'd say, because we see here her remains surrounded by royal thrones carved (though very primitively) from oak trees. *Obviously* Tamsen Wingfield was actively engaged in some puberty rite when everything was suddenly buried under lava. All oxygen was of course excluded, and thus we have these perfectly preserved bones of the young Queen Tamsen and her carbonized wooden thrones.

There were people who spent their whole lives dealing in such stuff. They sat in reading rooms like this one, only much much larger, with thousands upon thousands of books, and they persuaded themselves that something had happened that had been so important they had to write it all down so that young folks would appreciate how real it was. And the funny thing, or maybe the bitter, future-poisoning thing was that it *was* real, more real for instance than anything the President of the United States had ever said. Like—her eye skimmed the page—

Clark was also honored by the naming of the beautiful flower, clarkia, after him, as he was the first to discover it near the Clearwater River.

What a trip! Imagine being the first one to find *any*thing anymore. That was what was so deadly boring about being young nowadays. Who'd ever name a flower after you? There was nothing new unless you were in geriatrics, helping bored old people live forever. Tamsen felt like those beavers whose unused teeth got so big they couldn't eat and actually starved to death. She needed something more than all this library stuff to whet her teeth on, a whetstone of real life, that's what she needed. And first of all, some fresh air.

It was 4:30 when she left the library. The couple from Bonners Ferry were just settling down to a book full of diagrams and sketches on *How to Build an A-Frame*. Probably they're still living in a wigwam, kid and all, thought Tamsen; but she'd prefer a wigwam any day herself, to living out of a car. She'd rather die than live that way again.

Outdoors she stood still for several seconds, shaken by the sudden transformation in the world. Indoors it had been warm, the milk-globe light soft and immutable. But meanwhile outdoors an inch or two of snow had been accumulating, twilight had begun to darken the hillsides. Already the houses along McKinley Avenue had turned on their Christmas lights. The air was cold, but there was very little wind. Tamsen unlocked her bike and walked it along a few yards, leaving a trail through the fresh snow.

The early evening sky seemed to be moving, shifting about its puffy bags of lavender cloud; the red green and blue Christmas lights mingled with the crepuscular light, softening everything. She could almost get used to this weird place. It was all so serene, it was a landscape which lacked . . . (she grasped for the word with her new clarity, seized it) . . . *vindictiveness*. There, *that* was something she'd put in her term paper.

She decided to ride home along McKinley Avenue, a somewhat longer route, but she preferred anyway to arrive home as late as she could, when Josh had had his evening bath and dinner was ready, and Reffie had rested up and read his newspaper. Altogether, everyone seemed in a better mood by then.

The few cars heading home had already made comfortable tracks in the snow for her bike. As she passed first Smelter Heights, then Deadwood Street, she began to follow the path alongside Larchwood. It was a little less smooth here, irregular and uphill. She got off her bike and pushed it along with one hand. Amazing how even at this time of year there were gardens in bloom, they grew such hardy plants here. And the brilliant hues: in the fall there had been red dogwood with their bluish white berries suddenly turned red and purple and gold. Even now, lying on a few graves here and there you could see shining right through the snow, as if trying to brighten up the place, the reddish-purple petals of what they called here the false-bittersweet.

Suddenly a huge dog ran toward her from out of nowhere, barking furiously. Lord, there were dogs everywhere in Silver Valley, you couldn't walk half a mile without some dog questioning your right to be there. *Who are you?* this one now demanded to know, his mouth looking angry and evil. He might not be hydrophobic, he wasn't foaming at the mouth or anything, but he seemed to have a definite longing to sink his teeth into her. Tamsen opted for cutting across the cemetery, avoiding the dog entirely. She devoutly hoped that whoever owned him would call him and get him back on his leash. Quickly Tamsen hopped back onto her bike and, giving the angry dog the widest possible berth, headed straight across the cemetery. She hated to do that, crossing like a wheeled apocalypse over the heads of the dead, but that beast was scary. For a moment, as she picked up speed, she thought he might make a rush for her wheels, so she rang her bicycle bell to attract the attention of someone she saw standing in the distance, who looked to be the dog's owner. No, it was not a person but a couple standing together beside the Kellogg plaque. A snowflake fell across Tamsen's face. As she brushed it away, she recognized Julia in the arms of a man she had never seen before. At once Tamsen silenced her bell.

To her own surprise, she did not head straight home to denounce Julia to Reffie. Instead Tamsen knocked on her neighbor's door and said she had locked herself out. Could she stay with him a while? She could see that Sean was overwhelmed; he'd been inviting Reffie to everything he could think of in order to get to know Tamsen better. Tamsen had had no trouble understanding that, but had ignored him as part of the unfavored landscape. Now she looked at him appraisingly, wondering if he were suspicious of her sudden appeal for help.

"Should always leave an extra key with your neighbor," he murmured, unable to conceal his delight at her presence. "You want me to try a window?" Then, precipitately, as if he feared she would accept his offer, and he'd be deprived of her presence, "You're welcome to stay as long as you like."

"Where're your folks?" Tamsen looked around. The house was spotlessly clean, and full of new furniture which shone into one's eyes, like the glossy pages of a color catalog. Tamsen took in the wall-to-wall carpeting, hundreds of feet of it extending all the way to the kitchen and beyond.

"They've gone out," Sean said after a pause, as if suddenly remembering he was required not only to stare at her, but to answer her.

"What a bummer," said Tamsen. "I always do some dumb thing."

He rushed to defend her. "Everybody forgets their key once in awhile. I've forgotten mine lots of times." It was a lie, and they both knew it. But protecting her with this lie was as if he'd babbled words of love, *I'll lie for you, I'll do anything for you . . . just stay with me.*

Tamsen slumped into a chair. "I left my bike outside," she said irresolutely. He seemed so defenseless with his shock of innocent light hair and fern-green eyes, like some barefoot kid on a calendar. Tamsen was not used to unresisting surrender; she struggled to overcome her pity for his ignorance. But maybe if you grew up in Silver Valley and had never been farther away than Seattle, maybe you thought it was perfectly natural for girls to park their bikes on your sidewalk and visit you in your home after dark.

Without stopping to put on a jacket Sean hurried out into the snow-fallen night to rescue her bike. She heard him open the garage door. She was standing at the mantlepiece examining the family photographs when, having returned by another door, he suddenly reappeared at her side. "That's my father and that's my mother, and that's my two sisters—one of them is married to a supervisor at C & L, maybe you know him—Sidleigh? He came here to see if they could keep the mine from being shut down, and now he's married Darcy and he's moved here permanently. He's doing what they call a time and motion . . ."

Glancing around, already bored, Tamsen reminded him to close the door to their garage, he was wasting their heat. As he hurried to shut the door, he began telling her how many cords of wood he had cut. Nodding, Tamsen looked around for the stove. It was a great woodburner, he explained. Since they'd switched to wood, his parents were saving seventy dollars a month on heat. "But how's that broken leg?" he asked with sudden guilty embarrassment, as if she were still on crutches and he'd rudely failed to help her.

"Oh, it's O.K. now. Staying home with Julia was the worst part of it."

He looked solemn, his loyalty torn. He liked Julia. Lately, whenever he came over with one of his sacrificial offerings—tulip bulbs or venison—he'd sit down on the floor and play with Josh, trying to look as if he were talking to Julia or the baby while his eyes followed Tamsen around.

He suddenly looked radiant, as if he'd thought of something that would please her. "I got a new dog. Have you seen him? Shoshoni? A Siberian husky. You want to see him?"

After her encounter with the dog in Larchwood, Tamsen would have preferred goldfish, or at most, a haughty Siamese who would have ignored her. Besides, she had something more serious on her mind than dogs, but his pleasure was so pure and childlike, she couldn't get down to it. She considered for a moment the unhappy prospect that instead of helping her, he was going to give her real trouble. She needed someone loyal to herself but cunning and secretive with all others, like Too-lah and Malinche, she thought, grimacing at herself in the mirror above the mantel.

Uncertain whether she had consented, he repeated, "Shall I bring him in?"

"In from where?"

"Well, we keep him out back, in the yard. We got a big yard, you know. . . . " He seemed to be apologizing for something.

Tamsen removed her coat and sweater, making herself more comfortable. "Don't know if Julia would like my staying here," she called after him as he headed out the kitchen door into the backyard. But either he hadn't heard her or hadn't realized that this was his cue. She saw that she was going to have to be more direct with him.

Sean led the husky into the living room on a leash, standing to one side so that Tamsen could admire it better. He was beautiful, the mysterious Arctic-blue eyes set in the white face, his silver-gray fur brought an ache to your heart. A magnificent animal was such a simple thing, all you had to do was fall in love with it; but adultery—ah, that was complicated. Tamsen had not seen the face which had inspired such passion from Julia (*Julia's hands holding his face like a cup from which she drank again and again, intoxicating herself, and the warm breath rising from their mouths like their souls, into the cold air, and Julia nearly falling to her knees in the snow. . . . In another moment, maybe, if they hadn't heard the bell and the barking dog, they'd have made love right there, the snow melting beneath them. . . .*)

Such passion, like greed or murder, had been frightening. Tamsen had never seen such a look on anyone's face and thought she never wanted to see it again. Now as Sean stood in the living room, proudly showing his dog, a confused wave of emotions stirred her. Sean was so simple and guileless, his dog was so beautiful, Julia was so heartless, Reffie was so simple and guileless; and what was to be *her* place in all this? Tamsen's eyes filled with tears: it was all lies, nothing but lies. She had been cheated out of her natural inheritance, cheated first of all of Roseanne, then of Salinas, and finally of Reffie by this lying Julia who'd never—Tamsen now bitterly believed—looked upon Reffie with anything more than tolerance or affectionate boredom. And now Sean seemed to be feeling about her as Julia had felt toward Whoever-he-was. The enormous injustice of it, a totally unearned, gratuitous love thrust upon her by a boy she hardly knew—the very random and inexplicable nature of it all, filled her with an angry despair. "Christ," she blurted out, "What a beautiful dog." And inexplicably began sobbing.

At once he was on his knees, comforting her. "What is it, Tami? What is it? Did I say something?"

Violently Tamsen shook her head; as he took her in his arms to comfort her, Tamsen began explaining to him about Julia. He listened in amazement. Hours later, when Tamsen glided across the snow back into her own house— they waited until they saw the Christmas tree lit up and everyone home again—Tamsen had decided Sean could be trusted after all, he would be her lover, he would bend to her will, he was part of her Plan.

VII

Following Smetka's death there was an investigation. The rescue team had been unable to reach the two men. Why? Why, also, had there been no extra emergency shafts by which the men could have exited more quickly? Why had Smetka been working with an inexperienced man? Why had they been permitted to wander off to work separately from the rest of their crew? What had caused the rock burst in the first place? And above all, why had there been a lethal leaking of carbon monoxide? The insurance investigators, with an air of rational concern, like scientists asking about new life-forms on Mars or Jupiter, went around asking questions of everybody, including Smetka's wife. Their manner suggested that time and scientific examination of the facts would solve everything.

Finally the bereaved wife was paid her *danegelt*, the body was buried in Larchwood Cemetery. Reffie had not wanted to attend the funeral; he hated funerals. Every death forced him to think his life back to the beginning. It was like pouring it through a sieve to see what was left: his farm, his religion, his marriage to Roseanne, the kids, and now Julia and the new baby. Reffie believed that he had become thoughtful and philosophical, that it was useless to be angry with Life, that it only wasted your energy for fighting the real problems, like getting the crops in. But as he looked past Smetka's fresh grave toward the hillsides and beyond, toward the Bitterroot Mountains, he felt a new and hopeless bereavement, as a man feels when he's lost his religion. Smetka's sudden death, as if a man were as expendable as a timbering log, continued to shock him more than he understood why.

Shortly after the investigation, while Reffie was punching his clock after a day's work, he was accompanied out to McKinley Street by a man he'd seen at the funeral. He was Murray Sidleigh, the man said, and he'd come to the Valley last year to have a look around and start keeping proper records. . . . As he walked with Reffie he asked how long Reffie had been with C & L, how much seniority he had built up. At the word "seniority" Reffie turned toward Sidleigh in alarm: it had the motorized sound of tomato-pickers, yielding profit without the labor of men.

"Let's walk down Main Street to the Pizazz and have a beer," suggested Sidleigh companionably.

"I'm Ephraim Wingfield's grandson," said Reffie suddenly, as if that might explain everything. *Maybe he's on my side*, Reffie prayed. *Not every time-and-motion guy loves robots better than folks. But maybe this Easterner had never heard of Wing.* He was surprised to hear Sidleigh say "Yeah, I heard about him. He's got some old-fashioned ideas, Mr. Wingfield does. He thinks a corporation is the same as a Boss who's arguing over a nickel-an-hour raise. It's natural he should feel that way. How old is he now, your grandfather?"

Reffie managed to swallow the inference that Gramp's ideas were cranky and old-fashioned, a failure to keep up with the times. Sidleigh's casual dismissal of Grampa Wing's sixty years of union loyalty frightened him. *They must have a lot of power to talk like that; they must know something about us we haven't figured out yet.*

When the waitress at the Pizazz had served them, Sidleigh turned at once to Reffie, as if he'd waited a long time for this moment. "Look, Wingfield, let's be up front about it, O.K.?" He pushed his beer to one side and unfolded a paper napkin as if it were a rolltop desk. He scribbled some figures. The nib of his pen was exquisitely fine, Reffie hadn't seen one like it in years, it tore at the paper napkin. Sidleigh crumpled the paper, tossed it into the ashtray and tried writing on his placemat; but the plastic surface rendered what he wrote invisible. Sighing with impatience, he pulled an envelope out of his pocket. Reffie's eyes darted to the return address: *United Steelworkers of America. Is he for us or against us? Or is he working both sides of the street?*

Casually Sidleigh now asked Reffie how many hours he'd put in last week (*how come him to have the right to ask and me the need to answer?*) and wrote it down; then multiplied that number by some appropriate figure, compared it to what he referred to as "theoretical annual tonnage" and showed him that he, Reffie, was not personally profitable to the mine, adding, "But you're not the only one. C & L has to keep on a lot of miners like you, paying wages that have just gotten out of line, I tell you. But the union won't vote for any give-backs."

It was the first time Reffie had ever heard the term. It was all very baffling. What did Sidleigh want with him, especially? Reffie was new to the place, hardly knew his way in and out of the tunnels yet. Why didn't he bring these numbers to some oldtimer who could understand them better, maybe do some explaining to Sidleigh himself?

"You understand what I'm saying?" Reffie must have looked as if he'd drifted off on an idea of his own. "I'm telling you the truth. Back when your grandpa was young enough to shovel a couple of tons a day, C & L could haul tonnage through an adit at a cost of ten dollars a ton. Can you believe that? And as for raising a shaft—well, you can figure it out for yourself, look here. They were paying timbermen about five dollars a day when he started, right? Even the bosses hardly ever got more than eight dollars a day. So to raise a shaft in the C & L back in those days would have cost—" he scribbled some figures on the envelope "—about ten dollars a foot. And we're talking here about raising just *one* shaft. Think of the money that means today in terms of the whole operation. What could you develop today for ten a foot? What do you think the folks back in Pittsburgh, where the *real* power to keep this mine open really is, would say if C & L were to pay you guys five dollars a day?"

Reffie felt the wall of the cafe grow cold at his back. *He's sittin here tellin me I got to be dumped, that I'm costin the operators too damned much money.*

"Look, you're an intelligent man, Wingfield. I can see that. You haven't been underground so long that you count skip hoists at night to fall asleep." He chuckled at his own joke. "They're getting rid of a lot of feather-bedding around here this year . . ." He interrupted himself with sudden emotion. "We're trying to help you guys. We want to keep the mine open. But somebody's got to give."

Reffie felt his chest tighten with fear. "Then it's true what they say. They want to shut down the mine."

"Not *want* to. Never say *want* to. What *we're* doing is trying to keep it *open*. Drink up and we'll go to my office. I'll show you the numbers. You can make your own decision."

All the way to Sidleigh's office, Sidleigh's words rasped through his chest like steel chains. Reffie felt more cold and afraid than he had ever been. "Own decision" could only mean that he was about to be dumped and forced into some small investor's ten-man mining operation somewhere at Depression wages. Either way he and Julia would have to give up some of what little they'd gained in the past few months; he could not risk moving them down home again. He began calculating how little they could get by on if his hours or wages were cut. Cut how deep? In half? He could maybe sell his car, he didn't have to have a car (but there was little or no public transportation in Silver Valley, and how would he get to a job that was maybe twenty or thirty miles farther down the road?) He began wondering if there were Goodwill stores somewhere in the Valley where he could begin to buy up some warm underwear, maybe get some presents laid by for Christmas. For a moment, as they walked into Sidleigh's office, the idea seized him that maybe like other folks he'd heard of, he could move his family farther North, into wilderness country along the border. But he knew his womenfolk would not abide it. Tamsen was growing up; she would soon need . . . what a girl growing up might need extended before him in an overwhelming vista, like those stunningly beautiful canyons of the Southwest wrought by natural upheaval. . . .

"Sit down, sit down," Sidleigh was repeating, darting him a strange look. "I'm going to show you the numbers. Then you'll see the handwriting on the wall. Numbers don't lie."

Why me?

Sidleigh began pulling open filing cabinets, taking out oversized looseleaf notebooks, each page of which was protected by plastic folders. Many pages were carefully typewritten descriptions of working areas and transportation modes. Some were filled with diagrams, others were color-coded; still others seemed to be just long lists of specific occupations and working hours. It was all meaningless to Reffie, like idiot's dribble strung out in words.

While Reffie was trying to understand it all, the phone rang and Sidleigh, with an affable expression and a benign wave of his hand indicated that Reffie was to go on reading. As he spoke on the phone the man who had been talking to Reffie like an intimate friend became abruptly transformed. He sat up straight, projecting his voice directly into the mouthpiece. *He's telling the guy on the other end what to think and the guy better think it, that's what.*

Reffie tried not to listen. He was trying to make sense of the diagrams and numbers Sidleigh had given him to read. He had the frightened feeling that it was no exaggeration to say his life depended on understanding what Sidleigh wanted him to understand. He felt himself cruelly betrayed by his lost schooling; there were signs and symbols on the freshly typed pages that he had never seen before, much less could understand. What he did understand was that this was a new and updated report.

"Goddammit!"

In spite of himself Reffie raised his head to listen; he didn't really want to hear any more of that new voice, at ease with itself, full of authority.

"I told you guys, and *mistake me not*, you don't send new

workers down a shaft to fix a chain. The kid probably hadn't had more than a year's experience. We were going to let him go . . . Damn you all, if you're going to let an eighteen-year old from the palouse country climb down a circular shaft at a fifty degree angle, I'm just not going to be responsible for what happens. You're going to have one helluva lawsuit on your hands, and I hope to Christ they sue the pants off you."

In his exasperation, Sidleigh was breathing heavily, he seemed for a moment to have forgotten Reffie. Then abruptly he terminated the conversation. "Look, Frank, I got a . . . pal . . . here who's beginning to see the other side of the story a little, so I'll talk to you later, O.K.?" He listened a moment or two longer, his irritability increasing. "Yeah. Well, if they're too lazy to *wear* the glasses, that's not the company's fault. No, I don't buy that. They don't have a case."

He pushed the telephone roughly aside, as if it had rudely and intentionally interrupted him. He tried to smile at Reffie, but he was no longer affable. "What I want is . . . I want you and your grandfather to understand that the contract negotiations have just gotten out of hand. We're losing money running this mine. You guys are just pricing yourselves out of the market. How can you compete with the foreign markets? Hell, they've got *robots* in Japan that'll make you guys look like fairies . . . if you don't believe it come on over to my side of the desk. Come on over." He seemed about to drag Reffie physically over. "Look at these." Through all the dust of Sidleigh's little histrionic explosions a bitter allegation was beginning to be discernible to Reffie: that it was his grandfather's lifelong friends in the union who were impeding all reasonable efforts to cut costs, thereby keeping the mine from being shut down. So long as labor continued to keep wages artifically inflated by kneejerk contract increases— "COLA contracts" Sidleigh called them—then labor and management were on a collision course. "Now you can be with us or against us. As a *miner*, I have to tell you, Reffie, that I've been clocking you," he emphasized each word like bullet shots, "and *you're one real lousy hard rock miner*, but I guess you must know that. Still, you've got other talents. You can still help us. You can help us save money."

Reffie was silent. "How?" he asked at last.

"You know how to read and write, don't you? And you can press a stop watch, same as me. All you got to do is watch how long something takes to get done and write it down. Then we count up the hours, the benefits . . . like what I want to do right now is eliminate two powdermen. I wrote this up last week. See how it sounds to you."

Reffie listened intently as Sidleigh read aloud:

RECOMMENDATION: Reduce man-hours by two full-time powder-men:
(1) Since remaining cager helpers are not required during crew-hoisting, and
(2) The supply system in explosives often duplicates the other movement of supplies, the cager helpers could be used during some of their work shift to move explosives.
CONCLUSION: 2 powder-men for 8 hours a day x 250 days a year make 4,000 man-hours. These jobs may be eliminated.

"But C & L's already cut their work force in half. Used to be over two thousand people working here, Gramp says."

" 'Gramp says,' " Sidleigh mimicked. "You better forget what your grandaddy says and take this job I'm offering you. This mine is maybe going to be bought out . . . saved . . . by some big Idaho businessman, but only if we can show that it's still a profitable mine. And we're not going to let those guys in Pittsburgh decide whether this mine stays open. We're not Pittsburgh, you know, we're Idaho."

"But it's a *national* union, U.S. Steelworkers. . . ." But Reffie could already feel the anger rising up in the other man, so he added quickly, "this job you're offering me"? Sidleigh, in a dramatic gesture, now took the phone off the hook, as if what he was about to say were too important to risk interruption. "By this time next year we'll be down to less than 200 employees. But *you* got a chance to hang on for awhile, see if these Idaho businessmen can save the mine. Given a chance to negotiate with the workers themselves, maybe they can. Meanwhile, we need a lot of paperwork to show these guys back East how they're sucking the blood out of us with all these demands—OSHA problems, environment problems. You heard me just now on the phone. Accidents cost *money*. But do you think safety has improved any, for all these government regulations? Well,if you think so, you don't know much about the human factor. *Human beings* cause accidents, which are expensive, believe you me, they cost plenty . . . to say nothing," he added mechanically, glancing at Reffie, ". . . of the human waste. Do you know, for instance, what the chief cause of accidents is? Do you?" he insisted as Reffie remained silent. "*Walking*. Just careless walking. More than half of our accidents take place while the miner's walking or climbing." Sidleigh flipped open his charts, showed Reffie the typographical proof.

Not grasping the significance of the long lists of accidents accompanied by charts of tens of thousands of man hours, Reffie's eye dropped to the conclusion: Average Fatalities, October (Room-and-pillar method) 1.31. *Reffie thought he knew who was the one, but who was the 31/100?*

"What I'm saying," Sidleigh said, smiling collusively, "is that human intelligence hasn't increased with wages."

Reffie felt he ought to defend his grandfather and all the others, so he asked quietly, "And what about production?"

Sidleigh put the phone back on the hook, his voice became declamatory, "Well, we've always been pretty good on production. Till this year, with about 400 miners we always got our two thousand tons entering the mill every day."

"And now?"

"Actually we haven't needed that 400 for a long time now. There're machines that'll mine you a miracle a day."

"And you want me to see . . . how many hours a day. . . ." Reffie's voice faltered. *He wants me to be a company fink, that's what. And I'm goin to do it; I'm never goin to see my kids go hungry again. No matter what.*

"Well, it's not just goofing-off time you got to take notice of. You're not like a policeman, for Chrissake. What you want to notice, too, is any relaxing of safety regulations."

"But the Regulations Handbook says that any guy can be fired for breaking safety rules. If I tag somebody, he's gonna get fired." The idea was so stunning to Reffie that he had to say it out loud, as if by saying it, it would mean something different or Sidleigh would finally contradict him.

Sidleigh glared at him, as if he were a hopeless dammed fool. He slammed the looseleaf notebook shut. "Well, I guess you're really not trained for this sort of thing," adding spitefully, "you got a college degree?"

Reffie admitted he'd dropped out of high school in his last year.

"That's all right. Not everybody's got the talent for it. Guess I mistook my man," adding as if involuntarily, ". . . though I hardly ever make a mistake that way. . . ."

"No, no, you didn't make a mistake, Reffie assured him quickly, as if it were Sidleigh's life that was in jeopardy, not his. "I can do it. I'm sure I can do it." Feeling his intensity betrayed his need, he tried to add lightly, "Julia can help me type up the reports."

Sidleigh sucked his lower lip thoughtfully. "Better not do that. Just keep on checking in like you're working a regular day. Any irregularities, you *remember* them. Then come back here and write up your report."

"*Here*? In your office?"

Reffie saw him hesitate before he sealed their collusion. "And keep your mouth shut. Your grandfather being so strong with the union men puts me on the spot, you know?"

Reffie didn't ask why that was.

VIII

Since the afternoon Tamsen had driven through Larch-wood on her bicycle, she had begun to think of herself as a Texas wheeler-and-dealer. She had persuaded Sean to contract for snow-shovelling jobs on week-ends, from whose returns she divested her proper share as "manager and bookkeeper;" she persuaded Reffie to let her have a paper route: when she made her collections she managed to mention as often as she could that, her father might be unemployed next year, and how all her earnings and tips were going into her College Education Savings Account. In addition, she "borrowed" small sums from Sean or Reffie—a dollar here, a dollar there; neither of them ever spoke of it again. Then towards February she hit on the idea of selling greeting cards on the same evenings that she collected for the newspaper. She discovered that while folks merely listened in an absent-minded way if she talked about how Reffie had lost his farm, or how she'd broken her leg in the mine, they liked to listen to a pretty girl who chattered away while selling them something. It took Tamsen several weeks to realize that they hadn't believed much of what she said: they had paid for the performance. By these strategies she had managed to save nearly two hundred dollars.

In addition to the sweetness of money-in-the-bank, Tamsen had discovered the power of bearing a secret. Amazed at her own self-control, she'd not mentioned Julia's betrayal to anyone but Sean. But Sean was in love with her so he would not tell unless she wanted him to. From what Tamsen had seen so far of Love, it appeared to be a kind of demonic possession. It wracked you with joy and pain; it caused strong men to groan and women to faint; it gave you over to someone else's power: it had made Sean her vassal.

She had decided early on that for her Plan to work, it would in turn be necessary for her to fall in love with Sean. Tamsen did not feel however that she was giving herself over to some awesome power, because she felt free to change her mind if she wanted to, *unlike Julia*.

Tamsen watched week after week as Julia's agonies intensified, her terrible anguish when the phone rang or failed to ring, her abject misery when her lover's grey VW failed to be waiting for her at the appointed spot (twice she'd seen Julia slip into the car right outside the post office), her nervousness on those days when Josh was too fussy to be left with Mrs. Parranni, so Julia could not go "shopping"—running instead to her lover's apartment on Bitterroot Street. Sometimes the daring of Julia's stratagems impressed Tamsen in spite of herself. Who would have thought, for instance, that a Respectable-Mother-of-Three would leave her family on Christmas Eve and rush out to exchange abandoned kisses with her lover? But Tamsen had seen it. Suddenly while they were still wrapping presents, Julia had looked up at the tree and declared that it needed more angel hair. She'd just slip out to the supermarket before it closed. Observing Julia's restrained excitement, and that Julia took care to put on her boots (the parking area outside the supermarket was always kept clear of snow), Tamsen felt certain she was going to meet her lover, so a few moments later Tamsen had casually remarked that she'd run down and join Julia, she had a couple of last-minute purchases to make herself—here she smiled at Woody. Sure enough, she'd almost run into Julia heading for her lover's apartment. Tamsen had stood behind a parked car watching her father's wife (*wearing that new coat Reffie bought her*) stumble through the windblown snow until she came to a lighted hallway. Then Julia took out her key and went in.

Tamsen had waited until Julia came darting out again, hatless, her cheeks flushed. She appeared to have been crying, but Tamsen couldn't be sure. Julia was already running across the snow-covered walk when a young man with dark hair and a crimson turtleneck sweater came hurrying out of the building after her. "Julia!" Julia turned at once, a look of sublime terror on her face at the sound of her name being called through the street. Her lover was holding her gloves. "You forgot . . ." With a gasp Julia ran back. At that moment Tamsen glimpsed the young man's face: a big square face with terrible eyes—he looked almost angry as Julia flew into his arms. Julia kissed the dark face again and again. "Goodbye. Be careful. And open it right away, Michael, will you open it right away? I want to think of you reading it tonight, while I'm thinking of you, you'll be reading it, won't you? I love you." She murmured through her tears, and ran.

Tamsen did not even hurry to get back to the Christmas tree. She did some last-minute shopping, arriving home with two or three gifts, including a small key-locking diary for Julia.

A week later Tamsen decided she was wasting time. She must hurry and make Sean her lover. It would have to be at her house not his, she reflected. She could plan it better that way. She chose a night when Reffie had announced that as part of their Christmas-New Year's celebrations the entire family, including Josh, would go to a movie. Tamsen checked the newspaper for the time schedule, and a few hours before the others were to leave she managed to simulate a listless, feverish look which allowed her to stay at home. When she was sure that nobody was going to return unexpectedly, she let Sean in by way of the kitchen. Tamsen began turning out all the lights, including those on the Christmas tree. Sean objected.

"But I want to be able to see you."

"You know what I look like. You've been seeing me every day."

"But this is different. How will I know . . . ?"

"Know what?"

"Whether you're, you know, wanting me?"

"If I didn't want you, why would you be here in the first place?"

He sighed. "Tamsen, you're too much."

Tamsen offered to compromise by bringing in Reffie's flashlight.

Sean stood diffidently near the door of her bedroom; he seemed unable to believe that this was about to happen. Tamsen tried to remember what she had heard or read about Love. All she could evoke was the memory of Julia's face, drunk with love. Sean did not look like that. She glanced into her bureau mirror to see how she looked to Sean: her lips were set with determination, her eyes wide and inquiring.

"I need a shower," Sean said at last.

Tamsen kneaded her lip; she knew exactly how long the movie would last. "Well, *get* one, then." She herself had been lavish with cologne, the way she understood she was supposed to be. When Sean returned, he smelled strongly of Reffie's soap; he held the towel awkwardly around his waist with his left hand. His arms and shoulders were still a little wet, so Tamsen brought out another towel and began rubbing him vigorously. He became suddenly excited at her touch and pulled her to him with a quick strong hand. They fell to the bed.

"It's cold—why don't we get under the covers?" Tamsen suggested.

He had propped up the flashlight so that it made a v-shaped beam on the wall. Outside her window Tamsen heard a passing car, then the crunch of someone walking on a cindered path, and, finally, the sound of a train in the distance. It caused her to think of how rare was the sound of a train anymore, and how wonderful it had been that time she'd gone with her mother by train from San Antonio to Nuevo Laredo; and she thought too of how astonishing it was that such memories came unexpectedly out of your childhood like ghosts dropping into Christmas-Present.

She wasn't sure what Sean was supposed to do, exactly. It occurred to her that he was waiting for something, maybe she was supposed to help. He lay on his side, trying to see her face.

"Tami, are you *sure* about this? That you want it, I mean?"

"Of course I'm sure."

"But you haven't said you love me, even. You do love me, don't you?" Tamsen studied the v-shaped beam projected on the wall like a bare bright screen waiting for pictures.

"Of course I love you. What a question." She lifted her head from the pillow and pressed her mouth firmly to his.

"Well, if you . . ." He groaned, returning her kiss. Then he broke away from her for a moment, reaching for his clothes. "I guess I need to wear . . ." Delicately he turned his back. Then Tamsen felt an odd papery sensation between her legs as if Sean had applied scotch tape before entering her. He now plunged quickly, with a kind of frightened determination, as if he both feared to hurt her and feared to stop hurting her. As Tamsen gasped with pain, he promised, "It's better just to get it over with, it'll not hurt the next time." He turned his head to one side as if he were listening for something.

As Tamsen waited for something remarkable to happen she felt certain that this could not be what had sent Julia breathless and weeping through the snowdrifts, risking hell's damnation and a husband's fury. Maybe it was just another one of those mysteries people lost their lives for without ever understanding. Sean seemed very pleased with her though she felt she had done nothing. She had once or twice tried to behave in a manner which she thought might be erotic; but he'd been crushing her upper arms. She stretched them now, looking for bruises. She felt very wide awake, as if she'd like to get up and read a good book.

But Sean now wanted to begin again. He vowed it'd be much better for her this time. Secretions from their bodies had made him gluey, however, and the condom would not slide on. He excused himself to go to the bathroom taking the flashlight with him.

When he returned he said tenderly, "That was the most beautiful thing that ever happened to me. Being in love with you has changed my whole life." Tamsen agreed that being in love was the most wonderful thing that could happen to people. She thought that it might be all right then to ask, "Why don't you turn off that flashlight, Sean? It's hurting my eyes."

In the dark Tamsen listened carefully and tried to help him more, because she was beginning to understand that sex was a serious undertaking which took your entire attention; you could fail at it just like at anything else.

By the time the others returned, Tamsen had lit up the Christmas tree, she and Sean were listening to carols being sung from cathedrals all over the world. When Woody rushed in, breathless and excited, wanting to tell her and Sean all about the movie, Tamsen was eager to listen. It sounded real exciting, she said.

A birthday party for Woody had been planned for Saturday night, and because it was also February, Julia had thought it would be nice to have it around Valentine's Day. She promised to bake some cookies for Woody and decorate the house with red-paper hearts. On the morning of the birthday party Tamsen wakened late to the sound of moaning in the bathroom. Julia emerged, looking pale and shaken. Woody, wanting to be helpful, particularly since it was his party, had already set out orange juice and dry cereal for everybody, and had even set Josh in his high chair with a biscuit. "*Thank* you," breathed Julia with relief and sat down. She was still in her bathrobe.

"What do you think, should I call Lamont?" Woody asked. "Even though it's sort of at the last minute? I mean, will he be insulted do you think?"

Julia nodded feebly. "Sure. Call him."

"Yeah, call him," agreed Reffie. "Guy named Lamont needs all the friends he can get."

Woody flew to the telephone. Julia pulled her bathrobe close to her body and sat hunched over the table, watching Josh gnaw at his biscuit. She lifted her glass of juice with great care, as if she were afraid to spill something.

Reffie looked at her with concern, leaning over to feel her forehead. "Any fever?"

Without answering, Julia rose suddenly, her hand to her mouth and rushed to the bathroom. Reffie started after her, then thinking better of it, stood outside the door until she came out again. Julia leaned against the wall weakly, a kleenex to her lips.

"You oughtn't to be tryin to have a party for Woody with the flu coming on," said Reffie.

"Everybody'll *catch* it from you," said Tamsen.

Woody stood by, torn between what he thought he was expected to say and the impossible idea of cancelling his party. "She could just lie down somewheres. Me and Tamsen could do everything, couldn't we, Tamsen?"

"Oh sure, sure. What else could I have to do on a Saturday night? And what about Josh?"

"What about him?" demanded Reffie.

Unable to stare down Reffie's stern look, Tamsen faltered. "Well, he'll need his walk, won't he?"

Reffie looked relieved. "Just let him play in his playpen until it's time for his nap. I'll take Julia over to the doctor. I got to stop by and see Sidleigh anyway."

"You mean you're not going to be here *either*?" Tamsen complained, overwhelmed by the thought of all that would have to be done before Woody's friends came.

"And who're you to ask questions about where and when I have to see somebody? Dammit, somebody asks you to do something around here once in a while . . ."

Tamsen felt a rush of anger like liquid fire surge up her spine. "'Once in a while! Once in a while!' I do a lot of things around here. I do my own laundry, I do *all* the dishes. And besides *that* I have homework, and besides *that* I have my paper route. Am I supposed to work *all* the time? I'm home a lot more than *she* is!"

Reffie had taken a step toward her and perhaps would have slapped her, which he'd never done before in his life; but Julia was moving again toward the bathroom, her hand touching the wall as if for support. With an angry glare at Tamsen, Reffie strode to the phone to call the doctor. He began relaying information through the door to Julia. "If you can come right away, he can maybe squeeze you in before he goes to the hospital."

He picked up his metal briefcase and stood by the door waiting for Julia, rebuking Tamsen by his silence. As they drove away, Tamsen realized he hadn't even said Happy Birthday to Woody.

"Now look what you've done," said Woody mournfully. "What did you have to say that for?"

"What have I done?"

"Just ruined my birthday, that's all."

"It's not ruined. We're going to have it. It's just *us* going to do it, not her." It occurred to Tamsen that "since Larchwood" she never referred to Julia by name anymore; Julia had become the anonymous *she*.

Tamsen tried conscientiously to save the day for Woody. She fed Josh his breakfast, bathed him in the kitchen sink the way she had seen Julia do hundreds of times and let him play in his playpen until be began to cry *Ma-ma*. She tried to explain to him that Ma-ma was gone but would be back soon; but his totally unreasonable demand that Mama reappear wearied Tamsen of his complaints, so she decided to put him down for his nap an hour earlier. He balked at this as if he knew what time it was and began calling out from his crib—at first in annoyed, persistent yelps, then with self-pitying little cries.

After an hour or so of cleaning house, she and Woody sat down to make party favors. "How many kids are coming?" she asked, trying to be friendly. But her ear was tuned to the bedroom, where Josh was still whimpering. It was Julia he wanted, not her. Twice he'd thrown his bottle out of the crib; twice Tamsen had picked it up and cleaned the nipple before returning it to him. She resisted the urge to shake him as she repeated for the tenth time, "Ma-ma will *be* here in a minute. Go to sleep. Naptime!" she tried to call gaily, as if she were offering him something.

"Fourteen kids? Do we have enough cookies, do you

think? Maybe you'd better just run out and buy some more. I can't bake any and do everything else too."

Obediently Woody ran to get his jacket. "Got any money?"

"Damn. They forgot to leave us some money. Well, I've got some." She set aside the party favor she was making and went to her room where, first shutting the door carefully behind her, she took a five-dollar bill from her savings.

As she handed Woody the money she said, "Be sure to tell Reffie I lent you that. I need to have it back."

"Aw, for crying . . . You'll get it back."

She and Woody were working on valentines for the party when they heard Reffie drive up with Julia. Josh had finally fallen asleep and was lying diagonally across his crib as if he'd been through a terrific struggle and finally been overcome. Woody was singing under his breath, "Happy Birthday to me, Happy Birthday to me/Happy Birthday, dear Woodrow, Happy Birthday to me." The table was set for the party, complete with a party favor for each child. Tamsen had at the last moment even decorated Woody's birthday cake, adding, *We love you, Woody*. She felt tired, but not too tired to go around with Sean to collect for her paper route. She always felt better about doing this while Sean stood by, not more than a foot or two away in the darkness. He was not a heavy-weight fighter, but he would (she knew) have thrown himself on anyone who. . . .

She and Woody were now making up verses for the kids' valentines. Together they'd cut out red hearts, then with a felt tip pen Tamsen had inscribed a little poem for each. For one of the girls Tamsen had laughingly written, Roses are red/Violets are blue/Abie loves Patty and I love her too/Boo hoo hoo/What shall I do? Woody had at first objected, then upon reconsideration had decided, with a blush, that it was not a bad way of wooing his lady. There were still several valentines left to do. Tamsen was drawing a heart pierced by Cupid's arrow when Reffie entered, smiling broadly.

"She's all right—nothing to worry about," he announced before they asked. "Doctor given her this prescription." He laid it carefully on the mantelpiece. "How's everything for the party?"

Woody said, "Tamsen did *everything!*"

"She did, did she? Well, well. That's good. Julia, you hear that?" he called to Julia, who'd gone into their room to change clothes.

Julia came out in her robe, looking tired and subdued. She glanced at the set table, at the party favors and birthday cake; then sat down, looking at her hands.

"You just lie down a while till the party. You see Tamsen has got everything done for it. Nothin to worry about . . ."

The phone was ringing. Parents began calling to see if they had the right time, to ask when the party would be over, to ask when they should pick up their children. Then Sean telephoned to ask Tamsen whether they'd be going out to collect for her paper route.

"Tamsen," remonstrated Reffie, do you *have* to do that this evening?"

"I do," said Tamsen, compressing her lips. "I've been in this house all day. And afterwards Sean and I are going to a . . ."

Julia said, "Really, Reffie, it's all right. I'm . . . fine."

Reffie smiled at Julia. "She's fine," he said. "Just fine."

As if wakened by Julia's voice, Josh began babbling to himself. Julia seemed grateful for the distraction and rose to get him before he had called out to her. Still half-asleep, and with an air of surprise to find Julia hugging him close as if he'd been lost and found again, Josh blinked at them all.

Reffie bent his head to ask, "Hi there, young Joshua. Fit yourself any battles today?" Suddenly he burst into song, *O Joshua fit the Battle of Jericho, Jericho/O Joshua fit the Battle of Jericho/And the walls came tumbling down!*"

Josh smiled ecstatically; it was his favorite song. Then Reffie peered into the baby's eyes as through the mist of an oracle and asked, "How'd you like to have a baby sister, Josh? How'd you like that?"

Tamsen stared at Julia who stood patting down Josh's hair with an absent, rhythmic motion.

"Hey now!" exclaimed Woody. "On *my* birthday party too! At which Reffie burst into laughter, Josh bounced into his father's arms and Julia busied herself with fixing them sandwiches before the party began.

Tamsen bent her head, continuing her work on the valentine. On one side of the pierced heart she inscribed, *Julia*, on the other *Michael*. Then she slipped it into an envelope, addressed it to Bitterroot Street, licked it, and pounded the table till it sealed shut.

PART II

IX

As he left the birthday party Reffie felt a deep, almost religious pleasure. He thought of the new baby as proof that one's own life was not yet such a burden that the gift-of-life would only add to your misery instead of easing it. So he had believed, so he meant to go on believing. He hoped that in time Julia, too, would come to see it his way.

He was mulling over the possibility that Julia might, however, *not* come to see it his way when he became aware that Grampa Wing was walking toward him. Wing's cheeks were red from the cold, but he was walking straight as a rod and not even puffing for air. *He's gonna live forever,* thought Reffie with admiration and this too seemed somehow in harmony with the events of the day.

"You headin for the party?" said Reffie, slowing down.

"Yeah, I was. But no hurry. I'll walk along with you to Main—you goin that way?"

"Ummm. Got to get a few things." It had not occurred to Reffie that Gramp might reverse his direction and go along with him.

Gramp glanced down at the metal case in Reffie's hand. "What you got there, Reffie? You look mighty like a big wheelin-and-dealin lawyer from Houston with that . . . *box.*"

Reffie was silent. He could tell by Gramp's sharp look and the tone of his voice that these were not idle remarks. He continued walking slowly down the hillside as if he were in fact going to Main Street.

They came to a section of icy walk where Reffie instinctively shifted his briefcase to his other hand and put out his arm toward Wing who clutched it as if determined not to let him go.

"How come you never come by my place anymore, Reffie? I done something? You mad at me about something?"

Reffie shook his head, smiling. "What could you do to make me mad, Grampa?"

Soberly Wing looked into his grandson's eyes. "Lots of things a man could do." Abruptly he added, "Reffie, come on over to my house. I want to talk to you."

Reffie felt the cold fear of a boy caught with his hand in the till. "Gramp, I can't just now. Really I got to go and get some stuff for Woody's party. Just think of it, would you believe that kid's twelve years old today? *Twelve years.* Would you believe?"

"I'd believe," said Wing laconically. "Reffie, I don't want to make trouble for you. I just want to talk to you. And bring that damned box with you." Gramp shot a look of contempt at the briefcase.

He knows. "Gramp, couldn't we make it some other evening? Like tomorrow night, even, would be better than just this minute. Really . . ."

For answer, Wing clutched Reffie's arm fiercely and they turned the corner together. *I can't very well push the old man down and cut and run.*

"Won't take but a minute," Wing assured him.

They turned up the path to Gramp's little Cape Cod. The snow had been freshly cleared from the walks. "That Sean does my walks for me. Gettin too old to shovel snow," said Gramp in a tone which indicated he thought giving the job to Sean was nothing but charity; he could still do it himself if he wanted to.

Feeling trapped, Reffie sank into a chair in Wing's living room and looked around him. The floor was covered with the same braided rug; the Indian snowshoes on the wall and the wooden chairs with rawhide seats were the same; but Wing had added an aquarium and put in a new wood-burning stove.

"You can get all the free wood you want," explained Wing, following his gaze. "The state lets you pick it up free from their land. They want you to help clear off the fallen trees. Guess you know that?"

Reffie confessed he didn't know, adding that he wished he *had* known it, he could have saved some money on fuel bills, maybe. He hoped Wing would keep the conversation at this level. He didn't mind being found guilty of not knowing wood was free and abundant. A man couldn't know everything.

As if echoing his thought, Wing said, "Well, you can't be expected to know all the customs of the country. Guess I should have told you. But it's a lot of work, believe me, cuttin up wood. You wouldn't want to be doin all that choppin after you've been down the mine eight hours." He paused, looking sharply at Reffie as if waiting for Reffie to explain why he was working shorter hours underground these days.

But Reffie was looking at the aquarium. He didn't recognize any of the exotic fish except the angelfish. Wing had outfitted the aquarium so as to give the fish a constant temperature and a continuous supply of artificial light. Now and then a fish would glide delicately downward, appear to nibble something at the gravelly bottom, then swim gracefully upward. Reffie found himself wondering what they added to Grampa Wing's life, these silent creatures flowing like so many silk fans, opening and closing.

He realized suddenly that Wing was reminiscing, something he rarely allowed himself to do. Gramp considered himself a hard-nosed man of the Present; the fact that as a kid he'd worked half a day for the price of a sack of potatoes was—he was in the habit of emphasizing—*irrelevant.*

But now Wing was saying ". . . been here all my life. I can remember when the first conveyor belts were installed back in the thirties. They was only 500 feet long then, they took the ore from the scrapers to the skip-loading pockets at the shaft. And it was not an uncommon thing, I tell you, for a man to shovel twenty-five tons of ore on a shift. And what was our wages?"

Reffie roused himself, realizing this was a challenge. Reffie could not avoid this battle, he had not brought it on, it was Wing who had brought him here, and he was not going to flinch. He had a family to support. Maybe in a minute he'd let Gramp know about how Julia was going to have another one; but now he simply said as amiably as he could, "Gramp, what good does it do to dig up all those numbers? Houston and Pittsburgh don't care about what guys *used* to do. They want *cost effectiveness,* and the mine don't produce enough anymore. That's why they're going to . . ."

"What? What do you mean—not produce enough?" demanded Wing. "We still produce 16% of the country's refined lead, dammit. And only a couple years ago silver production was *up.*"

"Yeah, well according to Sidleigh, it's all been downhill since."

"Ah . . . Sidleigh . . ." Gramp leaped to his feet, *like a tough old armadillo,* thought Reffie, and ran to fetch a box of papers. "Now you mention Sidleigh, I *understand*—I understand what you been up to. But what I can't understand is how my own grandson could do such a thing, bitin the hand that fed you. And you not even havin a job when you come here. I'm the one, I'm the damn fool who took you in on account of you were starvin—you and your family . . ."

Reffie stared at the angelfish which puckered its mouth. "Well, that's it. You done said it, Gramp. I was starvin. My family was starvin. And I don't mean for them ever to be hungry again. What's more, we gonna have another baby soon . . ."

Gramp stared at him in helpless rage and exasperation. "Damn fools," he muttered. "Just look here at *my* statistics, before you go writin up any report about how we're not working enough."

"It's not that the men are not working enough—it's that the machines can do it a lot faster. Like the mechanical scrapers."

"Yeah, and they gonna mechanically scrape you right off the face of the earth, Reffie, you better believe it! And all those write-ups you done for "Prohibited Behavior." Just where the hell you get off at, writing up other guys for so-called "Prohibited Behaviors": Goshert, Wronosky, Farrier, Mangeone . . ."

"It says in the Handbook, don't it? 'Authorization is to be obtained from Industrial Relations before attempting to solicit . . . *or distribute any material* during working hours on C & L property.' Mangeone didn't have a permit."

"And Wronosky?" demanded Wing, resting his palms on his papers, as if for support.

"Wronosky was carrying a gun to work: 'Possession of firearms is prohibited.' " Then, defensively, before Gramp could sound the litany of names of those men who had been furloughed or terminated in the past six weeks, Reffie named them himself. "Goshert—found asleep on the job; Hernandez—falsification of employment application; Farrier—*stealing.*"

"Stealing!" exclaimed Wing wrathfully. "He did no such thing."

"They found *matériel* in his lunchbox. Where I come from, taking Company Property, even if he says it's 'borrowed,' is stealing."

But Wing seemed suddenly overcome by grief. Shaking his head as he looked down at the old records he had brought to show Reffie, he repeated softly, "Who would have believed it? Who would have believed it? I been here over sixty years fightin for the miners, and now its my own grandson workin . . . a *fink* for the company. Sixty years . . ." Suddenly his eyes flashed. "And that's exactly *why* Sidleigh chosen you . . ."

"What do you mean by that? He offered me a job. I'm no miner by trade."

"No, nor by heart *either,*" said Wing, white with rage. "And you so dumb you can't see that's exactly why they chosen you. 'Cause you *are* my grandson."

Reffie scowled and rose to his feet. "O.K. If you think I'm so dumb, what're we doin here? There's nothin else to say . . ."

". . . it's 'cause you *are* who you are that they chosen you," repeated Wing. "That way they can divide us. The guys will say, 'How can we trust anything the old man says? How do we know he's not tellin everything to that grandson of his—a company fink—his grandson . . .' "

Reffie turned to leave. "I guess that about wraps it up, don't it?"

Wing appeared to struggle for self-control. "Reffie, just look here at these records. This is the way it was. We've gone a long way to health and safety and gettin decent wages. Just look at this record," he demanded, "and don't forget," he added in a broken voice, full of pride, "it was mostly just dynamite and jackhammers in those days."

Reffie forced himself to move to the table to read what Wing was pointing at. But he was afraid of his own weakness, he steeled his heart:

1937: Mining costs per ton including development were: Labor, $1.43; explosives $0.08; other supplies $0.08. Compensation Insurance $0.12. TOTAL . . .

"Think of what that means, Reffie—*think* of it and don't sell yourself short. Think of what twelve cents a ton for *compensation insurance means.*"

Reffie tried to move away. He didn't want to see anymore, he had his own report to do, and his time was running short. But Gramp was virtually holding him back.

Reffie read aloud, in a monotone, feeling remote from his own voice:

When working on steep slopes, drillers should be supported by ropes and safety belts; jackhammers are practically the only drilling machines for such conditions . . .

His eye wandered to the bottom of the page:

. . . during 1930 on a basis of all underground labor, 3.04 man hours were required per ton of ore . . .

With a heavy sigh Reffie moved away, buttoning his jacket as he walked toward the door. "Wing," he said, "what you been showin me are nothin but dinosaur bones. And that's just it. C & L is gonna be *extinct*. But until it *is* extinct, I got to put bread on the table. I ain't no angelfish. Ain't nobody goin throw me some feed and keep me warm in a nice little glass house." As he opened the door, he added in a tone which was meant to say that he was sorry but that was the whole truth of it, "And I don't mean to die like Smetka."

After leaving Grampa Wing Reffie went directly to Sidleigh's office and, before his will could waiver, wrote up his report. This time it seemed couched in much better language than he'd ever managed before. He thought he was getting the hang of it. He paused for a moment to consider what final recommendations to make; then decided to leave that part of the report to Sidleigh, who would also correct the report for any spelling and typographical errors.

A few days after Woody's party Julia stopped Tamsen just as she was leaving for school. "I want to speak to you," she said.

Tamsen stood silent, her books in her arms. She was wondering where Sean would be an hour from now when she would need him.

"I think you know what I want to talk to you about."

Tamsen watched her, waiting to see if she would weep or beg or confess, but Julia did nothing of the sort.

"Sit down, please."

Insulted that Julia should feel she still had the right to command, Tamsen stood rooted to the floor.

With a great sigh Julia took the valentine and its envelope out of her pocket. "Do you recognize this?"

"Are you interrogating *me*?" demanded Tamsen.

"No. I just want to know what you think you're doing."

Tamsen spoke reflectively to the ceiling. "She wants to know what *I* think I'm doing. Now that takes a lot of . . ."

"I mean, I want to know if you . . . if . . . somebody's trying to break up your father's marriage by this kind of thing."

"Are you trying to say it's *me* who's breaking up your marriage when it's you who . . ." Tamsen waivered, glancing at the envelope in Julia's hand.

Julia sank weakly to the sofa, her hands between her knees. "So it *was* you who sent . . . I was hoping perhaps . . . I was hoping it was *any*body else. And the diary. A *Christmas* gift. Given me—" her voice rose interrogatively with disbelief "with the evil intent to . . ."

" 'Evil intent!' It's not *me* who goes running round in the snow . . . and the lies you must have to tell Reffie—it's sickening . . ."

Julia suddenly sat up straight. "I've never lied to your father."

Tamsen turned on Julia with what she meant to be a bright bitter jet of laughter. She was still clutching her books as if she meant to go to school, as if today were like any other day.

"I mean by that, that Reffie has never once *asked* me . . . if I were happy with him."

"Well," Tamsen observed coldly, "I guess he deserved to be punished then, for not asking. Guess every miner working his head off down there's got nothing to do but bow and scrape and shuffle and ask if little Missy is happy today."

"Stop that. Just stop that. You know what I mean. I want to know who said anything to you . . . where did you learn . . . get his name?" With an almost imperceptible movement Julia touched the envelope. When Tamsen remained silent, she went on. "I knew him . . . before I met Reffie. I loved him before I loved . . . anything or anybody. But he was ill."

"Yeah," Tamsen observed maliciously. "He looked *'ill'* when I saw him."

"You saw him?" A stunned incredulous look came over Julia's face.

"Yeah. I saw you. I saw you in Larchwood Cemetery. I saw you at the supermarket. I saw you at the post office. I saw you on Bitterroot . . ."

Julia burst into tears, her hand pressed to her mouth. "How could you be so *low*? Following me . . ."

"Low? *I'm* low? Well, *you* have a nerve . . ."

Sobbing, Julia sank her head into the pillows of the sofa. "To think you've been following us . . . all that time, watching us, and counting the times . . ."

"Yeah. Counting the times. But I couldn't count good enough to know for sure about this new one . . . Is it gonna be Reffie's cute little darling baby girl, or Woody's sweet little baby sister, or Michael's adopted . . ."

"Stop it! Stop it!" screamed Julia. "Stop it or I'll . . ."

"Or you'll what? *You'll* stop me? From telling Reffie? Nobody'll stop me from doin that if I want to . . ."

"Go ahead then. Tell him," Julia said, hot with rage and still sobbing. "Go ahead and tell him how you've been watching us, spying on us. Give him all the details, so he won't ever want to see me again—*or you either,* you wicked bearer of ill . . ."

"Those high-toned literary expressions . . . but it's nothing but clear-cut lying and cheating. And to cheat my father who's been laying down his *life* for you, leaving the farm and everything . . ." But here Tamsen felt she was getting out of control, she didn't want to exaggerate. She felt she had enough cold killing evidence to bring Julia down without exaggerating. "You've made a damned fool out of my father, and I hope to high *hell* he kicks you right out of the house into the street when he knows . . ."

". . . and you're going to tell him! Well go ahead. Go ahead and tell him then. If you want to kill your father, that's the way to do it. If you want to kill us all. . . . May God forgive the suffering you want to bring down on us," Julia sobbed.

Tamsen spoke to the ceiling again. "It's always these hypocrites who go around crying about God."

"I don't have to stay here to listen to you."

"No, you don't, that's true. You can to go Bitterroot and *stay.*"

"I'll do that. I'll just do that. And you'll have yourself to thank for breaking your father's heart."

"To stand there and accuse *me* of breaking Reffie's heart. While *Michael's* probably waiting for you right now, less than a mile away."

"Get out of here, Tamsen, I mean it. Just *get out*. Come back tonight when your father's here, and tell *him* whatever you want to say. But while I'm still in this house I don't want to lay eyes on you."

"You don't have the right to tell me to get out of my own house. I'll leave when I want to not, not when a . . . not when a . . . *thing* like you tells me . . ."

Julia advanced toward her as if she would forcefully shove Tamsen out the door. But suddenly bursting into a keening wail, she herself ran out the door, coatless, crying aloud, "I don't care. Tell him. Tell him if you want. It doesn't matter anymore. Nothing matters anymore . . ."

Tamsen stood at the window watching as Julia ran heedless along the snow-covered hillsides. At the incline she stumbled, but picked herself up again. Tamsen waited several minutes to see if Julia would change her mind, but she never looked back.

With elaborate care Tamsen put her books down where Reffie would be sure to see them. It was only eight in the morning. Josh had slept through it all. Tamsen called Mrs. Parranni to come and take care of Josh, then she hurried into her room to pack.

She was surprised to find that she was trembling. She wanted to go, she feared going. She wanted to hurt *them,* she feared hurting herself. She thought that having spent weeks in planning this flight, that when the time came she would be calm and methodical. But after a few minutes she found she could give no explanation for what she had packed. She was taking things with her that had no practical use and would only take up space. She found herself leaving behind her best clothes and piling her favorite records at the bottom of the suitcase. She'd have to repack those at the airport in Spokane, else they'd be banged out of shape by the time the plane landed in Mexico. She took out several albums in order to make room for a stuffed kangaroo Reffie had given her one Christmas: from its marsupial pocket hung a baby kangaroo recklessly suspended by its fingertips.

From its small metal frame Tamsen removed a snapshot

of herself and Woody and Reffie (holding Josh), taken by Julia during a moment of hope or maybe of indecision at Puget Sound. Standing on the pier, the vast blue horizon behind them, they appeared to be afloat on a spar in the sea—the only survivors of a shipwreck, doomed to stand there forever, suspended between the blue water and the deserted pier.

Tamsen looked around her room, saying to herself that she would never see it again: the old-fashioned flowered wallpaper, the armchair with its straight wooden arms; the bed in which she'd taken her first lessons in sex and love; and the maple bureau, its horseshoe mirror secretly shedding quicksilver like hair. From one of its drawers she removed her turquoise ring, the wristwatch given to her by Reffie and Roseanne when the farm was still flourishing, and her five-year diary. She still had nearly a whole year left in it. It was unnerving to realize how few things she had accumulated. It seemed a failure on her part somehow, leaving her more vulnerable . . .

And finally, money. She stuffed her savings firmly into her wallet and packed it away in her worn old Mexican handbag. It was one of those handmade fringed bags you saw everywhere in Texas, but maybe not in Spokane—maybe there it would draw attention to her and Sean. If, for instance, Reffie should call the police and begin describing her . . . But she didn't expect that. She began mentally composing a farewell note for Reffie which she imagined him reading, "Well, I'll be damned," he'd say. "She's gone and run off." "Who?" Woody would ask. "Tamsen," Reffie would say. *"Tamsen?"* Woody would repeat incredulously. "Yep," Reffie would say. "Her and that boy, Sean. I reckon they gonna get married," Reffie would add after a moment's thought, hoping to preserve her respectability. *"Married!"* Woody would exclaim, torn between scorn and disbelief. "But she never even *mentioned* him!" And then Reffie, sagely, maybe forgetting his grief as he savored his apothegm, "You don't have to *mention* a person to marry him."

An hour later, suitcase in hand, Tamsen stood for a moment on the front porch. It had snowed during the night and their sparse lawn was crusted over with a fresh layer of snow which glistened in the sunlight. As she descended the steps Tamsen stopped to stare. Someone during the night had urinated on their lawn, shaping with his hot melting insult the word FINK. Tamsen gripped her suitcase firmly. *Well, that's their problem,* she thought, and hurried to meet Sean.

At the bus station Tamsen didn't ask Sean what he had told his parents. She felt she couldn't risk softening her position. He had wanted to come with her; he'd said more than once that he'd follow her to the end of the world. Now, smiling and laughing nervously as they stood by the window to purchase their tickets, she reminded him of having said this. They laughed joyfully.

"Where to?" asked the ticket lady.

Tamsen began to giggle. Sean smiled broadly. "The lady wants to know, *Where to,* Tamsen. Answer her."

Doubled over with laughter, Tamsen replied, "To the end of the world."

"*Well,*" said the ticket lady, and took their money.

PART III

X

When Reffie and Roseanne and Woody and Tamsen took their vacations in Mexico, they would go in Reffie's station wagon. They would move along at a comfortable pace into the vast country, mile after mile, gradually absorbing the sunny land and soft ambiguous smiles of *los mexicanos,* until with one final spurt they would arrive at the capitol. After the long deserted stretches between towns they were not unhappy to find themselves surrounded by vehicles in the roaring traffic, watching the anarchic struggle from behind the air-conditioned sanctuary of their car: anointed Texans going guilessly into their vacation as if it were written in the Book of Fate that Reffie should prosper forever. On those vacations Reffie had not reckoned every gallon of gas nor cursed the greed of the hostelers offering shelter at Reasonable Prices. They had lived every day of their luck as if accepting their reward for the good they had wrought in the world.

On those trips Tamsen had been bored by everything that wasn't totally different from anything she'd ever seen before. Looking up from *The Call of the Wild,* or from some card game being played with Woody in the back seat, she would complain as they crossed the mesquite and cactus-covered land that there was *nothing to look at* and would demand to know why they hadn't gone to Orlando or Canada instead. What did Canadians look like? she wanted to know. And Roseanne and Reffie had merely smiled at one another at these complaints, feeling the luxury of choice. With youth and health and money, they believed they were free to go anywhere . . .

But arriving by plane, Tamsen discovered, was quite another thing. Early that morning she'd been walking along Main Street to the bus station, suitcase in hand. The town had been so quiet—only the sound of her own boots suggesting what life after death might be like, when you would lie forever under a quilt of silence, invisibly breathing. The only other person in the street had been Arimeo the barber, shoveling snow in front of his shop. And the bus station, except for Sean and herself, had been deserted. No one in Silver Valley going anywhere in any direction.

But by late tonight, she and Sean had been turnstiled into bedlam. It was as if they'd fallen from their empty planet into God's Population Center, from which human beings were being sent everywhere to inhabit the universe. No longer sheltered in Reffie's station wagon, Tamsen had found herself On Stage and forgetting her lines while all around her vendors, moneychangers, taxi drivers shouted at her the forgotten cues. Their unwavering attention forced upon Tamsen the knowledge that she and Sean were identifiably *foreign*. It was a shock to her self-esteem, Tamsen had always thought of herself as unique. Suddenly she was merely part of an easily recognizable species, as conspicuous as a leaping kangaroo on Main Street. *If Reffie really wanted to find me, all he'd have to do is call all the airports and describe us. We look like a couple of clowns, me small and dark, Sean tall and blond. With his tight jeans and orange backpack and expensive sneakers Sean's like a neon sign flashing U.S.A.* Maybe they'll deport us right away . . .

But no such international crisis occurred. The immigration clerk simply stamped their tourist cards, his face a curious mix of boredom and contempt: *a month or two of The Way We Really Are,* his face seemed to say, *and you'll be running back to the Hilton.*

But they weren't headed for the Hilton. Sean had an address given him by a friend in Silver Valley, who'd once stayed at an inexpensive (he said) posada in the city. But neither Sean nor Tamsen had the least idea where in the vast city this particular posada might be.

"I'll phone them," offered Sean. And after what seemed an interminable wait while he went first to exchange their American money into pesos, and then again to exchange a few pesos into centavos for the coin-operated phone, he managed to call the posada. But there was no answer.

"Let's just stay at some hotel downtown, Sean. There's *lots* of hotels." Tamsen was sure of that much, Reffie was always saying it. She recalled Reffie arranging the credit cards in his billfold, good for A Thousand and One Nights, he said.

Looking tense and anxious Sean brushed his hair back. He said he thought they ought to go straight to this place recommended by his friend. "Just *go* there and maybe just sit on the doorstep and wait." Adding diffidently, "I'm not worrying about the posada. There's *millions* of posadas . . ." He looked out at what must have seemed to him a city of people buying tickets, rushing home, pushing their luggage around with their knees to make room at the phone lines, ticket lines, taxi lines . . .

"Then what . . . ? Money?" She thought of her money securely hidden at the bottom of her handbag. Except for her bus ticket to Spokane, Sean had paid for everything.

"Well yes, but not even . . ." He said he didn't want to raise too many problems at once because he didn't want her to worry, he didn't want her to change her mind about him, he wanted to keep his Tami with him *forever*, even to the end of the world. As if to convince her of this, he bent to kiss her.

"Yes, yes, I know that. But then, what's worrying you?" She was afraid he was about to confess he'd forgotten something essential—his passport perhaps. They weren't supposed to need it, a tourist card was supposed to be enough, but still—somebody might pop up like a jack-in-the-box and demand to see your passport, too.

"What I'm wondering about—it's not really *worrying* me, I'm just wondering . . . is, what we'll do when those cards expire . . ."

"Oh, *that*. With relief, Tamsen explained how they could dash up to Salinas a while, then renew their tourist cards and . . ."

"'Dash up'? That'll cost . . . a lot, Tami."

"You just said you weren't worried about money."

"Well. I'm not, but still, that'd take . . . that's like a *fortune*. Like to fly up there and back, you mean? And like stay at a hotel in Salinas?"

"No, no, no. We'll just go up and stay with friends." She tried to think of who in Salinas might still be her friend and would take them in, but could not remember anybody offhand. "Well, I know what. When we've done our thing here, we can go up and stay in one of the border towns. We can go back and forth every day if we want to—live cheap. Reffie always . . ."

"Yeah, but even *cheap* costs *money*."

She stared at him with exasperation.

"Tami, it's not me who cares about money. It's the guy selling burritos on the corner, *he* cares . . ."

"Well you don't have to spoil everything on our very first day, worrying about . . ."

"Let's just take a taxi right to the posada," he said quickly, as if to prove that money was of no concern to him. And as if to emphasize his indifference, he did not even ask *How much?* before they climbed into the taxi. But all the way there, for mile after mile, Tamsen saw how attentively he listened to the ominous ticking of the meter.

The so-called inexpensive posada recommended by Sean's friend turned out to be just another small hotel, about fifteen blocks from the Zócalo. The sign above the hotel clerk's head indicated *Precios Modestos*, but the rates had not seemed modest at all to Sean who complained that it was robbery, sheer robbery. But exhausted from the long day they were ready to accept a bed at any price.

In the morning Sean knocked a dead cockroach from his spotless Nikes, shaking his head with disgust. Then he sat on the side of the bed, staring at Tamsen with what seemed to her sorrowful reproach.

"What're you looking at *me* like that for?" she demanded. "*I* didn't bring em here. What's the matter—didn't you think they had roaches at the end-of-the-world?" she added more lightly, hoping to make him smile.

But he remained downcast, looking around the hotel room with a thoughtful air. Then suddenly he began talking to her in a tone of heavy seriousness. He pointed out that they were right in the heart of the city, which might be great for those who lived and worked here, but a scary luxury for those like themselves who did not. If they stayed here in the city, their money would evaporate. Their pesos, he argued, would go farther in "the interior."

"God, Sean, you'd think this was darkest Africa or something. *'The interior.'* We can live here just as cheap as anywhere and nobody'll *look* for us here either. And if they *did* look for us they'd have a hard time finding us among all these millions of people . . . finding *me* anyway," she added plaintively, glancing at Sean's hair.

"Whaddya want me to do, wear a helmet? Or a big sombrero, maybe?"

"Don't be silly. People don't wear sombreros in the city. Unless they're Indian or something. Or beggars." She spoke from what she considered the superior knowledge of her childhood—trying to remember whether this was really so.

"I still think someplace cheaper—maybe down by the coast."

She sniffed scornfully. "Yeah. How about Acapulco?"

"No, no. Maybe just some small village. A fishing village, maybe."

"Sean, we don't know any *Spanish,* much less *Indian,* and you want to go into 'the interior.' "

But Sean was not listening; he had been scribbling on a scrap of paper, converting their dollars into pesos. "O.K. Here it is: you can see for yourself," he showed her his arithmetic, "if we keep this room, it'll cost us *minimally* two hundred pesos a day. And we got to *eat* too, don't we? I don't know any *clean* cheapie restaurants and we can't just eat at Sanborn's all the time like *you* used to. We should try to find a place where we can cook."

"*Cook?* I don't know how to cook—do you?"

"Well, we could economize. We could fix sandwiches or something. Tami, we *have* to be practical."

"Practical!" Tamsen giggled. "Oh yeah, you're sure one practical guy, Sean. Oh just a very prrr-act-ical hombre . . ."

"What's so funny?" he demanded. He hated it when she laughed at him. Then pocketing the scrap of paper with the figures, he sighed. "Aw come on, let's go have breakfast."

Tamsen leaped up from the bed happily. "Where? Where'll we go?"

Sean hesitated. He had already begun to have symptoms of an upset stomach, and several times during the night he had lurched down the hall to the bathroom.

"Some place *clean*," he said, managing to look at once dignified and affronted.

After breakfast they wandered around the teeming city, uncertain how to take advantage of their freedom. Now and then Tamsen tried to imagine what Reffie might be doing to find her; it would have been very easy, she felt, if he really wanted to. More often, she resigned herself to a sense of injury and abandonment, remembering with envy the descriptions of love-maddened parents kidnapping their children and hiding them out in the wilderness.

After several hours—more exhausted from their aimless walking than either of them would have admitted, with Sean complaining nearly all the while of a headache—they sank down on a bench in the Zócalo to rest. A group of children passed them, each one selling something. The eldest, a girl about ten, seemed to be shepherding the younger ones along as they offered their wares, then suddenly all three abandoned their combs and chewing gum to the sidewalk while they played a game of Flying-spinning themselves till they became dizzy, then dropping to the ground like fallen butterflies.

Tamsen drew closer to Sean. "I like it here, Sean, don't you? Don't you like it here? I'm *never* going back," she declared with sudden defiance.

Sean sighed heavily. "Well, come a time we'll run out of money. They city . . ."

"Sean, you've thought about nothing but money since we got here," she exclaimed with annoyance. But at the sight of the unexpected anger she saw harden in his eyes, she stood up, saying, "Let's walk a little—it's windy here."

"Yeah . . . I always thought it was warm 'Down Mexico Way.' "

It irritated her that the only thing he seemed to know about Mexico was an old song he'd heard on a jukebox; but she said nothing.

He handed her his windbreaker, remarking that his clothes were getting sort of neglected-looking and that his sneakers had dirty streaks on them; he'd tripped several times on the sidewalks and the surprisingly high curbs at the intersections. "Not like Shoshone County," he added good-naturedly.

"We *are* getting kind of grubby-looking," she admitted. "Police will think we're hippies."

"Hippies! There's no more hippies. What they *might* think is we're smuggling drugs."

Tamsen watched the children spinning. They were again falling to the sidewalk after their ecstatic dervish. She frowned. "You really think . . . ?"

"Nyah . . . we don't even have a car and they could go through my backpack in thirty seconds if they wanted. And now you've sold that fancy suitcase you had, you look like an honest Injun, especially with *that*." He pointed to her shabby Mexican handbag.

"Yes, but he'd only give us a hundred pesos for it and *he'll* probably . . ."

"Well, the main thing is," Sean emphasized, "you got *rid* of the damned thing and you got some money for it."

"Did you notice those other two Americans in the lobby, watching us?"

"They weren't watching *you*. What do they care about your suitcase? They were just registering, just like everybody else. I'll bet they were Mormons. They looked like Mormons. They were so clean . . . He looked down at himself with chagrin. "Right now I'll bet Shoshoni's cleaner than I am."

"Hey, I hear music. There's some Indians. Let's go see." She didn't want to hear a word about Home.

Sean followed, a look of misery on his face. "Tami, why don't we go somewhere where . . . where I can wash my hands, some place where there's hot water . . . and toilet paper." He averted his eyes as he spoke. She understood that it would have been sheer anguish for him to say he had diarrhea; it was as if such a word would not have been uttered in Silver Valley.

Suppressing her irritation she exclaimed, "In a minute, in a minute. Let's just walk up and see . . ."

An Indian, his face seamed as a dry arroyo, was playing the flute and dancing; he danced in a circle, at a slow, unchanging pace, as if he could have danced that way forever. Around his legs clacking nutshells accompanied the mournful flute. He wore a ceremonial headdress of yellow, pink and blue feathers, very worn and dirty—rather like dyed baby chicks bought for a season and not meant to survive through Easter. Beside him stood a small boy of four or five, half-asleep, offering his cup to the onlookers. He took a step toward Sean and waited, holding up his cup.

Sean stared resolutely into the distance.

"Sean, *give* him something!" whispered Tamsen.

Sighing with annoyance, Sean placed a ten-centavo piece in the boy's cup. Tamsen angrily took a quarter out of her handbag and pressed it into the hand of the boy, who had already turned to go.

Sean shrugged. "If we feed every beggar in *Mexico* . . ."

"They weren't begging, they were *dancing!*"

"Well, if you're not going to be sensible . . ."

"Sensible! *I'm* sensible! He's an artist, that's what that man is, an *artist.*" She did not know why, but she felt like crying, she was ready to fight fiercely over the definition.

"O.K. O.K." Sean clearly wanted to avoid quarreling in the street. "He's an artist. Anything you say . . . Let's go see some more *artists.* Let's go to a museum and see lots of *artists.* Then maybe I can use the . . ." His voice trailed off.

They began walking in the direction of the museum, which they'd been told was on Paseo de la Reforma. They'd walked nearly twenty blocks when, wearily, Tamsen demanded, "Did you look at your map first? Just where *is* this place, anyway? And why are we *walking* there? I'm so tired I could die."

Sean went into a camera shop to ask someone how far they were from the museum. Weary and exasperated, Tamsen stood outside watching through the window. She didn't know any Spanish *either*, it would just add to the confusion. The young man Sean was talking to appeared surprised though anxious to assist. He pointed and gesticulated; Sean listened attentively, trying to understand.

He came out looking dejected. "It's still a long way. What'll we do?"

They agreed they wanted to go on to the museum. Both had a sudden longing for clean well-lit rooms whose purpose was clear and familiar to them. They decided to splurge on a taxi. "And it'll be warm and dry there," added Sean, looking up as a drop of rain fell on his thin shirt. Carefully he counted out what he hoped would be enough money for the cab, then shoved his billfold down into his backpack.

The cab driver was a friendly, handsome young man, but he spoke almost no English. Tamsen tried to remember a few words of Spanish from Reffie's days-of-affluence, but could recall only *muchas gracias* and *adiós.* She now added *por favor* to her repertoire, as she and Sean indicated on the map where they wanted to go. Sean sat hunched over, gripping this throbbing head all the way, not even looking out the window. The driver talked amiably in Spanish; he seemed unconcerned that Tamsen was able only to smile or nod approvingly, but kept up this one-way conversation with her during the entire ride. Suddenly they were there.

Bent over with pain, Sean climbed out of the cab. As he paid the driver, the young man shot him a look of disdain. She saw that Sean had failed to tip him enough. To compensate for what she considered Sean's meanness, Tamsen took out a dollar bill and handed it to the driver, who smiled. Tamsen tried not to smile back but simply to say in her most mature manner, *muchas gracias, adiós,* the way Reffie would have done.

When the driver had pulled away, Sean turned toward her angrily. "Here I was sick as a dog and you just sat there *smiling,* listening to all that flattery . . ."

" 'Flattery!' "

"The two of you going on like lovebirds. You acted as if you'd known him all your life. You acted like a . . ."

She stiffened with rage. "Go ahead and say it, why don't you? I'm just waiting for you to say it . . ."

Suddenly Sean seemed overwhelmed by what he had meant to say. He stared at her in unbelief. "Tami, for Christ's sake, let's go in. We shouldn't be fighting like this."

"Who's fighting? I'm not fighting. It's you who're being unreasonable. So *childish* . . ."

He was about to make some angry *riposte,* but suddenly he stood motionless, assaulted by a shocking pain. "Let's just go on in, Tami. Let's not fight, hear?" Awkwardly he climbed the steps of the museum. "Who's Tamayo?" he wondered aloud as they entered, his voice echoing through the galleries. Then at once he found his way to the men's room while Tamsen waited. He was gone so long she began to get worried. *Suppose he'd fainted, or was stabbed by a thief? Strange things could happen* . . . With relief she saw him walking slowly toward her, looking weak and pale.

"Sick . . ." he said, and shut his eyes a moment as if to get his bearings. "Sit down a while?"

They found a corner along the staircase where Sean felt they would be less conspicuous. He was breathing heavily.

"Is this what they call . . . ?" He paused; it was clear that his symptoms were too humiliating for him to name.

"Looks like it." Tamsen tried to keep her voice neutral. Once Tamsen had used the word 'urinate' and he had appeared shocked, as if people who made love together did not use such words. Besides, she knew his symptoms could be devastating. Woody had had it bad, and it had nearly ruined their vacation once; they'd gone home a week earlier because Roseanne said, You couldn't take chances with kids, you couldn't be sure it wasn't amoebic.

But Sean was now trying to change the subject. He pointed out to her a group of visitors, making the rounds of the gallery with cameras and interpreter. The tourists, speaking French or German to each other, Tamsen wasn't sure which, turned to stare at them as they passed. She and Sean must have looked strange to them, looking more as if they were hiding behind the staircase than looking at paintings. There seemed very few identifiable Americans around, although in another month or so the students would begin drifting down, thousands of them, looking very much like Sean, with their sneakers and backpacks, their wallets full of credit cards or travellers' checks. But she and Sean—Tamsen became gloomily aware as she watched the foreign tourists—were a special case. Neither students nor smugglers nor vacationers nor exiled Americans.

Leaning forward, his head between his knees to overcome his vertigo, Sean said, "Gee, I hope they remember to take Shoshoni in for his shots . . ." At the recollection of his dog, Sean's voice changed, he was nearly crooning with homesickness. Tamsen, recalling Sean's spotless home, the photographs on the mantelpiece, his beautiful dog, could sympathize. But she also envied him. At least he had something to be homesick for, whereas for herself she believed there had been nothing. Everything had been stolen from her by Julia—her father's and Woody's love, her rightful place in the world. Still, she tried to share Sean's feelings. "Do you suppose Woody took over our paper route? He went with me a couple of times. He knows everybody on the route." She saw how Sean raised his head, listening attentively in spite of his vertigo. *He's listening for a sign that I want to turn around and go home.* Fiercely she shook off their mood. "Let's move on somewhere else. That security guard's beginning to look at us."

Groaning, Sean rose to his feet. They wandered aimlessly through the galleries. Neither of them knew anything about painting. Sean, however, was intrigued by some of the ancient artifacts, so they lingered there. Tamsen stood before an exhibition case trying to read the Spanish legend. "Look, Sean," she called to him. "Seems like the God of Love has no sexual organs . . ." Her voice echoed through the corridor as through a conch.

"*Sssh!* Do you have to have the whole world *hear* you when you say something like that?" Irritably he smoothed down his hair.

Tamsen shrugged, indifferent to his embarrassment. But he became insistent. "Well, for God's sake, Tami, you want us to get arrested? You *look* like a ten-year old, and you *talk* like a. . . . You see that kid there—*that* one—" he pulled her around so that she could see a little girl wandering around the gallery while her parents looked at the paintings, "Well, what would *you* think if that kid stood in front of what's-his-name—" his tongue stumbled against the god's name as into a brick wall "—and said in a great big loud voice, 'Oh gee whiz, lookee here—Xochiquetzal ain't got no *penis!*' "

Tamsen giggled, but it troubled her nevertheless. Had she been loud? The idea had never occurred to her before. Now, in a soft whisper, as if to set her an exemplary model of self-control, Sean read to her. "'God of Death. Cultura Clásica de Veracruz. 1100-1521 B.C. Hey, where's Veracruz?"

Suddenly Sean felt another attack coming on. He left hurriedly for the men's room. Resigned to another long wait Tamsen sank down on a bench. This time he was gone even longer than before. Maybe they should find a doctor—but where? Maybe if they went back to the posada someone could tell them where to find a doctor. She had a frightening sense of being forced to rely on the kindness of total strangers. She remembered Seattle, their sense of abandonment, the long last ride from the coast to Silver Valley . . . following Reffie down the mine . . .

She became aware that for some time she'd been looking at the painting of a fallen body. It appeared at first to be just another pietà; around the body of Jesus were many men who appeared to be His disciples. Idly Tamsen strolled into the adjoining gallery to get a closer look at it. In the foreground there was the usual lifeless body; but the painter had distorted the other figures so that the men looked shocked and angry—not grieving but furious. In another moment it seemed the men would bury the dead and rise up to destroy the surrounding mountain, stone by stone. And there was, as always, the anguished mother. It all seemed familiar, as if it were a place she'd been. Tamsen drew closer, trying to read the plaque, but it was in Spanish. Still, she understood that it was about a mine, an accident. She looked closer at the fallen body. *Ah . . .* she burst into tears of rage. She hated the picture. She hated the flesh sacrificed for bread; she hated the mother who had not had it in her power to save the fallen figure but had allowed him to be crushed by a downpour of fire and stone.

When Sean returned she was still crying. He began at once to complain that he'd been looking for her. Why had she wandered off like that? But at the sight of her tears, he asked, "Hey, what's wrong?"

Tamsen shook her head. "I want to get out in the air, Sean. I *have* to get out in the air." She felt as if she were suffocating.

Looking worried Sean led her quickly to the exit; he began chafing her hands as they sat on the retaining wall. "Do you feel sick, is that it? Do you feel faint?" He himself looked deathly pale. A heavy rain had begun to fall, and he looked up apprehensively. "Tami, just wait here a minute, will you? I left my jacket inside. Here, hold this while I run back. He handed her his backpack and ran to find his windbreaker.

The rain fell steadily, Tamsen stood up, uncertain whether to follow him back into the museum, out of the rain. The vendors were protecting their booths with plastic sheets; they stood beside their merchandise, the rain falling on their brown arms. Suddenly a child, about four or five years old, began wailing and ran across the lawn; she had become separated from her family. She stopped in front of Tamsen, murmuring something in a high musical voice, like a bird chirping in the rain. Tamsen did not understand a word of it; ashamed, she shrugged, unable to hide her ignorance. With a solemn look of disappointment and reproach, the child poked her thumb far back into her mouth and ran away.

When the Wingfield family had visited Mexico, Tamsen had scarcely noticed the children. Herself a child, the world had been for her full of grown-ups who helped you through the ruthless traffic, who never themselves got sick, who bought you a regular American hamburger if you wanted one, who insisted on going to Sanborn's to protect you from germs, who carried you into the hotel room if you were tired and they thought a hot shower and nap were just what you needed, who would fly you quickly home again if you developed a fever, as Woody had done, and might really be sick. But now—Tamsen could not recall ever having felt so cold in Mexico. She thought longingly of the warm coat she'd tossed aside for the sake of her stuffed kangaroo. The coat would have been perfect, or at the very least Sean could have traded it for something else, the way they'd traded her suitcase. Sean was showing a gift for handling such practical matters which she could never have foreseen in Silver Valley; he did not seem to mind that he was sometimes an object of suspicion or curiosity or both, or that his appearance made him conspicuous. As for herself, however, it was as if in the weeks of planning and wrenching herself free, her own usually stubborn Will had tired itself out. Last night she had even turned over her savings, the whole two hundred dollars of it, to Sean to keep safe in his backpack. She'd hoped that that would ease his mind a little, but it had seemed rather to alarm him. Maybe he'd hoped she had much more. He'd pointed out lightly, that he himself had withdrawn his entire savings. "I figured that way my family would know I was having a good time and not going off on a suicide trip." That Sean was capable of thinking in such terms had surprised her, and although he spoke jokingly, she saw that he was not happy at the amount of their combined savings.

He was running toward her through the rain. She noticed that he seemed even paler, if possible, than before, and that he was already wearing the windbreaker. He seemed not to notice that Tamsen was soaked to the skin. He was shivering and his hands were cold as he took the backpack from her. "Let's *run* for a warm place . . . I saw a restaurant . . ." he said through clenched teeth.

They ran through the rain to a small restaurant not far from the museum. It turned out to be a crowded, noisy place where middle class families met for their mid-day meal. Fathers and mothers and sons and daughters were gathered together to share the huge quantities of rich fragrant food on oval-shaped platters such as Tamsen had not seen since their steak-and-barbecue days in Texas. She and Sean, awkward and dripping with rain, stood diffidently near the door beside the cashier's counter. Sean observed at once that it would cost them as much as a night's lodging to eat there, but he conceded that it might at least be clean.

"Jesus, Sean, you're really getting a thing about 'clean.' It's so . . . *American,*" she added irritably.

Rebuked, Sean remained silent. She noticed however, when they had finally been given a table, how carefully he examined the water glasses. Then slowly setting the glass down on the white tablecloth he said, "Anyway, we can't afford dinner here. It's too expensive . . ."

"Again!" exclaimed Tamsen, flaring. "I thought after last night . . ."

He in turn was angry. "Do you really think two hundred dollars pays for . . . ?"

She sat stunned and silent. *Strange how you don't know anybody in this world. People are like the sand dunes on Padre Island, they shift under and away from you even while you're walking alongside of them.* Nevertheless, she tried to be conciliatory, he seemed to be in bad shape and his voice had grown hoarse. Was he going to get pneumonia or something from running around in all this rain? To humor him she said gaily, "Well, if it's too cold for you here, I mean, if you don't like it here, why should we stay? We're free aren't we? We can go anywhere . . ."

He stared. "Yeah, well. If you call it free . . ."

"You know what let's do? Let's go where it's warm. Maybe you're right—everything's too expensive here. Let's go somewheres cheaper . . ."

But he had become bitter and resentful. "Like where? Bonners Ferry?"

"Well, we wouldn't be any better off in Bonners Ferry than we are here, would we? I mean, if money . . ." She watched as he began to dry himself with a balled-up handkerchief.

The waiter brought them menus and stood looking at them with open disapproval. Tamsen's wet hair plastered to her face made her look like an Indian; on the other hand, Sean looked like himself: a teen-aged American with chrysanthemum-colored hair, down on his luck. The waiter seemed baffled by their appearance. *"Café?"* asked Sean. "Can we get just *café?"*

Muttering under his breath the waiter snatched the menus away, set down two coffees, and slapped the bill down on the table.

Sean whistled. "They sure don't want us taking up any of their space, do they?"

Should have bought our dinners and been done with it, thought Tamsen resentfully. *And after I gave him my whole two hundred dollars too . . .*

By the time they had finished their coffee, sipping it as slowly as possible, it had stopped raining. The sun was out and the face of the city was transfigured. They began walking back in the direction of the posada. "Are you feeling O.K. Sean? Are you all right?" Tamsen asked every third or fourth block. She had a vague feeling that neither of them knew exactly how to get back to the posada, but she didn't say anything. After about fifteen blocks they paused to rest a moment, leaning against a kiosk and staring into the window of a travel agency. The window was filled with posters of alluring young bodies lying on sunlit beaches, attended upon by waiters in spotless white jackets. Against the horizon of white *casitas* the azure sea, velvety as the gown of Our Lady of Guadalupe, seemed to smile and bless the happy land, the glistening bathers.

"See, it's just like I said," Tamsen remarked lightly. "If you don't like it here, we can go . . . someplace else."

Hunched over in his windbreaker, Sean observed with heavy sarcasm, "Yeah, where? Australia?"

Tamsen pointed to the posters. "*Any*where. Pick one. See? Cancún, Cozumel, Mazatlán, Veracruz, Oaxaca, Tampico . . ." She was gratified to see the expression on his face change to comic surprise at her efforts to pronounce the names.

He laughed. "They all sound the same to me—we could draw straws."

Delighted to see him friendly again, Tamsen clapped her hands. "Wonderful! Terrific! Let's *do* it!"

Wild with delight—feeling instinctively that a change of place promised, at the very least, a change of problems, they sat down at the curb beside the kiosk. From out of her handbag Tamsen pulled her five-year diary and began ripping out blank pages from the final year and tearing them into strips, some short, some long. Then she began copying out the names of all the places they saw in the posters. "Wait, wait. I want to get the spelling right. I think it's supposed to be bad luck to misspell an Indian name." She had soon inscribed ten names. "'Oh one little, two little, three little Indians . . . ten little Indian names,' " she sang happily.

All the while Sean had been staring with a sort of weak astonishment. "But Tami, what'll we *do* when we get there? I mean, sure I want to go someplace cheaper . . . but . . . we don't even know how much it costs to *get* to one of these places . . ."

"We'll go right in and ask. Right in there. But now *choose*. Five long, five short. Whoever gets 'Long' first, wins. *Choose,*" she repeated joyfully, holding the diary shut tightly over the paper slips, protruding like bookmarks. "But don't complain to me afterwards!"

For a moment he too seemed caught up in the game, it was as exciting as gambling. Affecting an expression of profound deliberation, as if this were indeed some ultimate choice on which the fate of his soul was being wagered, Sean pulled a long slip.

"You win! You win!" cried Tamsen with delight, leaning over and kissing him on the mouth. "What did you win?"

Sean looked down at the slip of paper in his hand to see what he had won. "Veracruz," he said. "I've won Veracruz."

Together they examined a map to see where it was.

Tamsen found she was able to enjoy the bus ride, perhaps because while she was moving she could believe she was really going somewhere. The excitement of leaving one place for another, the continuous movement of the bus, gave her an illusion that she was Returning: to Salinas, perhaps, however changed and unrecognizable.

But Sean was wretched. He had made the mistake of buying second class tickets (he claimed it was ignorance on his part, but Tamsen believed he had wanted to save money). He complained endlessly about the dirty bus; he had become obsessed with germs and dirt, he wouldn't hold on to the seat in front of him as the bus careened around mountain curves, but tried instead to balance himself with his feet, his elbow thrust against the window. "You'll break your arm if he stops suddenly," Tamsen warned, but Sean shrugged his indifference.

Virtually from the moment they'd stepped onto the bus, it seemed, some line of communication had broken between them. Sean had stood beside the driver's seat a moment, plainly stunned, mumbling, "Hey, wait a minute!" while the driver urged him in Spanish to advance to the rear of the bus. Tense and angry, he'd climbed over baskets and babies and old women already settled in for the long ride, their wrinkled hands clasped as if in prayer:

Silent and forbearing, they glanced up at him as he bumped against them with his backpack. At last he and Tamsen had found a narrow space to the rear of the bus. Sean was feeling an urge to vomit and sat for a while holding a brown paper bag to his mouth. When the woman in front of them broke pieces of dry tortilla for her children—who sat chewing slowly, their mouths tightly shut as if they were concentrating on creating saliva—Sean groaned aloud and shut his eyes. He was so damned hot and thirsty, he said, that he would have sold his soul to the devil for a cold Coke. Then suddenly he began to talk about Shoshoni, what he fed him, how he took him to the vet's regularly; how he never barked at people who lived in the neighborhood but only at strangers; how he knew he must have his cod liver oil every day and took it without complaint; how because of the way they kept his fur carefully groomed, he never had fleas burrowing around his head or chest; about how once, when he'd needed an expensive hernia operation just like people did, they'd had to drive him to Spokane for the surgery, and how it had taken months for him to recover the use of his hind legs; how they'd taken turns carrying him outdoors to "do his duty." But how one morning he had overslept and had not heard his whimpering complaints, and when he came to take him out he had already "wet the floor . . . pitiful," he added. "Just pitiful, how ashamed he was. He was so smart—housebroke him in three days . . . *Cleanest* dog we ever had. Cleaner than . . ." He shut his eyes as if he were about to faint from the exhaust fumes; then he rose abruptly and in spite of the heat, pulled the window shut, then sank back into his corner as if exhausted from his sudden effort. Tamsen noted how the window had been cracked by a small bullet hole from whose splintered center radiated dozens of lines glinting in the sunlight like prisms.

Now and then the bus would stop at a deserted spot along the highway, and one or two people would silently step down and disappear for a few minutes. But Sean remained stubbornly in his seat. Tamsen, recalling her nights of torment in Reffie's car, felt sorry for him, his embarrassment seemed keener than hers had been. Suddenly she remembered a story she'd read once about fighting in the jungle—whether it had been Grampa Wing's war or some other war she didn't know—about men squatting, about how humiliating it had been for them. She thought she knew how Sean's pride would be lacerated at such an humiliation—*he'd almost rather die . . .* So when after about four or five hours Sean rose and descended with several other passengers to disappear for a few minutes, she knew that in his own mind he must have crossed some psychic Rubicon. When he returned to his seat, he seemed shocked speechless by this insult to his self-esteem. He turned away from Tamsen and pretended to sleep. Affronted, Tamsen decided not to care, she preferred to enjoy this momentary freedom from what she regarded as Sean's private obsessions. In spite of the uncomfortable ride, she would have liked the trip to last weeks, months. The bus in motion was a voyaging space ship, it had nothing to do with her life on earth. It was a place they would never find her. As through the cracked window she caught sight of a snow-crested volcano, she felt a deep peace descend on her. Suddenly she wanted nothing, nothing at all. What a joy to want nothing, not your comfortable home with its clean beds and hot water, nor your dog Shoshoni, nor your friends, nor money or food or love. Nothing. How exquisitely the Past dropped into an endless free fall, into the Nothing as into the breathtaking valleys below; all you needed was a little air, a little breathing in and out.

From somewhere in the bus rose the soft hum of a child playing a song on a comb. You could imagine the humming multiplied by thousands, becoming the sirenic chant of the Salinas cicadas . . . Then suddenly there came a clap of thunder followed by a cloudburst, and all Tamsen heard for a while was the soft pelt of rain falling on the rooftop. She dozed. When she awoke the landscape had become subtropical, banana and eucalyptus trees and a few thatched roofs. Now the sun emerged, a waterfall of light cascading down the rainwashed leaves of the banana trees. Suddenly the bus stopped and the driver stepped down to exchange a few words with some women and children who were selling iguanas. Then he came back into the bus to announce that there was something wrong with one of his tires, that they were not to get out of the bus, he would be back in a few minutes. He disappeared down a dirt road, into a small house in the distance. A woman who had been watching the bus driver until he entered the house, turned toward her daughter, *"Choza de sus padres,"* she said, and pointed out the thatched roof.

The bus windows were steamed up from the rain and the heat of the many passengers. From their own cracked window Tamsen received an oddly distorted view of the vendors, women's and children's heads forced into the radiating lines of the glass, appeared severed from their angled bodies. Tamsen shifted position, sitting up straight and narrowing her eyes in order to bring the two parts of the image together, the splintered iguana vendors smoothed into focus as into a kaleidoscope. She saw now that they were not only women and children but also a few old men. They stood along the roadside with their iguanas—some of the animals seemed dead but most appeared to be alive—suspended by a piece of rope, their reptilian jaws tied shut. The vendors were at first silent, they seemed not to expect the bus passengers to buy iguana, they were waiting, perhaps, for the tourists who would be stopping with their hired guides. But when they caught sight of Sean—almost sunken in the back seat— they approached the broken window. Sean refused to open the window for them, but Tamsen, stubbornly reaching past him, slid the window open, and gave the children a few centavos. Then she sat stunned by the scene she had created by this gesture. All the vendors surged toward them. The women, their faces withered as iguana skins, lifted the animals up, swung them before Tamsen's eyes. They had nothing else to sell, they seemed to say, thus they stood offering up these animals as if in some degraded ancient ritual; the seamed tails of the iguanas lashed desperately. They were not yet reconciled to their sacrifice.

A woman sitting near them indicated to Sean by nodding her head with enthusiasm and bringing her finger to the mouth that the iguanas were good for eating. *Comer, comer,* she repeated. Sean did not respond. Folding his arms across his chest, he burrowed into the farthermost corner of his seat. He looked as if he would have liked to hurl himself from the bus.

The driver reappeared and made an announcement in Spanish. From the murmured responses of the passengers, Tamsen understood that their bus was taking a slightly different route, through a seaside village. A few passengers objected, but one could see that their objections were purely a matter of principle; they had no choice but to remain with their driver. When someone tried to question him, the driver would only nod and smile and then shrug agreeably as if he agreed with them that life-was-difficult. Then he would go through his pockets as if looking for something he'd lost. But it was clear he was waiting.

Presently an elderly blind man with a boy at his side came out of the *choza* and slowly they made their way toward the bus. As they approached, the iguana vendors parted to make way for them. It was apparently for the sake of this old man—who perhaps was the driver's father, Tamsen couldn't be sure—that they were making the detour. Silence fell on the passengers, You could almost hear them blessing themselves, thought Tamsen, thanking God that they did not have to be led by the hand. Again she was struck by how little you needed for joy; you needed not to be blind, you needed not to be selling iguanas, you needed only to sit dozing, accepting, letting the bus take you where it listed.

An hour or two later, Tamsen had lost her sense of time, they reached the village near the sea. There had been another rainfall; orange flowers were blooming everywhere. After the long months among the fir trees of Silver Valley, the broad-leafed banana trees were a strangely physical relief, an easing of pain.

"Where are we?" asked Tamsen with delight.

"In Xoshi-something, where else?" On the way out of the city Sean had amused himself by trying to pronounce Tlaxcala, Totalco, Tlaxco and Tlapacayan, vying with her for the wildest attempts; but during the long bus trip he had become more and more sullen at their inability to remember, seconds after they'd passed a highway sign pointing in all directions, whether it had read Teziutlan or Tecolutia or Tlapacayan. Declaring that they all sounded alike to him and were utterly unpronounceable anyway, he had lapsed into silence.

But now his spirits revived. Delighted with the idea of being near the ocean, they chattered and laughed easily together. Sean waited impatiently as the passengers descended one by one; first the blind man with the boy, then the others. There was no hurry, only the resigned rhythm of people moving slowly down the aisle with their baggage, their children. Scarcely glancing around them, the passengers climbed into another bus, going on to Veracruz. She and Sean looked at one another, united for the moment in perfect understanding. What was the point of going farther? Here was exactly the little village Sean had imagined, where their money would turn into loaves and fishes.

Their bus driver had walked away into the village, leading his blind father. A new driver was now honking his horn at Sean and Tamsen, waiting with impatience for them to climb on; Tamsen called through his window for to explain that they were not coming, they were staying. She waved a friendly *muchas gracias y adiós*. The driver stared, at first mystified, then stiff-jawed with contempt. He shrugged, revved his engine loudly, and began pulling away. The bus, belching fumes, abruptly reversed its direction. As it moved away, Tamsen restrained an impulse to run after it. During its endless rocking she had felt safe, she had felt joy . . . as they'd driven across the endless landscape, she'd known there had to be a future some-where, a Plan, but there'd been no immediate need to find it. Now, suddenly, they were no longer travelling toward somewhere, afloat in time. They had arrived at their perfect place, their fishing village by the sea. Their future was now imminent.

They began looking around for a restaurant or a gas station where there might be a toilet facility, but could find none. Sean was the first to notice several men coming out of what appeared to be an abandoned house with boarded-up windows; it was a cantina. Moving from the bright sunlight into the cool darkness of the cantina was confusing. At first Tamsen could see nothing, then she realized there were no other women in the cantina. The men stared at Sean as he began threading his way around their small tables. Tamsen stood awkwardly near the door; she felt the eyes of the men upon her, measuring her with a shrewd look. It made her feel as if she were a saddle they meant to buy for their horse. It was unnerving, a flutter of fear rose to her throat. She stepped back out into the sun-light. In the open air she felt better; she turned her back upon the door of the cantina and stood gazing at the few thatched roofs nearby, breathing in the salt air of the sea. She was that there were no paved streets, only a sandy path leading to the sea, and dirt roads gullied by trucks or buses, now reflecting pools of light from the afternoon rains. Silence lay over the village; there was no traffic in the dusty roads; the villagers seemed to have hidden themselves away from the afternoon sun . . . Suddenly Sean was standing beside her. She turned quickly, sur-prised at her relief that it was only Sean.

He was complaining about "the filthy cantina." He hoped, he said, that he hadn't picked up some horrible disease. He'd taken a bar of soap along with him into the "washroom" but there'd been no water. He was so angry he hardly glanced around the village as they walked down to the shore.

The sea was nearly at high tide when they reached the beach. No one was swimming. They stood for a moment, awkward and indecisive. Not far away were a group of people talking together as they rested on worn wooden benches sheltered from the sun by a thatched roof set up on poles in the sand.

"Let's get away from these people," said Sean. "Up farther along the beach." He pointed. "There . . . see where that boat is?"

He continued to grumble about the cantina. His hair was matted and there was dirt around his eyes. He'd cut himself while shaving hurriedly somewhere the day before, and the cuts had become infected. He fingered them gently, remarking that the salt water would disinfect them. With a groan of exhaustion and relief at having arrived at last, they stretched out on the beach. Then for a long restful hour they let the power and beauty of the sea overwhelm them. They felt at peace with one another and the world. On the other side of the horizon lay Eternity, you had merely to let it envelope you and you could escape everything except for the blessed sound of the rolling sea. At their feet the whitecaps swelled, at first threateningly, then breaking, they unravelled into soft curls of foam.

When Sean felt rested, they decided to go into the water. Sean buried his backpack and Tamsen's handbag under the rotting rowboat. Tamsen ran joyfully toward the water, still wearing her jeans. She plunged in, then bent down a moment in the water along the shoreline while she stripped off her clothes. She flung first her jeans, then the rest of her clothes onto the beach.

"Hey, Tami what are you *doing?*" he objected. "You can't *do* that." He glance around to see who might be watching them. The people who had been sitting on the wooden benches were still gazing at the sea. Then someone stood up and began collecting driftwood, perhaps to prepare a fire; his head was down, staring at the sand.

"Oh, but it's wonderful, Sean! Just wonderful! The water's not even cold. Come on in. Come *on*. Who cares, anyway?" she added with impatience as she saw that he was affronted by the casual way she'd flung her clothes aside.

Finally with a resigned sigh, he waded in up to his knees, stood watching the waves a while, then from the pocket of his jeans he pulled out a bar of soap and began lathering his hair.

"Terrific! Throw me the soap!" cried Tamsen. "Break it in half, break it in half," she added as she saw his reluctance. When he had rinsed his hair, he tried to break the soap in two. It did not break evenly. He showed her the broken soap, obliging her to choose. To please him, Tamsen took the smaller piece.

His jeans were wet to the hips and Tamsen urged him— since they were wet anyway—to throw them onto the beach. "We'll be in the water . . . who'll see you?"

Involuntarily Sean glanced behind him to see whether the people were still sitting on their benches. They were gone. Slowly and cautiously he peeled off first his wet jeans, then his shorts, and threw them on the beach beside Tamsen's. Then they swam together parallel to the beach, Sean repeating in an awed voice over and over, as if he could not believe in their great good luck as he sluiced through the water, "Wow, this is neat," adding, as a dog came up toward the water's edge, "Shoshoni would have loved this." Tamsen, moved by a kind of pity, wanted to ask if he'd never swum in the ocean before. But she'd learned that he was resentful when she asked questions which seemed to suggest that Silver Valley was the outback of the universe. Once or twice she'd even caught him in little fibs. "Of *course* we have plenty of libraries. What do you think we are, Indians or something?" And once when she'd asked why his folks had gone all the way to Portland to see some particular doctor, he'd snapped, "Because Silver Valley is just a mining village and there's not a real surgeon for a hundred miles."

They swam until Sean suddenly announced that for the first time since leaving the city, he felt really hungry. He said he still had a Coke and some saltines left in his knapsack which would hold them till later. "Let's split the Coke, then find a place to stay. Gee, that water makes you feel clean." They swam lazily back toward the abandoned boat.

Tamsen was surprised at how awkward she felt about walking out of the water, but she resisted the impulse to cover her body like some exiled Eve hiding her nakedness. Sean on the other hand, in his desire to be discreet, squatted down and scuttled out of the sea to where they had flung their clothes. He reached out his hand, his eyes still blinded by the water. There was nothing. Their clothes were gone. He glanced around in shocked disbelief, hoping perhaps that some grinning child, screaming with delight at having played this trick, would suddenly appear and throw their clothes back on the sand. But the beach was deserted. With the energy of terror, Sean ran to the boat and lifted it half out of the sand. The thieves had taken it all, his knapsack, Tamsen's bag, their wallets, passports, tourist cards—even Tamsen's kangaroo.

Tamsen had never fainted, but now ocean and sky seemed to merge and whirl; for a moment the blue sky darkened, she turned to see the now-menacing whitecaps rush upon the sand, curling upon themselves, preparing for a new assault.

"What'll we do? What'll we do? Oh *God*."

Sean began cursing all Mexico. Then he turned upon her with sudden rage. "Of all the crazy ideas! I *told* you these people wouldn't like it." He seemed to be trying to hide his nakedness and to dry himself at the same time; his arms flailed in a frighteningly absurd motion. His eyes, which she had once thought warm and innocent, were cold with rage—the dark-green of the sea toward dark.

On the beach someone was approaching. It was a woman, carrying a basket. At the sight of their naked bodies, she stood stock still with fear, then turned quickly in order to avoid them. But Tamsen called out to her, sobbing with fright. "Señora, señora. Help us, please. Please help us!"

There was no mistaking the terror in Tamsen's cry. The woman put down the basket and waited for Tamsen to come to her. Sean remained crouched against the rowboat, overwhelmed. Tamsen ran toward the señora repeating, *"Robbers, robbers,* everything—*todo*—they took everything . . ."

"Ay! . . . robado? The señora shook her head in a mixture of shock, sorrow and rebuke. Discreetly she turned her back on Sean. Then slowly she pulled her rebozo from her shoulders and covered Tamsen's nakedness. She arranged the shawl into a loose-fitting garment, knotting it at the ends, tugging at Tamsen gently, as she would have pulled a small animal by the collar. In doing all this she did not touch Tamsen's cold bare flesh shivering with fear. *Anda, Anda,* she commanded, indicating that Sean should follow behind them. Lifting the wicker basket to her hip, she led the way up the narrow path back to the cantina.

It was now early evening; many barefooted children stood watching from their doorsteps. Others, with the hobbled gait of hunchbacks, were hurrying home, carrying plastic jugs filled with water. The children on the doorsteps began whispering and laughing among themselves at the strange procession: one figure looking rather like themselves and wrapped in a rebozo, the other looking as if he'd been kidnapped and held a naked hostage. When they arrived at the cantina, word had already spread around the village; children were now everywhere, smiling and gazing. Sean was at once sequestered in the washroom of the cantina while Tamsen sat waiting at a small table, hardly daring to look around her. The men in the cantina joked quietly among themselves. In spite of their audible cluck-cluck of sympathy, as they shook their heads their eyes shone with merriment. Tamsen felt that for them these moments were the show of the day. Events like this—not tragic nor involving life or death or hunger— were for them a comedy in which the clumsy trespassers had got themselves stuck in the cowpads. Still, in spite of their open enjoyment of the trespassers' predicament, the men, with many high-spirited observations, began to contribute articles of clothing to cover Sean's nakedness, which they tossed into the washroom.

When Sean reappeared, he was startling: wearing a ragged shirt and shorts absurdly too tight, so that his entire body seemed diminished—a slender, boyish epicene god-of-Love. But the look on his face was frightening. He was pale with shock and humiliation. The bright bronze head set on the slender body had become a great Greek mask of Fury.

Someone had gone to summon a policeman, hoping that the Law would resolve the problem of what to do with the strangers. The policeman now took charge with great energy. He spoke rapidly, asking questions of the people standing around the cantina. Tamsen was relieved that there seemed to be no feeling among the men in the cantina that Sean and Tamsen should be arrested, but rather there seemed a pervasive air of acknowledgement among the people that she and Sean had been stupid, rude—*brutos*—but not criminal. The policeman, who knew some English because (he said) he'd once spent a few months working in Los Angeles, now tried to carry on a conversation with Sean. Since Sean knew no Spanish at all, their exchange was of barbaric simplicity. At last with a theatrical sigh, the officer pushed Sean in a hearty patronizing way (clearly wanting to express his own and the villagers' sense of tolerance of Sean's abysmal ignorance) toward the telephone behind the bar. Pointing at the phone, the officer repeated several times that Sean was to call ". . . *larga distancia, larga distancia.* Your Mama? Your Papa?

Tamsen sat in dejected silence, feeling that under the circumstances they had no choice. Sean would call Silver Valley; their escape would be instantly aborted; they would be returned home, perhaps in the custody of some official person, like this policeman. The idea filled her with shame, it was not what she had meant to be her Plan when she'd parked her bicycle at Sean's house that snowy night.

After Sean had made several unsuccessful attempts with *larga distancia,* Tamsen realized with mixed feelings of relief and anxiety (her freedom seemed always to have burrowed within it some worm of fear) that for some reason they were unable to make the connection to Silver Valley. The señora was trying to explain to Tamsen, her fingers imitating the falling rain, that the telephone lines were broken down because of the heavy *lluvias.*

At last the policeman, becoming irritated, demanded of Sean, "Where do you want to go, exactly?"

It seemed to Tamsen the most deceptively simple of questions. Pulling the *rebozo* more tightly around her, she sat stock still, waiting for Sean to explain it all. How— actually—they didn't want to go anywhere in particular, they merely wanted to swim in the ocean *and live* thought Tamsen inconsequently, *like the lilies of the field which toil not, neither do they spin.* But to her surprise Sean had a much better answer. Tamsen marvelled at his cunning inventiveness. He managed somehow to convey the idea that they had good friends in Mexico City, that he and Tamsen were just heading back to the city when they'd decided to take a swim, and really, there was no need for anybody to be concerned . . . here Sean's voice trailed away. He was not sure how much of what he had said, the policeman had understood. He had cleverly refrained from mentioning the loss of all their money and clothes. It seemed to be understood between the officer and himself that Sean could not expect his things ever to be fully recovered, that to pursue the thieves would prove futile and— very likely—only create further trouble.

The officer nodded approvingly; it was clear that he preferred to have them get out of the village, the quicker the better. He did not want them on his hands. He asked them to wait a few minutes while he went to discuss the matter with a friend, he'd make some arrangements. When he returned, he explained that his friend, an avocado farmer, was driving to Puebla tomorrow morning to pick up a brand new VW at the Volkswagen factory there; thus he had been able to arrange a ride for the *americanos* that far, at least. His friend would come by for them at Señora Valdez's house with his pick-up truck. The officer nodded toward the señora who had brought Sean and Tamsen to the cantina. The señora nodded back in agreement. Señora Valdez then lifted her basket to the bar, emptied her shrimp basket, received some pesos from the owner in exchange, and indicated to Tamsen that she and Sean should come with her.

"Lock em up good!" called the policeman to the señora as they left the cantina. Then chuckling with satisfaction, he sat down and ordered a drink.

Señora Valdez appeared to live alone. There was no question of privacy or prudery; it was understood that Tamsen and Sean would sleep together on the floor of the señora's bedroom. The house itself was so small they could hear every sound as Señora Valdez walked back and forth, moving her chairs, preparing herself for sleep. There was electricity in the house but no water, and several times they heard her go out—the outdoors seemed to be an extension of the house—returning with a metal pail filled with water which she set beside the stove. When she had arranged her own bed, the señora brought them a blanket and with a mingled look of disapproval and amusement, shut the door.

They had hardly stretched out on the floor—exhausted, but relieved to be rescued at last from the public eye—when she and Sean began arguing in angry whispers as to whose fault it was. In a voice of barely-controlled fury, Sean accused her of having brought this humiliation upon them by *insisting* on swimming nude. Tamsen retorted hotly that he didn't *have* to swim nude if he hadn't wanted to, and besides if he hadn't *stupidly* made such a big deal about it all, drawing attention by *hiding* their stuff under the rowboat and everything, nobody would have noticed them.

"So, *I'm* stupid!" choked Sean, shaking with insult. "And whose *stupid* idea was it to come to this filthy country in the first place?"

They stared at one another, drawing back in shock. Having called each other stupid, there seemed nothing else to be said: If she had screamed that she hated him, if he had been furious with jealousy and struck her, if they had wept with mutual betrayal, it would have been less chilling; there might yet have been a reconciliation between them. But to say your lover was stupid, Tamsen thought, was to say that you had been totally deceived, that he or she had never been worthy of your love, it made *you* stupid as well. It was the poison in Hamlet's drink by which you died as you had meant to kill. Coldly, Sean lay down on the blanket and turned his back to her. With one arm curved under his head, the other between his legs, he became a remote, disdainful stranger.

During the night the thieves had thrown Tamsen's old handbag up against Señora Valdez's door. For some reason they had also shoved Tamsen's kangaroo head first into the bag, the baby-joey now missing from its pouch, and Sean's wallet, empty except for a snapshot of himself with Shoshoni, across which someone had scrawled contemptuously, *Chinga su madre!* For a while Sean sulked over this further insult, growling that if he ever laid hands on the thieves he'd. . . . But his spirits revived when Señora Valdez asked if they'd care for some hot coffee.

As they drank their coffee Tamsen and Sean were reserved and polite with one another, needing to forget the hot insults of the night before in order to survive—to remain in collusion against the whole world, if necessary. They appeared openly affectionate in the presence of others, smiling at Señora Valdez and at the neighborhood children while they awaited the truck driver who was going to take them back, back to hot showers and telephones that worked. But they did not speak to one another concerning the hard question of what they would do when they got back to the city, for fear last night's anger should break through their temporary alliance.

As they waited, Tamsen tried to express her gratitude to the señora in some small way—by arranging a chair, folding a blanket—but never had she felt so useless. There was nothing she could do for this woman into whose house they had come like beggars. As the señora sat at her table cleaning shrimp, she explained to Tamsen in slow, measured phrases that the shrimp were for the owner of the cantina, that somebody was having a birthday, and the family had ordered a whole basketful, that she herself had no refrigerator so she would have to take the shrimp over before the heat of the day, that she would only wait until the farmer had arrived to take the *americanos* to Puebla, then she would go. As Señora Valdez explained all this, Tamsen, with a thrill of surprise, realized that she had understood most of it. *If we stayed here, maybe I could catch on, maybe I'd never have to go back.* But when the truck driver arrived, and Señora Valdez began speaking to him in a rapid birdlike chatter, describing the events of the preceding day and the predicament of the *americanos,* Tamsen understood nothing. Sadly she realized that the señora had been speaking to her in a kind of pidgin-Spanish. Señora Valdez now handed Tamsen some warm tortillas wrapped in newspaper. Tamsen could not imagine ever being hungry enough to eat dry tortillas, but accepted them gratefully. *I've done nothing for her to deserve all this, she'll probably never see me again in this life or any other.* Tamsen found herself thinking again how kindness or love was as random as violence, a thing which unpredictably and undeservingly happened. Awkwardly she embraced the señora and, folding up the borrowed *rebozo,* tried to return it to her with thanks. But the señora shook her head, almost with violence, waving her hand. *No, no, no. Un regalo. Buen viaje, buena suerte.* And almost laughing with the pleasure of having given a gift to someone she would never see again, the señora hurried away, walking close to the houses in order to keep the shrimp in the shade.

The avocado farmer who'd come for them in his pickup was not openly impolite, but he maintained a cool distance, silently shaking Sean's hand when they were introduced by the señora. Plainly he seemed not to accept the village's interpretation that they—she and Sean—were just a couple of *locos.* And as if to declare his refusal to communicate with the suspicious-looking *americanos,* he turned up the volume on his radio, drowning out all possibility of a conversation. Sean, sitting between Tamsen and the driver, stoically folded his arms, pointedly allowing the driver all the elbow room he might need, while Tamsen dozed, her head bobbing against the door.

As if to emphasize that he felt absolutely no curiosity about them, the farmer, without asking them where they were going, pulled his truck to an abrupt halt right in downtown Puebla. "O.K.," he announced with a heavy sigh, obviously relieved to be rid of them. He watched as she and Sean clumsily climbed down from the cab, tying up traffic as Sean unexpectedly turned to shake hands. "*Muchas gracias y adiós,*" Sean called to him. Smiling faintly, the farmer leaned over in the cab and accepted Sean's hand while behind them drivers leaned on their horns. Then tipping his straw hat—it was at once an ironic dismissal and *vaya con Dios*—the farmer disappeared in the traffic. Dazed by the sudden change, from the silences of the village to the teeming sidewalks of the city, they stood on the sidewalk opposite the cathedral, trying to get their bearings.

"Well, what now?" Sean demanded of her, with open hostility.

Tamsen stared indecisively.

Sean opened his palm, showing her three large coins. With a flutter of anxiety she realized she did not even know how much they were worth.

"Where'd you get those? I thought all . . ."

"I traded off my class ring with that farmer—he could tell how much it was worth, that sonofabitch—while you were sleeping," he added accusingly.

It occurred to her it was the first time she had heard Sean call someone a sonofabitch. *Why is he so angry about my having fallen asleep?* But it was no time for useless questions which might end in a quarrel. They were alone in a strange city and they had to combine forces against the unknown.

Sean nudged the pieces of money around in his palm as one would have nudged small animals, to see if they were alive. "It's enough for . . . one day, maybe two. So you'd better decide, just in case we . . ."

"Decide what?"

He sighed with exasperation. "About calling Silver Valley. We can't stay here without money. Who will it be? Your folks or mine? Mine would have . . ."

"*I* don't have any folks. Not anymore," she murmured in an injured tone. "Why don't we go somewhere and sit down and *think* a minute?" The thought of returning to that dreary town of slag heaps and railroad tracks, a town of three thousand bored and boring people, a town with a Main Street, two movie houses and one library—above all, the thought of returning to the house in which she would be expected to perform daily rituals of repentance made her want to sink to the sidewalk in despair. Silver Valley to her was nothing, nothing, nothing. On the other hand, if she and Sean could somehow get together enough money to return, not to Silver Valley but to Salinas . . . she had friends in Salinas. . . . Diffidently she expressed this idea to Sean.

"Yeah. *Salinas*," he echoed with cutting irony, as if she'd suggested the moon.

They straggled along for a few blocks until they reached an arcade where there was no vehicular traffic, only benches in the center of the walk, with shops on either side. Wearily they sat down to share Señora Valdez's tortillas while they considered their options. Tamsen secretly hoped that for the moment, at least, Sean would forget their situation: She herself would have liked to forget . . . everything.

Not far from their bench shoppers were gathered around an exhibition of posters, some displayed on the sidewalks, others suspended from improvised clotheslines or taped to wooden boards. All the pictures were of children—some with straight hair and aquiline noses, others with red or blond curls and blue eyes, their skin a soft pastel of rose or beige. From out of the posters the children gazed at their buyers with sad luminous eyes. On each child's face, regardless of color, the artist had drawn tears: On these tears was lavished an artist's love. Each tear fell, radiant and distinct down the beige or rose-colored cheeks. Passers-by paused to buy these posters as gifts, or as souvenirs to be framed and hung above their mantelpiece; then they passed on to another shop, another vendor.

Vendor, vendors everywhere. They installed themselves as shops-in-front-of-shops. One might survive, Tamsen saw, by selling shoelaces or prickly pears or posters of children, or if one had some special talent, like singing or dancing. Their problem—hers and Sean's—was that they had nothing to sell, no posters, no flying monkeys with streaming feathers, no windmills or stuffed toys. If for instance, they only knew how to draw, they could sketch the throngs of shoppers and earn their living. Or if Tamsen knew their native dances, she could dress up like an Indian, learn to play the flute . . .

She became aware of what she thought was the high piping sound of a flute—and saw now that a trio of blind musicians had entered the arcade and begun methodically to arrange themselves on the sidewalk in front of a shop (one of them, Tamsen noticed, touched the wall with his back to confirm his position). At their side a girl who might have been their daughter stood facing the street. Her glance rested a moment on Tamsen and Sean, then looked away, her face solemn and expressionless. Her blind companions bent their heads to their instruments, listening and tuning them; they smiled occasionally, exchanging a few words with one another, but they did not speak to the girl who stood slightly apart, staring silent and expressionless at some invisible spot just above the heads of the passing crowd.

Tamsen sat mesmerized by the girl's blank and expressionless face.

"We could be beggars," Tamsen said.

"What?"

"We could be beggars," she repeated, without looking up. "You could be blind, and I could be . . . I could be . . ." Her imagination faltered.

Sean replied as if he believed that she was indulging in some sort of tasteless joke. "Well, *I* don't look much like them, but *you* . . ."

Sean looked down at her. She felt a shock at his cool appraisal. With sudden self-consciousness she began rubbing away the dirt she imagined he saw on her face. Nervously she made an effort to moisten her sun-cracked lips, but the tortilla she was chewing had turned her mouth to dust. Her hair, she now remembered, had not been washed since they left Silver Valley, and she could feel now how coarse and matted it had become from the salt sea water. In spite of herself, she felt ashamed. . . . Looking down, she saw as she lifted the tortilla to her mouth, how the lines of her hands, in her knuckles, her fingertips, the very lifelines of her palms, were filled with dirt. She stopped eating, handing over what was left of her tortilla to Sean.

He nodded. "Yeah. If you tied that *rebozo* around you real tight, you could get away with it." He stretched his legs out in front of him, leaning his head against the back of the bench as he added, "Why don't you try it?" He yawned wearily, half-closing his eyes.

"Try what?"

"*You* know. What you just said . . ."

She thought a moment, trying to recall what she'd just said. "Oh, *that*. I didn't mean . . ."

"It's not such a dumb idea, really."

She stared. She saw now that he was serious. "But how . . . ?"

"You could slip into a ladies' room somewheres and make yourself even more . . . try to look like one of them. Like that girl we saw—where was it? On Reforma? Or was it Insurgentes? *Whatever* the street was—you remember?"

She didn't remember. Her heart was pounding with fear. Suddenly it was possible to believe that Sean was capable of forcing her to do this if she refused. Though his voice remained steadfastly light-hearted she saw that he was serious. Tamsen laughed nervously.

He echoed her laughter, but added, "What do you say,

Tami? Shall we do it?" Suddenly he seemed more like himself, full of the spirit of adventure. He exclaimed, "Let's go check out the possibilities. Hell, we don't want to work *any* old corner."

Laughing together they crossed several *calles* and *avenidas*, looking for what they called their Perfect Place. At last they thought they had found it—just outside a corner church, five or six blocks from the zócalo. In front of the huge wooden church doors with its ancient iron hinges squatted an Indian woman, dressed in rags. She sat nearly motionless, seemingly oblivious to the thousands of people in the streets, to the rags she wore, to the flies she waved away with a repeated, absent motion. There were no other beggars sitting beside her, no one questioned her right to remain there forever if need be. She seemed to have rightfully inherited this piece of the world's property. She dozed. *Impossible to tell how old she is, as young as Roseanne, could be,* thought Tamsen.

Tamsen and Sean crossed and recrossed the corner, observing the church from several angles. Sean wanted to remain within sight of the Indian woman, but not too close, he said. Suddenly a gaping hole in the sidewalk which neither of them had noticed before appeared under their feet. "Lucky we saw it this time or we'd have broken our legs for sure," observed Sean. Peering down into the two-foot drop, they congratulated themselves on their good luck. It was a hole easily overlooked, as it was being rapidly filled with garbage and old newspapers, either deliberately thrown in to fill the hole or blown there by the wind. Squatting down, Sean reached in and pulled out several folded newspapers which were dirty, but not wet.

"How about right here? Right outside the church, just like *her*. Not *too* close, but just so that they think you're with her. And if *she* doesn't complain about your being on her turf. . . ." he concluded with triumph.

Tamsen was astonished at his liveliness, his inventiveness. He seemed almost happy. For a moment Tamsen wondered if he were high on something, maybe the men had slipped him some stuff, either as a joke or in male solidarity. *But no, he's just enjoying himself, he's enjoying tell-ing me what to do, what I HAVE to do.* She was overwhelmed by a sense of helplessness; her stomach churned, not in hunger but with fear.

As they stood by the gaping hole suddenly the heavy church doors swung open, one could see the altar, bril-liantly decorated with orange and white flowers. Above the altar, gazing down the nave of the church into the street, stood a sculptured Virgin, wearing her blue robes, her flesh-colored ceramic hands held out to the empty church.

Tamsen could hear Sean chuckling as he spread the newspaper on the sidewalk for her. Tamsen sat down, her eyes lingering on the church door, but from where she sat she could no longer see the ceramic figure. Sean, in a final gesture of inspiration, now wrapped the *rebozo* around her bare feet, tying it in knots as one would truss a turkey.

"My God, Tami," he exclaimed with pride in his work. "You look like an Indian papoose!"

This time Tamsen did not join in his laughter. She was suddenly tired and sleepy. She wished she could lie down on the sidewalk; she felt she could have slept forever. But Sean was instructing her, arranging matters of importance. Tamsen opened her eyes, tried to concentrate her atten-tion. She could not reply to his instructions but merely nodded, it was such an effort to speak. . . . Sean was ex-plaining where he would be waiting for her; he promised he would be in sight at all times, walking back and forth, or standing beside the kiosk just in front of that restaurant—*there* (he pointed). With a great effort Tamsen turned her head. She saw the small restaurant with its open door, its few tables and chairs, the kiosk just outside the restaurant. She understood that Sean had found a sanctuary. He assured her that she was not to worry, everything was going to be all right—tomorrow, maybe, they would be able to take the bus back to Salinas. But it was precisely his gentle soothing tone that worried her; it seemed to make promises that only she herself could keep. How could Sean promise her Salinas when he had never had it?

"Ready?" He smiled down at her. With a sudden, in-spired gesture he drew Tamsen's kangaroo from out of her handbag and pushed it under her *rebozo*. Its inquiring eyes looked out upon the passers-by.

"Oh," she murmured gratefully. Tears sprang to her eyes. "Oh," she repeated and was about to thank him but he motioned her to silence. With a collusive wink he bent and solemnly laid a peso in her cupped hand. Then he tucked the old newspapers he'd retrieved from the side-walk and walked toward the kiosk. He stood there several minutes, pretending to read. Tamsen tried to wave at him, to prove to him that she was game for the game, that she truly believed it was possible that tomorrow they might be in Salinas. But he did not return her gesture, his eye was on a newspaper. She realized he was not pretending to read, he was *actually* reading. Disappointed, she dropped her hand to her lap. A coin fell into it. Tamsen looked up at the señora who had given her the peso. She dared not speak. *Muchas gracias y adiós,* she thought, as she watched the señora disappear, feeling suddenly that she *knew* the woman, knew exactly what motive of penance or charity had stirred her. Tamsen couldn't afterwards recall how long she'd been sitting on the sidewalk when this feeling of *knowing* became frightening. It was as if she had sud-denly reached some level of altered consciousness where truth ignited in her head—incandescent, hallucinatory; as the people passed before her, she seemed to see an aura round the head of each one; she had become suddenly afflicted with this awesome power, that she could tell who had Evil in his heart . . . it was terrifying knowledge, she wanted to reject it, but it imposed itself upon her. She sat now watching closely as people passed, noting the mark of Cain on their brows, inhaling the soul's corruption. And then, in a sudden sun-blinding vision, she could see God, not as Roseanne had described Him, but as a Radi-ance, a Cortés-on-horseback, full of beauty and manliness and youth and vigor. Suddenly she thought of Reffie.

The vision faded. She became aware that Sean was no longer where he had been standing beside the kiosk. A flood of panic gripped her. Suppose . . . ah, there he was, with a bag of bakery rolls in his hand. With remarkable disingenuousness he first strolled past, dropping a coin in her lap, then tracing his steps as if overcome by her plight, bending to offer her a roll. The bread was still warm and fresh; at the smell of it, sickness gripped her, she trembled with the desire to vomit. She looked up at Sean with astonishment and terror. There was no aura, only a dark cloud out of which his head seemed to emerge as from the eye of a tornado. She drew back in fear.

Sean bent toward her inquiringly. He wanted know how well she was doing. Tamsen shut her eyes, she was unable to speak.

"*Mañana*," he promised. "Salinas *mañana*," he repeated, and moved away.

Tamsen sank back on her ankles, dropping the bread to one side. She could not imagine ever wanting it, biting into it, chewing it. It was getting cool now, she had no idea what time it was, how long she had been sitting there. Suddenly she found her chin resting on the long ears of her kangaroo. She pulled it out from under her *rebozo*, began rocking it tenderly, crooning an old song Roseanne had sung. She felt overcome by pity for it. A few children who passed stopped to stare, pointing at the kangaroo. A woman paused, folded some pastel-colored paper money and slipped it into the marsupial pouch.

There was a lull in the traffic, some shops were rolling down their metal gates. Tamsen tried to free herself from the *rebozo*, she felt as if she had waked from a long coma. She wanted to move her deadened legs, but pain shot through her at the effort and she sank back onto the sidewalk. With relief she saw Sean—no longer beside the kiosk but returning from the farthermost end of the arcade—was walking slowly toward her. She saw him pause to glance into a shop window, she struggled to call to him, to help her. At that moment a passerby bent down to her, speaking in English. "Señorita," he said. "Aren't you lonely down there, all alone on the sidewalk? Where is . . . where are your . . . *familia?*"

Frightened, Tamsen dared not speak, she prayed he would go away.

But he bent closer, looking into her eyes. "What beautiful eyes," he murmured. "You're a beautiful girl, you know that? How would you like? . . ." He bent closer, showing her the top of a folded ten-dollar bill.

Tamsen reared back in shock, she began struggling like a roped calf to free herself from the *rebozo*. The man's face now became angry, as if Tamsen had meant to lure him into some well-known and ancient trap. He glanced around fearfully. Tamsen looked desperately toward Sean who was still strolling slowly toward them. Ah, there he was, he'd come at last . . . But Sean seemed not to have noticed the man who, in his fear and confusion, let fall the folded money. Mechanically Tamsen picked up the money and pushed it into the kangaroo pouch.

Sean stood before her, smiling and triumphant. "Hey, good job! You did great. You could of fooled me. How much?"

They counted the money. Tamsen knew before he told her that there would not be enough to bring them back to Salinas. "Well, shall we dine first?" he asked cheerfully, "and then you try again? The late afternoon should be better. People going out to the movies and stuff." He averted his gaze.

"*No. No.* I'm not going to do it again. We got to go back, Sean. We got to go back." Her voice rose faintly. "Can we get back to the airport in Mexico City? Sean, can we? There's a Travellers' Aid at the airport. Maybe they can . . ." She thought she was screaming, but she was barely whispering. She was still holding the kangaroo pressed to her bosom. Sean tried to take it from her as he helped her to her feet, but she shook her head violently. "*No,*" she said. "*No.*"

Tamsen had at least earned enough money to get them back to Mexico City by bus. Exhausted and feeling remote from it all, she left everything to Sean, who this time bought first-class tickets for their return. *He's feeling easier about money now than when we had all his savings, like now money's not a problem anymore.* But she said nothing. She sat motionless and indifferent, holding the kangaroo pressed to her as if Sean might try again to take it away. When after the two-hour ride from Puebla they arrived at the ADO bus terminal, Sean led her deftly through the throngs of people. *He's glad to be going back to Silver Valley,* thought Tamsen dully, feeling only a dizzy revulsion at the milling crowds of hundreds of people, selling, begging . . .

But at the International Airport Tamsen felt somewhat better. For some reason it was quiet, nearly empty of people. The immense expanse of shining floor was somehow reassuring to her, a guarantee of control, of life not getting out-of-hand. Someone was in charge; the floor would be polished a thousand times a day if need be by the cleaning woman with her shredding mop; the trash can would be emptied; the water shortage in the restroom would be taken care of; the offbeat moneychangers offering pesos for dollars would be warned by the police to take their business elsewhere. The same uniformed policeman with his gun who would be terrifying were he to approach you in your nakedness on a deserted beach belonged here to a dream of justice. Here in the great airport, a city-within-a-city, where thousands of people were coming and going, running away and returning, loving and despising, hating and forgiving, here the uniformed officer was part of the sacred concept of law and order. Here you saw how all you thought of as Civilization was suspended by fragile, invisible cords which could easily break—a bridge of San Luis Rey. For the moment however, she could walk on it, this webby bridge of Civilization. If she didn't look down into the abyss she might make it across; if she didn't ask herself how these multiplying millions would get their drinking water, nor ask herself whether the same man or another was at that moment perhaps approaching another girl very like herself, Tamsen, murmuring in a language the beggar would finally be forced to understand, *"Señorita, you're a beautiful girl, you know that?"* But all this was Knowledge earned at gunpoint; Tamsen didn't want any of it. What she wanted was to go back to Salinas, not to be deported to Silver Valley.

"Let's go," Sean now commanded her, and she followed. First he approached an Information booth, then walked over to Travellers' Aid. He began to explain at once why they had no money. The clerk looked up at him with interest, but did not smile.

"Ah," she said finally, regarding them sympathetically. "So it's true. We heard about a couple of . . . some kids. Stranded down in Veracruz, they said. So it was you." She stared at them with concern, but seemed reluctant to offer any help. "But I can't help you without identification, you'll have to go to the embassy. You'll have to explain . . ." She made an effort to smile now, somewhat more encouragingly. "You shouldn't have any trouble. I'll call the embassy first. They'll know you're coming. The consul will get in touch with your family, he'll make arrangements. You shouldn't have any trouble," she repeated. "Here, just let me take down all the information." Quickly she scribbled down on a small piece of notepaper, their names, their families' names, their addresses, their phone numbers in the States. Watching her deft fingers, an identity seemed to emerge before Tamsen's eyes, a safe identity which would save her forever from the assassin, the procurer, the unpredictable madman.

As she dialed the embassy, the clerk turned away from Tamsen and Sean, as if for a more private conversation, while at the same time sitting up very properly, *as if there's some professional posture you take on when you call the American Embassy,* thought Tamsen. Again and again, the clerk nodded deferentially to the voice which spoke now in Spanish, now in English. Then with a sigh, as if she had made a prodigious effort on their behalf, she wrote out the

address of the embassy in a large firm hand and gave it to
Sean. Tamsen became aware at that moment that not once
had the woman spoken to her. It was understood here that
Sean had all the authority, he was not only male, he was
visibly American. Whatever Tamsen might be was not
clear. Several times the clerk had glanced down with an
offended look at Tamsen's dirty feet, but now, inexplicably,
she rose and placed in Tamsen's hand the money for the
taxi fare to the embassy. Glancing down, Tamsen saw that
the bill was the same pastel color as the money she had
earned in the streets. Sean now signed a receipt for the
amount, called out cheerfully, *Muchas gracias y adiós*, and
they fled, fearful their appearance would finally incense
the officer who stood not far away and that he would decide to arrest them.

At first the consul was openly angry. It was as if he'd
known all along that they would have to come to him, and
he'd become more and more exasperated at the very
thought, so that by the time they actually appeared he had
lost all patience. He moved around his office in short nervous steps, with undisguised indignation. Now and then
he glanced at their ragged dirty clothes with disgust. He
did not ask them to sit down; he asked only formal, professional questions; he seemed indifferent to Sean's personal answers. He was not interested in whether Sean and
Tamsen were married or not, he said, nor in what they
might say was their real reason for being there at all. What
concerned *him*, he said, was their breach of conduct in
having shed their clothes right under the nose of villagers.
"You insulted them, you crazy kids. You insulted their *mo-
res*. You think you can go around doing anything you want
down here, like you're at a rock party in Fort Lauderdale,
high on drugs. *Basically*," he emphasized, "we . . . the
Mexican people are very *chaste*, I want you to know. Who
the hell did you think you were, jumping around the
beach, showing your bare . . ."
Sean spoke hesitantly, trying to explain as one American
to another, that he and Tamsen had just felt tired and dirty,

that they'd been worn out from that damned *bus*, that they'd meant no offense, that they hadn't realized . . .

"You hadn't *realized!*" blazed the consul. "It's your *responsibility* to realize. And drugs—you're lucky you didn't have any drugs on you. You didn't, did you? No . . . thank God for that much. Listen, if they'd found any drugs on you I couldn't help you at all. . . . Dammit, I *heard* a rumor about a couple of *locos americanos* running up and down the country, hitchhiking home in their bare skin. The first thing I thought when I heard about it, was 'Serves them right.' "

Tamsen was moved to protest. "We didn't do that. They . . . the señora . . . gave us some clothes."

The consul turned his attention to Tamsen for the first time.

" 'They *gave* you'!" he snorted. "They should have given you a swift kick!" With sour disapproval, he added, "I *wondered* if you could speak English. I thought maybe your . . . he was smuggling back some Indian girl." Abruptly his manner changed, as if he had just realized the depth of their ignorance. "I can see now, you're both just plain *ignorant*, but I tell *you*—" he paused to take a deep breath as if extinguishing the flame of his anger with a heavy sigh, "—such ignorance is *criminal*."

He's scolding us, just scolding us, like we were a couple of neighborhood kids climbing into his backyard. It's like he's yelling, 'Hey you kids, get off my fence,' but wouldn't hit us or call his dog or get the police on us.

"*Now*," said the consul, pushing a sheet of paper toward Tamsen, "give me your parents' telephone number. Whereabouts *is* that?" he demanded as Tamsen wrote down her Silver Valley number. He seemed not to expect that they would have come from such an improbable place. "They don't have many Mexicans up there, I guess," he added, nodding in answer to his own question, as if that explained everything.

As he dialed Tamsen's number the consul kept his eyes on the slip of paper before him as if he thought it might disappear if he did not give it his entire attention. He leaned forward, a look of intense concentration on his face. It was this *intensity* which suggested to Tamsen, almost for the first time, that what she and Sean had been doing was serious, that what the consul had found it necessary to do for them would be of the utmost importance. Instinctively she stood closer to the desk, as if wanting to be a part of his mission. She did not want to look at Sean who stood beside her; he had become somebody only remotely connected with all that was happening. Suddenly the only person who could be involved in her hope of anything at all—food, home, water, air—was this perfect stranger with his expensive suit, his neat graying hair, his smooth mustache and manicured nails. Tamsen could now hear the phone in Silver Valley ring again and again. As it rang she turned absently to the photographs on the consul's desk. They were arranged in a careful semi-circle facing outward, so that anyone approaching the desk might see at once that the consul was a married man with a large family. One of the portraits was of a pretty dark-haired woman. Her children stood around her in various poses, some leaning against her negligently, one—the eldest perhaps—standing behind her, his hand on her shoulder. Two of the children, sitting on a piano bench seemed to be about Tamsen's age: Their eyes shone, warm and intelligent. In a separate frame stood a girl greatly resembling the dark-haired wife, wearing a bridal gown. Guilt and shame suddenly flooded Tamsen as she stood beside the consul's desk, in her beggar's clothes. It was as if the consul had arranged these photographs to reveal to her the orderly progression of Honor and Respectability: nursery school, kindergarten, nuns' school or military academy, the foreign university, Bonn, Oxford or Rome, all meant to point up to her the undeniable fact that Tamsen should have begun from the very beginning, *Here* at this first portrait of the pantheon, where the proud father might be holding her above the baptismal fount so that she might end up *There*, at the farthermost end of the parabola, wearing lace dresses and satin shoes at her daughters' weddings, her sons' graduations, her grandchildrens' confirmations, until at last when she had died, all the people in the portraits—grown to mythic size and utterly unassailable—would return to honor her in her passing, to swear that she had been the best, most revered, most beloved of parents. . . .

Finally the connection had gone through. The consul briefly explained the purpose of his call; he sat waiting, listening. The voice from Silver Valley seemed to burst from the receiver, ricocheting against the consul's cupped hands. It was Grampa Wing's voice, coming to her in fragments. She could not make out his words, but the consul's mournful response was very clear. "Oh," he said, and then again, softly, with pain and realization, "Oh." He sat knitting his brows and frowning into the receiver. His vigorous, efficient posture changed. He slumped back now into his great leather armchair looking strangely smaller, as if he too might disappear. "Oh, I see. I see. Of course not. Of course not." There seemed to be a sudden need for the consul to say everything twice, as if the truth stated only once would never be enough. "Yes, yes. I'll see to it. She'll be back. She'll be back. Oh, don't worry about that. Don't worry about that. That's O.K. That's O.K. That's what I'm here for. Just doing my job. To the U.S. Embassy. Make it out to the U.S. Embassy. I'll get them myself." Tamsen heard the word *tickets* repeated over and over like a time bomb. Then the consul gave Grampa Wing his phone number, and the address to which Gramp should mail a check. There was a heavy silence. At last the consul asked, "There anything else you think she ought to know? If there's anything I . . ."

Fear rose in Tamsen's stomach. She didn't want to hear whatever else it was the consul and Grampa Wing thought she ought to know. She didn't want to know *any*thing: knowledge hurt. Knowledge was what had been forced down her throat as she sat in the streets begging. Knowledge then lodged forever in your stomach, it made you sick as if with maggots, crawling, crawling, in the indigestible fiber of what you had learned; knowledge made you so sick you never wanted to smell bread again, never wanted to break bread with humanity again. Instinctively, at the threat of this force-fed knowledge Tamsen reared away from the desk, huddling against the wall nearest the door, as if preparing to flee. But here her shoulder jarred still another portrait in the family pantheon, this one not a photograph but a painting. She looked up, frightened that her awkward flight had set the portrait swaying. It was the face of the consul, white-haired and grown strangely old, whose gray eyes gazed steadily at the consul's desk and seemed to say forever, "Well done. Well done, my son."

Somehow this portrait, too, frightened her. She felt surrounded by well-intentioned but somehow threatening figures; from out of the benevolent painting leaped the astonishingly simple realization that not only the consul, but tens of millions of people had hidden away somewhere in their memory benevolent eyes-of-love which repeated *Well done. Well done, Consul, my son, my son.* And the shock of this revelation was somehow borne out by the knowledge Tamsen now sucked in with the bitter air, that she would never see their flowering mimosa again, no, not the least bud of it; and this terrible knowledge lay strewn about her life like so many crushed and fallen petals even as the consul turned toward her, and laying his hand gently on her shoulder said in a voice which had become a whisper, "Tamsen, sit down. I want to talk to you," and taking her hand in his big hands sighed heavily, murmuring, "My child . . ."

The consul had said that Gramp had said that the miners had said they had no idea how it happened; they could not imagine how Reffie had died. But Tamsen had no such difficulty. She could imagine it over and over. She could imagine it even as, homeward bound, she and Sean sat in the plane, Tamsen leaning against the window, her eyes fixed on the banked clouds along which they moved as smoothly and invisibly as a yellow railcar thousands of feet below the earth. She could imagine Reffie, dressed in the coveralls and hard hat she had worn herself, descending from the elevator. She could imagine him climbing into the yellow railcar and disappearing into the tunnel, far far beyond the reach of the Delphic warning: *Respirators, Safety Toe Boots and Hard Hats Will Be Worn Beyond This Point.* She could imagine him in a vaulted grotto so hot your skin would first steam, then dry, then finally be flayed from your body in coarse leathery strips. She imagined how Reffie might be with several other miners. They would prepare the dynamite. The men would drill holes into the rock face; they would stuff explosives into the holes; they would back away from the blast. But now her imagination faltered. The other miners had disappeared. Where were they? Ah, they would be somewhere nearby, perhaps. Silent and angry they were perhaps slashing the long white plastic sausage of air, while one of them was inscribing FINK on the walls in white chalk, to which a third man perhaps would object, shaking his head and rubbing out the epithet, wanting the death to appear accidental, a failure of the ventilation system. She could easily imagine how during the first few moments maybe Reffie would not have noticed this slashing and diversion of air, maybe he would simply have felt a little more tired, his breath would have come a little harder. Then, looking around, he would have seen that he was alone, that the rest of the crew had moved off to another part of the tunnel. He would have remembered, perhaps, how on the day of the rockburst in which Smetka had died, he and Smetka had been separated from the others by a crumbling wall. But this would be another sort of rockburst, a burst of vengeance. And backing away from the explosion area Reffie would perhaps have begun to wonder, begun to fear, because he would know that he had reason to fear, would know that he was a marked man upon whose lawn the men had not disdained to leave their yellow badge of hate. Then, as the dust of the blast had died down, Reffie would have become aware of a suppressed sound, a malevolence, as of an enemy breathing, letting him know he was there in the silence. Then certainly Reffie would have panicked and begun to run . . . Tamsen failed to imagine in which direction, only that it was along a blue-veined

wall in an underworld where men who were yoked together like blood brothers turned upon you with the fury
of fratricide. In his panic Reffie would have stumbled, perhaps, even as she herself had stumbled, sliding into the
mud, or would have tripped over a hose, or would simply
have become weak, dizzy, leaning against the wall for support, as close as possible to the broken oxygen system
which was already draining him of his life. Finally he
would have sunk to his knees, lain on the ground
until . . .

The cloudbanks, visible below the wing of the plane,
began to quaver and dissolve at this point as if melted by a
mighty conflagration. Tamsen huddled against the window, listening to the steady roar of the plane. It was a
reassuring sound; it meant they were still humming with
life, whereas Reffie, she imagined, would have been choking . . .

Choking: She too was strangling for air. She flung her
seat belt away from her, stood up, heaving and gagging.
Air, more air. I'm suffocating. Alarmed, the stewardess ran to
assist her, passengers turned to stare. Tamsen sank back
into her seat, the stale odor of her own body, of its fears
and deprivations, enveloped her, she felt herself slip into a
sort of void where the darkness was soft, velvety, endless
as the August nights of Salinas. But Sean was insisting on
waking her, chafing her hands, asking her if she was all
right. Such persecution enraged her, she would have liked
to *bite* him. But the stewardess was standing in the aisle,
calling to them above the roar of the plane as if they were
in a storm at sea, her voice full of professional concern but
also a real urgency, until Tamsen shook her head at last, in
impatient refusal. But Sean was cruelly persistent; he repeated what the stewardess had said; he too felt Tamsen
should eat, drink . . . He too seemed to have developed
this strange urgency in his voice, Tamsen could hear the
frightened pitch of it as he repeated over and over relentlessly, "Eat. Eat *something." It's not that he loves me, it's that
he's afraid. And to think that he was going to go to the end of the
world with me.* It was enough to make you throw up, how

quickly Love could go full circle—from awe to contempt, from tenderness to trash in the streets. It was a matter of amazement to her that she did not leap at his lying throat and sink her teeth into him like a mad dog. They would have had to tear her away, chain her up with his voice locked in her teeth. But instead, finally, wearily, she shrugged and pretended to sip at a glass of water as all around her passengers began their ritual of survival, their drooling, their smacking, their swilling. They devoured their dinners, peeling off the plastic covered plates like skin, examining and sniffing the contents like dogs. And then (Tamsen shut her eyes against the nausea of it) like attack dogs temporarily unmuzzled, they devoured the meat covered with a sauce so thick it oozed like the slime of the C & L mine, suffocating you. . . .

She opened her eyes. This time, instead of turning away, she watched with the fascination of revulsion as people ladled food from their styrofoam trays to their gaping mouths—like skip hoists carrying waste rock to the acid-filled rivers of their esophagus, their stomach, their intestines, their . . . at last, by fixing her gaze heroically upon it all, the sight neither revolted nor interested her: She was indifferent, it had nothing to do with her. Now she could simply gaze out the window at the endless white highway above which they soared like fantasy folk from Star Trek in their space ship, going to planets she did not even know existed. She could wipe out her loathing forever, she need not even speak to them. Like a wise nun taking her perpetual vows, she'd prepare herself for eternity by silence. The eternal highway brightened with sunlight, the iced drinks tinkled around her; Tamsen leaned back and found, yes, that she had no trouble at all, no none, imagining again and again, Reffie coming out of the elevator, Reffie climbing into the railcar, Reffie disappearing into the tunnel as into an horizon. At last she shut out even the bright white light of sunlight rebounding from the wing of the plane, folded her hands as if to sleep, and followed Reffie down the elevator, down down, into the mine where he. . . .

From her bed in the Kootenai Hospital Tamsen could hear Grampa Wing's voice in the corridor. He was whispering, either to a nurse or to Woody, she couldn't be sure. Or perhaps she was still dreaming; she had lain awake all night dreaming dreams as soothing as the sound of the surf; they rolled toward her, an endlessly murmuring sirenic song. Sunlight streamed down on waves as she dreamed, they became mirrors reflecting first the sky, then unwinding reels of film loosing her dreams upon the un- furled sea. Then one afternoon as she lay motionless, the sound of the sea grew softer, she recognized it to be the sound of mimosa leaves stirring in the April air, a sound so faint she had to hold her own breath for long moments, listening, listening. *Now* she could hear the other sound with it. By an act of supreme attention she could hear moving toward her across the winding air, Roseanne's breathing—again and again while she sat reading under the flowering mimosa. And Tamsen could clearly hear Roseanne agreeing with her, Tamsen, as she breathed and breathed again, that never had there been a lavender so delicate, a flowering so perfect. In all The Southland no tree, surely, had borne such porcelain petals, had worn a corolla as delicate as the human ear, listening. Even their stamens and pistils listened. One could see their nerves straining with memory and longing, listening, waiting for the flowering to come.

Someone was urging Tamsen to swallow. Water brushed her clenched lips. But Tamsen had learned that the coarse ugly sound of swallowing detonated in her eardrums, roared down her throat, drowned out the sound of Rose- anne's chair rocking under the mimosa, of the leaves per- forming their miraculous photosynthesis, of Roseanne's breathing. . . . She had learned she could control even her need for water, you could learn to sip less and less, till finally you took none at all. They might fill your veins with glucose, flood you with all the horrors of their I.V. bottles like ugly douche bags, hanging—but it was the water that decided, after all. If you did not need water, you could survive on air. The secret was to learn to breathe in and out, in and out, inhaling dreams, exhaling the past. You'd always thought that like the mimosa tree, you needed your share of water, but you could give that up too for the sake of the music of Roseanne's breathing, for the cherished song humming through your instrument of hollowed flesh.

It's all a matter of will, Tamsen silently consoled the defeated hand, which put the water aside. It was like the story Roseanne had read to her and Woody once about the Mama-llama in the Andes, or wherever llamas lived, who had refused to carry her too-heavy burden. In the story the Mama-llama had simply lain down on its side, refusing to rise again. The Indians had beat it and begged it and crooned to it lovingly, but it had lain there, its gentle llama-eyes full of resignation, its slender, agile legs folded beneath her. The recalcitrant llama, knowing what it wanted, knowing what it could not have, had refused to move until. . . . But Tamsen could not remember the ending, perhaps she had fallen asleep while Roseanne read; but she remembered the silly argument she and Woody had got into about what the llama *should* have done. Woody had said it should have *bitten* its owners and run away; Tamsen on the other hand had defended the llama's action, saying it was what any sensible animal should do, being tied to its heavy load forever. . . .

She didn't know why they wouldn't let Woody come in to see her. Grampa Wing was a babbling old fool, she didn't want to see Grampa Wing. He would only begin again, talking about how much they loved her, and how this would have broken Reffie's heart. The reason Grampa Wing could talk that way was, he hadn't known *Roseanne,* he couldn't know it was not Reffie's heart but *Roseanne's* heart that would have been broken if she'd seen Reffie married to that-Julia, and seen Julia with that . . . but here again the music of the mimosa miraculously interposed and Tamsen didn't have to deal with all that, she had only to listen attentively to the rocking chair and the stirring leaves. But if only they'd let Woody in, she could laugh about it all, she'd remind Woody of the Mama-llama, and she'd say, "Now see? Wasn't I right." And he'd have to admit that she was right. Because who could deny how easy it was? You simply lay down, you set your teeth and turned your head away, and nobody would force food down your throat either, unless they held you down, and Gramp wouldn't let them do that after the one time they did it. . . . "Maybe she'll hear us," he'd said, "if we just keep on saying over and over that we love her, we love her," and Gramp had left the hospital room sobbing. For what? wondered Tamsen. An old man, why should he sob, so near to his own time as he was? He should simply, like the llama, lie down and neither eat nor drink . . . but of course not many like herself had the will to resist water. When you resisted water, your body became hot and feverish, even the soughing breeze off the Gulf barely cooled your tongue, the burning of your kidneys was a fire, a self-immolation. But at least you would never again have to squat down in the back seat of a car nor have to be lifted up, leaning against the nurse and listen—not to the sound of the mimosa through the air soughing, making *music*, *music*—but to the sound of your ugly wasting body making waste, making urine.

Tetany! It was a pretty word. They said it might set in. Well let it *set!* Tamsen shrieked gaily, silently, moving closer to the sheets which seemed to become colder every day, a curious thing—her body was hot but the sheets were cold. Maybe it was, as They said, because the calcium level in the blood was so very low, it was like lockjaw, They said. *No, no,* she liked Tetany better. Lockjaw was an ugly *swallowing* kind of word. In Mexico Sean was always worrying that he'd get lockjaw because he hadn't had a tetanus booster. . . . She slipped her hand across her body, under the cool sheets, reaching now for her kangaroo. It must have slipped down to the foot of the bed. Her hand passed over her body as she reached down, feeling her way. . . . How beautifully thin she had become. Like an Alice in Wonderland she was, she had the power, the choice—to eat or not to eat of the magical Cake. She could become as thin as she had always wanted, a girl of luminous porcelain, her skin as transparent as the mimosa flower, through which you could see the sky turn rose-colored as if you were gazing through rose-colored glasses, through Roseanne-colored glasses.

Her burning hand now reached the kangaroo and pulled it upward by its long ears. Amazing how heavy it was, how hard to pull it was, it came up toward her slowly, as if it too, had become part of her dream, as if she were pulling it out of the sounding surf through deep, heavy water. Her arm ached with the sheer strenuous effort of it. As she cradled the kangaroo in her arms, she parted her lips with pleasure, opening wide her locked mouth that had not willingly yielded to anything in days or perhaps weeks, not even to say *muchas gracias y adiós* to Sean who had so cunningly brought her the kangaroo one day, hoping perhaps that she'd forgive him for everything, for the hideous sidewalk where people had passed her, murmuring abominations—so utterly unlike the breathing, soughing sound of the leaves and the rolling waves. But no, she would *never* forgive him, she had not and would *never* speak to him. He had trussed her up like a dead rabbit and set her in the marketplace to be sold; above all, what she would never forgive was the craven smell of the bread he had dropped in her lap, the smell of food for the starving. He had insulted her, he had believed she would do anything for bread, that the torments of her belly would force her to surrender her will, her freedom. . . . But she had not surrendered, she would never surrender, they might bring to her the fragrance of bread, of wine, of sweet liqueurs and exotic delicacies, nothing would ever tempt her again. Now she set the long ear of the kangaroo between her teeth like a blade, it tasted of her life, like the bittersweet salt of one's body wrung from the pain and exertion of loving, or running in terror, or sweating free of feverish illness, or of lying in the heat of a Salinas summer, breathing. . . . Its concentrated taste of life did not sicken her, its brine was the salt of the sea. She tried at first to nibble delicately at its ear, but her mouth was dry, it was impossible. . . . Then luckily the very smell of the kangaroo brought back so many memories that tears flooded from her eyes, wetting the flabby floppy ear, softening it, till it became soft, tender, malleable as a nipple, and Tamsen, groping in the darkening air while the seawind soughed and roared around her, set her mouth firmly around the nipple-shaped ear and closed her eyes, content.

Epilogue

Wing considered: Maybe he shouldn't have brought the boy after all. Maybe it wasn't something a kid should see. It was definitely not what he, Wing, would have wanted young Ephraim to see, and Reffie maybe wouldn't have wanted Woodrow to see it either. He himself would not have believed it. *If anybody had told me back when I beat the biggest bum rap in the world and come back to Silver Valley padded with money like a Chinese quilt-coat, that any generation would ever be like that again I'd have laughed him right off the stage.* And if you've survived a plague or a fire or a flood or a train wreck or a Great Depression, you don't ever expect to meet with one head-on again. In fact, you'd walk miles out of your way if you heard one comin. So Wing would damned well have preferred to walk away from what he was watching; but he'd come to the Steelworkers Local to have a talk with the guys, and the truck had begun arriving while he was talking to Woody about something else. Mainly Woody had been telling him about what he'd like to see and do in Pittsburgh once Gramp was through visiting with the guys in Braddock.

Wing was just wishing he'd stayed home. He'd accomplished nothing. The young men had listened with something like tolerance to his words of advice; then after a respectful silence, they'd proceeded as if he hadn't spoken. None of his suggestions had been taken seriously. The men were already living in Memory Lane—in that long-ago nostalgic era when they used to make twenty-six dollars an hour. With all the guys talking about their mortgages or their car payments or their hospital bills, Wing's tales of derring-do and stick-with-the-union had sounded in his own ears preachy and old-fashioned.

After three hours of listening and talking, Wing had signalled to Woody that it was time to go. He didn't want to get snowed in, they had a plane to catch, Wing explained to the men, and the kid there—he put his hand on Woody's shoulder—wanted to see the dinosaur before they left.

A melancholy glaze had settled on the faces of the men, and one of them had remarked that he'd not been to the museum in Oakland since he was a boy. "Yeah, I guess we got a pretty good museum there," he observed with what Wing thought was an odd sort of diffidence and pride, as if the place did not really belong to him.

Some of the other guys had started telling Woody what else he should see. "Tell Wing to take you over to Pitt—you can see all the Nationality Rooms."

"Yeah, especially the Polish—don't miss the Polish room," added someone, laughing.

"And take him downtown to see Heinz Hall . . ."

"Hey, wait a minute," Wing laughed. "You're talking to a man who's been seein things since Woodrow Wilson was a pup. I can't go runnin hither and yon like you youngsters."

At this designation, a faint gleam of hope and fear had gleamed in the eyes of them, many of whom were in their forties or fifties. One of them slapped Woody on the back. "Well, at least you ought to hear Hal the Robot on WDVE. He talks and sings every morning. He's . . . it's a disc jockey, you know? He's like Hal in 2001?" And some of the fathers of nearly-grown sons had looked dismayed at the realization that they'd seen *2001* nearly a generation ago, and that Woody had not yet been born . . . Woody apologized for not having seen the film, not even on a rerun. But one of the guys had laughed and reassured Woody. "*You* don't have to see it. You're gonna *be* it! When 2001 gets here, you'll be managing this place."

"Yeah—managing it all by yourself. Just one guy pushing a button. 'Cause the-robots-are-coming, the-robots-are-coming," sang out one of the younger workers, urging Wing to take the kid to see the Robotics Institute at CMU. "Interesting place . . . Ver—y interesting."

"*Can* we? Can we go Gramp, and see some real robots?"

"Sure—*take* him," said the younger man. "Let the kid meet the enemy face to face. By 2001 those fucking robots will be doing the work of seven million men."

"Aw shut up, Arnie," said someone. "You've just gotten to be a real hotshot know-it-all since they *retrained* you."

Wing was annoyed with the young man for talking that way in front of Woody, and was about to warn the guy to watch his language, when suddenly the trucks started arriving and Wing forgot everything else.

It was a convoy like you see on TV when they're telling the Cambodians to move on out or kicking the Moslems out of India into Pakistan. And that's when (after all the joking and friendliness) Wing had begun to understand from the expressions of shame and resentment that the men had not come that day just to discuss union matters, but for the food. They began lining up now to accept the bags of free groceries, at first with silent bitterness, then with grins and shrugging of shoulders at one another. *Food banks. That's what they call em now. We used to call em bread lines and soup lines and being-on-relief.*

On the sides of the trucks strange new letters were visible, not the multiple alphabets of some federal agency as in Wing's day—not the AAA nor the CCC nor the WPA nor the NRA—but letters indicating a strictly local group. But it was precisely the uncoordinated, stop-gap regional nature of the business that was more shocking to Wing than all the hand-outs of the Depression.

"What's that—PACS-FAB?" Wing asked.

"The Pittsburgh Area Concerned Steelworkers Food Assistance Board," answered the young man who'd been retrained.

"You mean there's some guys around here who *ain't* concerned?" snapped Wing angrily.

Somebody was now offering Wing a bag of groceries. Wing shook his head, but Woody asked if he could have the package of cookies he saw sticking out of the top of the bag. Wing scowled at his grandson, then relented, shrugging. *(What's a bag of cookies anyway?)*

"Run and grab that cab there, will you Woody? Goodbye now, fellas," shaking hands all around, "we got to go and see a dinosaur."

As they rode the cab into Oakland, Wing was surprised to see how close it was, after all. In *his* day, he remarked to Woody, he would have walked it easily.

"But Gramp, you just *said* you can't walk everywheres."

"Well, maybe *I* can't, but you *ought* to." At the absurdity of which he was pleased to see Woody laugh. He was relieved, too, to shake the memory of those hungry steelworkers out of his mind. He was too old, he told himself, to suffer every time he saw somebody suffering. And there seemed so much more *of* it everywhere—more even than when he was carrying buckets of water for the potatoes of Idaho. It was enough to wear your nerves thin.

So as he and Woody gazed up at the Tyrannosaurus, Wing was gratified to think that maybe he'd done the right thing after all bringing Woody, giving the kid a chance to see something besides Silver Valley. Good for Woody too, to see a school with so many people going up and down in elevators, learning things day and night (though Wing did think it peculiar that anybody would build a university like a mine, where you had to go up or down to get anywhere). Woody had wanted to see all the Nationality Rooms, but Wing said, *No way*—he was too tired. He just wanted to sleep. And he'd been relieved to see that Woody, too, was looking a little tired, leaning on Wing the way he did from time to time, a habit he'd picked up since the funeral.

Suppressing a moan that rose in his chest at the memory of Reffie's funeral, Wing asked tenderly, "Well, kid, had enough? How about we go catch that plane?"

Their plane was late. Woody chortled with triumph, "See, Gramp, they don't have *every*thing running perfectly in the big cities." So they strolled around the airport, picking up a news magazine which Wing didn't bother to read, and a puzzle cube for Woody which he couldn't solve.

"*Work* on it," preached Wing, dragging himself back to the old moralities.

"Why should I work on it, Gramp?" retorted Woody. "I'll just get a robot to solve it for me."

Wing shook his head threateningly. "You got to *work* even to make a robot work," he preached, but he had to laugh.

They wandered into a gift shop, looking for something they might bring back for Tamsen. Wing would have liked to bring her one of those life-sized bears, but they were too big and awkward to carry. He and Woody looked instead for something smaller, something Woody could put in his pack.

"How about a record album?" suggested Woody.

Wing shook his head. He didn't know whether Tamsen would like that. "And besides," he complained irrelevantly, "the kind of music kids listen to today!"

"Aw, we're not so bad," protested Woody. "Whaddye want us to do, listen to 'Bicycle Built for Two' on a wind-up phonograph?"

Wing was silent. He was being tempted by a beautiful stuffed mountain lion with gold-colored eyes.

"What do you think, Woody? Think she'd like that?"

Woody thought a minute. "How about a kangaroo?" he murmured almost to himself.

"What? A kangaroo? Another kangaroo? You think she'd like one just like the one . . .?"

Woody nodded thoughtfully. "Yeah. See can you get one with the you-know-what in the pouch. Ask the clerk what you call em."

But the clerk hadn't the least idea what you called them. She didn't have any kangaroos anyway. But she *did* have some very nice things from Australia. "Have you ever *been* to Australia?" she asked Woody.

Woody shook his head, ashamed. He felt he ought to have been at least to Australia. After all, he was going to be thirteen pretty soon.

"Well, I thought with your interest in *marsupials*," she added, pursuing her advantage.

Woody remained silent.

She now brought down from an upper shelf a koala. Wing's first reaction was to turn away from the hybrid-looking, snub-nosed thing. He remarked to the clerk that it looked like an unsuccessful cross between a fox and bob-cat. The girl replied that they were *very popular* in Australia.

Wing reminded her tartly, "But we're *not* from Australia," but immediately repented his irascible reply when he saw the injured look on her face. *Aw just a girl—making the minimum wage, most like.* "Aw hell, let's get it."

"Look what it says here, Gramp," said Woody, reading from the tag tied to the koala's long claws. " 'The aborig-ines believe that the koala bear is a reincarnation of the Spirits of Lost Children.' Hey, that's neat, don't you think?" Woody looked around for confirmation from the girl, but she was walking away as if indifferent to their conversation, and Gramp Wing was frowning and staring at the animal with a mixture of curiosity and fear, as if he thought it might bite him.

"You don't like it, do you Gramp? Well, *I* like it. I think they're kind of spooky, but I like it. And they're from *Australia*," he added, maliciously, glancing at the girl. "And they're *marsupial*."

"Hush, Woody." The boy would have to learn to be more discreet. "Hush." Wing turned to the clerk. "We'll take *two*," he said, trying to sound casual.

"*Two?*" Woody looked astonished and prepared to be in-sulted as the clerk wrapped the two koalas separately. "Aw for crying out loud, Gramp, what do you think I . . . ?"

"Just shut up and carry your own load. Here," He shoved the fancy shopping bag which said *The Total Toy Shop* at Woody. "Just keep it. Keep it. Make sure it don't get *lost*."

With a sober air Woody shifted his backpack so that he could carry the koala securely under one arm. When, an hour later, they were seated on the plane homeward, with Woody at the window where he liked to be, Wing watched as the kid slipped the koala free of its wrapping paper and set it beside him, where it sat all the way, looking out at the world with its gentle, inquiring eyes.